CAPTIVATING MELODY

EVERNIGHT PUBLISHING ®

www.evernightpublishing.com

CAPTIVATING MELODY

DEDICATION

To my author tribe—it takes a community to keep writing.

CAPTIVATING MELODY

CAPTIVATING MELODY

Discord's Desire, 1

Katherine McIntyre

Copyright © 2018

Chapter One

The stench of sweat, sex, and Chanel Number Five were never going to come out of Liz O'Brien's jeans. She frowned as her Keds gummed to the floor backstage for the five thousandth time. That was the last gig they'd ever do at Peekaboos.

She peered past the stage out to the main floor of the strip club where a plethora of half- empty TicTac white tables populated the place. The remaining folks embarked on the bump and grind journey that at one tender age might've shocked and appalled her, but by now, she rolled her eyes and shut out the moans. Liz winced every time her shoe stuck to the black-and-white tiled floor as she crossed the room. Pink lighting skated throughout the place, even post-show, adding to the seedy ambiance.

She raked a hand through her long chestnut locks, a couple pieces drying to her face from the heat they pumped through this place. Guess since their strippers were shedding clothes, the staff had to keep 'em comfortable.

Jett stood by the far door, giving her the 'I'm bored look,' which she'd come to realize happened about every two point five seconds when he wasn't onstage or getting laid. After playing the bass for their earlier show, he'd tied back his dark strands, and his light blue eyes had a familiar twinkle in them. Average girls would see a ladykiller who screamed sex from his pores.

Liz noticed the prettier-than-average looks, but she also saw the greenish tint to Jett's pale skin and the delicate gills along his neck. Since she'd never met her parents, Liz didn't know the 'why' of her ability, but she'd always seen past the fae glamour shielding normal humans from the weird.

Jett lifted his sculpted brow in a cynical arch he'd perfected, jabbing at his watch as if she dragged along at a snail's pace.

"The bar's not going to disappear if you're a couple minutes late," Liz called out, quickening her pace to close the distance between them.

"Lies. I know for certain there's an expiration date on the JD with my name on it. Six months on the road with us and you'd think you would catch on." Jett slung his arm around her shoulder, the familiar weight one she'd never expected from her former one-night stand.

"It's a miracle I've been able to put up with you lot for this long."

Even though the first time she met Jett they'd fumbled in a back alley together, Liz much preferred him as her tether of sanity and staunch friend on the road. After all, traveling with rockstars was bad enough. The satyr, siren, banshee, and incubus were the real deal when it came to sex gods, with powers that worked on every human except her. She navigated the regular folks to book their gigs, while they made sure she wasn't fae-bait to any supernatural who noticed her unique skill set.

Together she and Jett stepped out of the steamy room, which had begun to smell a little rank, and made their way down the narrow corridor leading to the front door. Neon pink lit the hallway, nauseatingly similar to the spotlights gleaming onto an opening act Liz would need bleach to remove from her memory banks.

"Good riddance," Liz muttered as they strode through the doors onto the concrete landing.

"You only have yourself to blame," Jett reminded her as he tugged out a cigarette, lighting it in one fluid motion. "You're the one who does the booking." Smoke trailed from him in a thick cloud floating up to greet the night sky, which filled with just as much smog. He sucked down the thing like his life depended on it, deep drags he hadn't been able to snag while they'd been playing.

Liz heaved a sigh, stuffing her hands into the pockets of her brown leather jacket as the strength of the breeze increased. "Thought you guys could use a pick-me-up. We've been on the road for awhile." After a week of rolling through bland and blander in the Midwest, she had an entire buffet of gigs lined up for the guys in San Francisco. "Not my fault the lot of you were getting crotchety."

"I needed space from Renn's snoring. Last couple of nights the idea of smothering him with a pillow has grown real tempting," Jett said as they ambled along the sidewalk. The neon greens backlit a sign for Shooters, the nearest bar to the strip club, and from the sportsball-related specials on the chalkboard outside, Liz made a wild leap at the clientele.

"Let's hope Kieran hasn't already gotten kicked out." She placed her hand on the bronze doorknob and turned.

Jett stepped behind her, flicking his half-smoked cigarette onto the asphalt.

The second Liz opened the door to the bar, her expectations faltered. A wrong tension threaded through the air, the sort she'd come to associate with fae. Jett straightened his stance, crowding closer to her in the protective way she'd come to appreciate. His body buzzed with the same nerves that flooded her.

The maroon carpeting crunched underfoot, and dim lighting cast the wood paneling lining the entryway in a buttery gold. A normal thrum of chatter flowed in when they opened the second door, but she expected that. Humans saw what the fae wanted them to. This time of night, not too many crowded around the oaken bar, and more than a couple empty glasses spanned the length with foam clinging to the sides. As Liz walked inside, she noted the groups clustered in the pleather booths along the back of the bar. Ensconced in shadows, those made the perfect meeting place for seedier sorts.

Not like her boys would be skulking around there. The bandmates of Discord's Desire were pretty boys who needed their egos fluffed on a constant basis. Thankfully, they hadn't hired her for that role.

In the corner, wedged into one of the back booths, Liz identified the source of the tension. A threesome of knobby-kneed skeletal fae who gave the rest a bad rap sat watching the bar. If average humans saw them, this place would be evacuated in screams, spilled drinks, and knocked-over chairs. However, glamour kept their pretty little eyes shielded. Not Liz. She'd spent years crying wolf in her foster homes, running inside because a shadow watched her from the street, or a brimstone creature approached in the woods. For Liz O'Brien, the monster under the bed was always real.

The malevolence in their stares as she locked eyes with them was the exact reason she'd hopped cities in the past, before her days of booking for Discord's Desire. Unaware humans made for easy targets, but the nightmares crawling through the streets found her interesting, and their scrutiny was worse.

"Come here often, beautiful?" a smooth, sexy voice drawled from behind her.

Liz folded her arms over her chest before turning around and fixing Kieran with a look. The man, given the chance, would flirt with himself, so she didn't ever take him seriously. His lips curved in a cocky smile made even more dangerous by the pointed fangs peeking out. He wore his stage clothes from the show—ripped jeans, a gray wifebeater, and a patched leather that had seen better days. Yet combined with the studs in ears, the streaked guyliner, and the labret piercing, the man oozed sex.

"Cool it, rockstar." She smirked, meeting his teasing eyes. "You've got a whole cavalcade of women who'd throw themselves at you in a heartbeat, already fallen under your spell. I'm immune to your hinky fae magic."

His fingers snuck up faster than she could follow to trail down the column of her throat. "Isn't that what makes it all the more interesting?"

Liz shivered under his silken touch, ignoring the hoarseness in his voice and the quickened pulse that followed in the wake. The incubus didn't need any powers to lure women. His voice alone would send them flocking, and with the attractive package it came in— well, he proved damn near irresistible.

Even though Liz had taken a tango with Jett the

first night she met them, after that she'd drawn a line in the sand. She joined on as their booking manager, and while the guys might find her ability to resist their charms alluring, she wouldn't get tangled into their webs. Even still, she couldn't quite stamp out the surge of adrenaline coursing through her every time he entered a room.

"Down, boy. You've got adoring masses to sate those needs," she sassed. Her attention returned to the table when those fae shifted in their seats. They focused on them with those filmy eyes, but whether their interest was territorial or curiosity, she couldn't tell. Kieran glanced to where she stared.

"They were already here when we arrived and haven't made a move, so they may be having a pint like us. More's the pity. All this post-event energy and I could use a good fight," he murmured, returning his attention to the three shots of bourbon he had lined up on the counter of the bar.

The air bristled with a fight on the breeze. Liz snagged one of the open stools, but she'd never been able to settle while fae watched her. Call it survival instinct, but without fail, no fae who noticed her spelled good news. The hiss of the naga who'd cornered her back in Tucson echoed in her peripheral sometimes, and the scars on her ankle from a boggart attack still throbbed on occasion.

"Two glasses of JD," Jett called to the bartender.

The guy rolled his flannel sleeves to his elbow and flipped the bottle, dispensing the amber dew. Liz tapped her nails against the lacquered hardwood, the click-click-click reflecting her nerves. Casual laughs ripped through the bar from the folks perched at their barstools without the slightest inkling of the threat in their midst. She accepted the glass from Jett and inhaled the rich fumes of the Jack Daniels in front of her before taking a deep swig, hoping the smooth liquid would settle the buzzing in her head.

Renn sat beside a big-haired blonde, his hand on her arm. The way the woman heavy-breathed, she was liable to bust out of her tight black tank top. His hair post-show tangled into a dark mess, but on the satyr it added to the wildness gleaming in his cocoa eyes. Though the blonde drooling over him couldn't see the obsidian horns atop his head, Renn didn't need glamour to lure a woman in. One flash of his blinding smile against his cinnamon skin and inhibitions flew out the window.

Trevor, their resident banshee, watched with a smirk on his face as the ice of his gin and tonic clinked against the glass while he swirled it. With the man's rich tawny skin and longer, silver strands, he had the type of unique looks to stop people in their tracks. However guarded he might be with his own secrets, his Southern drawl and the calm air about him tended to set people at ease.

Liz tipped back a little more of the JD, hoping to erase the filthy film of Peekaboos.

The sole of Kieran's combat boots tapped a tempo against the barstool but not with nerves like Liz's. She'd spent enough time with the boys to realize they didn't share the same fears—after all, those fae were a part of their race. Knowing Kieran though, the boy chomped at the bit for a fight.

Liz let out a sigh and ran a hand through her tangled dark tresses. She'd aimed for practicality in beat-up cargoes and a baby doll tee that had seen better days, yet Kieran scanned her up and down with a hunger reserved for the six-inch heel wearing broads they'd left behind at Peekaboos. She arched an eyebrow, and he laughed in return.

"Have to say, the fan club's intense tonight," Jett muttered beside her as he cast a glance to those hulking fae in the corner. He flipped one of his guitar picks between his fingers to hide his nerves.

"You boys part of a band or something?" the bartender asked while he popped down a tap handle to fill a pint for another customer.

"They just got done with their gig at Peekaboos," Liz said before taking another sip of her amber ambrosia.

"I heard. You're the punk band that rolled into town?" the bartender continued to make conversation, a welcome distraction from the group of nasties giving them the stink eye.

"You're part of a band?" the non-literal harpy beside Renn shrieked. Liz wrinkled her nose, sticking her finger into her ear to clear out the residual ring. If she had a dollar for the amount of times she heard that on the road, she'd have more ones than a stripper on Saturday night.

"Yeah, I'm the drummer," Renn purred as the woman proceeded to dry hump him, crawling onto his lap.

Liz grinned, shaking her head. After a few months touring with the lot of them, she ceased to be surprised at men and women alike flinging themselves at the foursome.

"He's talented at bursting our eardrums at four in the morning with his horrifying snoring," Jett called over as he lifted his glass.

"At least I don't spend an hour primping in the RV's one goddamn bathroom," Renn shot back. "No one's noticing each individual strand of hair while you're on stage." Renn's flavor of the night let out a loud giggle.

Liz patted Jett on the shoulder, trying and failing

to hide her smile. "Don't worry, babe. I notice."

Jett let out a mock sniff and tweaked his styled strands. "At least someone does."

"Why play somewhere like Peekaboos?" the bartender piped up again.

Liz restrained her eyeroll for Mr. Questions. "Because the boys like to indulge their vices." She didn't blink with her response.

The bartender gave her the up and down scan to her surprise, interest in his dark eyes. With his thick forearms and trimmed beard, he wasn't bad looking either.

"Why go out when a gorgeous girl like you is around?"

Liz stifled a laugh. The guys were laying it on thick tonight. "Right, they wish."

Faster than a blink, Kieran's chest pressed against her back, heat emanating from him. She glanced to him right as he placed his hands on her shoulders.

"She's got standards we can't even compete with," he said, the intonation in his voice making his 'back off' intent quite clear.

Liz lifted her brow, unused to seeing this side of Kieran directed toward her. The way his hands rested on her sent clear possessive signals as he squeezed her shoulders. A surprising warmth spread in her chest at the attention, yet as quick it burned to irritation. He had no say in who she flirted with.

"Maybe being surrounded by rockstars has me looking for a regular guy." Liz locked gazes with Kieran, challenge flashing in her eyes. The poor bartender was getting dragged into battles way outside of his pay grade.

Kieran bristled, those amber eyes of his flashing as he opened his mouth. Knowing the hothead like she'd come to these past few months, she guaranteed he'd say something he regretted. After all, the bundle of spitfire and vinegar had a heart bigger than her brittle black one. She wasn't backing down though. The boys weren't the type for monogamy, and she refused to contract a case of feelings only to watch him hook up with a different girl each night.

Before he spoke, his eyes widened as he focused on something in a different direction.

"Duck," he hissed, grabbing her by the shoulders and tackling her off the barstool before they crashed to the ground.

Chapter Two

Kieran had been waiting for the violence to explode from the moment he stepped into the bar, unsure of whether or not the creatures would make a move. On an average day, the pent-up energy thrummed through his veins, begging for release, and after a gig, he grew even more amped. So when those rakshasas in the corner stepped up from their seats, he was prepared. And when one of the bastards spit in their direction, he didn't even question if the glob was venomous.

Kieran tumbled to the ground with Liz, his grip tightening around her in a fierce way. The barstool went flying, and he hit the floor with a thud that shook his bones. Liz's body pressed against his, the silent thrill of her heat only diminished by the threat of the bastards trying to kill them. He had to keep her safe.

Pushing her back, he leapt up and whipped around to face the approaching trio. Already, energy pulsed through him, begging to unleash in the swing of his fist. Folks who'd been sitting near him skidded out of the way—average humans would see a barfight, and in a way they weren't wrong.

A click sounded beside him.

"Back down," Liz called out, wielding a pistol with the ease of familiarity. She had the muzzle trained on the rakshasas before them. "I'm the one you want, not him."

"When the fuck did you get that?" Kieran balled his hands into fists as he overrode the urge to get her out of the line of fire.

"A couple stops back. Jett took me to the candy store," Liz said. Even though her eyes took on the intense focus of fear, she maintained the same calm competency as always.

"Babe, scram," Renn dismissed his arm candy and cracked his knuckles. The girl took one look at the impending fight and almost knocked over her stool as she scampered away. "You lot want a piece of us?"

"Can we please have a drink at a bar *without* it ending in a brawl?" Jett complained as he pushed his seat in like a gentleman.

Trevor smirked, lifting his glass. "We wouldn't be very good rockstars if we came and went to places nice and peaceable-like." Even though Trevor hadn't left his seat, the man would launch himself into the fray when things grew serious.

Kieran didn't bother restraining his grin as he cracked his knuckles. He'd learned at an early age how to bend the rules of his incubus nature. While he drew passion during sex and women fluttered to his bed like moths to the light, he preferred siphoning from a different passion—violence. After all, starting with his own folks, people had wanted him dead or gone his entire life.

"We've no quarry with the rest of you," the rakshasa in the lead hissed out, his sounds flicking out with his forked tongue. "Only him." The creature's gaze locked onto Kieran, who raised his brows.

"Who'd you piss off this time, boss?" Renn asked, crossing his arms over his chest.

Kieran shrugged, ignoring the prickling down his arms. "I think they're trying to say I'm the lucky recipient of their undivided attention. I mean, we all know how desperate I am."

Liz snorted beside him. "We're not going to sit back and sip our drinks while you're busting in skulls."

Kieran couldn't hide his broad grin, even as he

tried to ignore how his heart beat a little faster. The woman didn't know how much she'd worked her way under his skin.

"Then you can get buried with him," the lead rakshasa hissed out.

Jett heaved a sigh and stepped beside Liz as he rolled the sleeves of his button-down. "Or you could deliver your doom and gloom message and take one to whoever sent you. Fuck off." His eyes gleamed with the challenge. "Do you need me to spell it out?"

The bony creature arched its back and reared its head. Kieran didn't have to be a genius to guess what would follow.

"Duck," he called out, grabbing Liz's sleeve and tugging her down again. He caught her annoyed glare but didn't care. His crew wouldn't get hurt on his account. A glob of venom sailed overhead. Except this time, it found purchase on the bartender in the middle of picking up a glass. The pint shattered as it hit the floor, and the man emitted out an anguished scream. The venom sizzled into his shirt and then hit flesh. Kieran let out a low curse. This encounter had already gotten too ugly. If the authorities weren't on their way yet, they would be in minutes. Chairs flipped as folks galvanized to action in order to get the hell out.

Time to start fighting.

Kieran rose from his crouch and with a push to take off, rocketed forward. One of the other rakshasas spat at him, but he brushed off the tingling globule. As fae, venom would only sizzle a little, just like poisons and flames needed insane quantities to do damage. Flecks dropped to the ground. He didn't stop in his tread, heading toward the lead one before it struck again to incite more panic inside Shooters. Kieran leapt into the line of sight for the beast, his hands latching around the knobby throat and gripping tight.

The creature gurgled and lashed out, those clawed nails scoring his arms as it fought to breathe. Humans might struggle against a rakshasa, but his kind possessed the skills and constitution to fight those bastards. Kieran squeezed harder. The rage clouded his vision, a building pulse in his chest begging him to go further. To destroy more.

Someone tapped his shoulder. "Brother, we might want to be questioning that one." Kieran's grip loosened for a heartbeat of a second as he whipped around. Trevor stood behind him, the man's dark eyes emanating perfect seriousness. Kieran cut a quick glance to the right to see Renn's cloven hoof smashing his rakshasa to the ground with the sort of bulldozing attack he expected from the satyr. He sucked in a breath. As the leader, he needed to keep a grip on his shit, even if he wanted to rip the spinal cord straight through this creature's mouth.

After all, they'd arrived here for him.

"So, who wants me dead?" Kieran asked, his voice low. The rakshasa inhaled greedy breaths as his chest fluttered up and down, the ribs protruding from its skeletal frame. The bar all but emptied at this point, the door swinging back and forth from the force with which everyone raced through it. The creature's eyes narrowed. "My patience isn't great," he continued. "So you either tell me who your bossman is, or I have no problem ending this job right here and now."

Silence filled the air for a brief bubble until gurgles filtered through the place from the guy Jett pinned to the wall with a fork through the throat. His guys were more than a little resourceful. Any fae trying to exist in the human realm outside of the Courts needed to be.

"He'll send more," the rakshasa said in a low,

gravelly voice.

Irritation flared in Kieran's chest. "Who?"

Before he asked again, the creature aimed a low kick, stomping on his foot. Kieran let go for half a second. In that time, the rakshasa dropped to the ground, but it didn't continue attacking. Instead, a slit opened in the carpeting, and it slithered into the portal to the Otherworld. Entering the fae realm that way—who knew where it ended up. Jett reached for the slit, but just as fast, his hand hit solid carpeting again.

"Damnit," Kieran spat, slinging a fist into the wall. Chunks of debris flew in the wake, and his knuckles throbbed, but the hit didn't take the edge off his irritation.

"Well, you musta pissed in someone's apple juice," Trevor said, clapping a hand on Kieran's shoulder.

"Haven't we all." Kieran cast one look around this tragedy of a bar, consisting of overturned tables, pools of black blood from the two dead rakshasas, and a dead, slumped over bartender.

"Boys, we better scram." Liz spoke as the voice of reason. Despite the carnage she'd witnessed, she kept a cool head on her. The woman was as much of a vet to piss poor situations as the rest of them, something she proved after one violence bender when his mother deigned to write him. He'd shown up back at the RV covered in blood, most of it not his. The guys let him do his thing—they all had their damage, but Liz? She had the balls to challenge him. Had the courage to care.

"Not like the police are going to bring us milk and cookies," Jett said, making his way to the front door.

Renn kicked the wall, his hooves carving dents in the wood paneling. "Looks like I'll be flying solo tonight." He stormed out the door next, followed by

Trevor who shook his head, trying to restrain his grin.

"At least keep it down this time," Jett called back, already outside. "Some of us don't find your guttural animal noises attractive. It gave me nightmares."

"Poor baby," Kieran called over, unable to help his smile. Even though the incursion weighed heavy on his mind, he'd dwell on it another day. Heaving a sigh, he jammed his hands in his pockets and strode out of the bar.

****

Kieran awoke from a whopping three hours of sleep to the enticing smell of bacon. He followed the scent into the kitchenette where Trevor stood by a frying pan, turning the sizzling slices.

Trevor slid a glance over to him and lifted the flipper in greeting, even though he didn't bother shifting from where he stood.

Kieran flung himself into the nearby booth along the opposite side of the bus and cracked a window as he lit a smoke. As far as human habits went, he liked the rhythm of this one. Though if Renn caught him smoking inside the RV again, he'd get reamed out.

"How 'bout you start telling me who the hell might be sending folks your way." Trevor piled the strips of bacon onto a plate and lifted it in hostage before Kieran snatched a piece.

He gave Trevor the side eye. "Like you're one to talk, Mr. Marked-For-Life."

"Now focus here, we're talking about you," Trevor drawled in his thick Louisiana accent.

Kieran sucked in another drag from his cig, letting the smoke trickle out. "Family hates me, but that's an old as blood grudge. As for up and comers, most bar brawls don't end in serious vendettas like this." He settled onto the worn leather cushion. Trevor handed him a piece of bacon, causing Kieran to lift a brow. "What am I, a dog?"

"Good boy," Liz said as she sauntered into the room. Her jeans hung low on her perfect hips, and the stained, torn-sleeve tee she wore couldn't be sexier with the band of tanned stomach it revealed. She'd tossed her tangled strands into a messy low bun that left her mischievous hazel eyes and full lips on display. Instead of beelining for the bacon, she dropped onto the couch beside him and plucked the cigarette from between his fingers.

Leaning back toward the open window, she took a drag, letting the smoke stream out.

She grinned before handing the cigarette to him. "Thanks, I needed that." Her husky voice from waking up caused Kieran to shift in his seat, aware his hormones started revving this early in the morning. The girl had an effortless way of turning him on.

Trevor crunched on a piece of bacon as he leaned against the lacquer cabinetry of their kitchenette. He offered the plate to Liz who hopped up and snatched a piece.

"So do you think your fan club's going to follow us to San Francisco?" Liz asked with her mouth full of bacon. The question in her eyes pierced him.

"I wish these fans of mine would make themselves known, because I have no idea how they've even heard of my work." Kieran locked eyes with her, making his meaning clear. "If they're mucking about though, I want you protected with more than just a gun."

Liz lifted a brow. "Never realized booking managers were so important."

She was. From the moment she'd crashed into their lives, Kieran couldn't get her out of his head. The way she cared for them, even when she didn't give herself the same attention made him want to turn the mirror around all the more. To make her understand how much her consideration meant in signing venues to keep them fed, how she brewed a full pot of coffee in the morning and kept a couple of mugs out. She'd sparked his interest from the start, and with each increasing day it intensified.

"Darlin, you have no idea what a mess we were before you joined," Trevor said, polishing off the rest of his plate. "We would drive to a town, pick a bar, and then get our rocks off. Now we've got a plotted route, a tour schedule, and someone who's willing to book strip clubs because we need a pick me up."

"So no going and getting yourself killed," Kieran jumped in. With the way those fae targeted him last night, more would come. The memory of the bartender lingered—if they'd made one wrong move the victim could've been Liz.

Liz rolled her eyes. "Yeah, I'm going to go toddle into traffic."

Kieran took another drag from his cigarette instead of responding. He'd never gotten this flare of protectiveness before, though he also hadn't bothered with many human friends. Hell, he barely had any friends at all until he'd met Trevor while fooling around at an open mic one night. After a shared drink and the need to escape their pasts, they'd formed the band then and there. The RV shuddered to a halt, and Kieran quick-flicked the cigarette out of the window as footsteps pounded through the place.

Liz's eyes met his, hers dancing as she helped him close the window. Both of them knew what a bitchfit Renn would put up after taking driving duty for the night.

"Pit stop, assholes," his voice resounded around the RV, causing a groan from Jett's bunk. "We're right outside of Berkeley." Renn stepped into view, dark eyes scouring the room while Trevor washed his plate. His gaze landed on the frying pan. "Did you char that shit? It reeks, man."

"True story." Trevor cast a glance over to Kieran with the hint of a smile. "Guess it's a good thing we're stopping somewhere with food."

"How's anyone supposed to sleep around here?" Jett called from the other room. A thump sounded, and a second later, a crash. "If I look haggard on stage tonight, I'm blaming you lot."

Liz snorted. "You'll be beautiful, babe."

"Thanks, gorgeous," his voice came from the other room as a few more shuffles followed. In moments, he stumbled into the kitchen area with the rest of them. His black hair lay in tousled strands, and he'd pulled on a pair of jeans and a black button-down that somehow wasn't wrinkled.

"You're making us look bad, Jett," Kieran said, gesturing to his threadbare camo cargoes and black wifebeater that had seen more than a couple of years.

"Oh stop." Liz thwacked him on the chest. "You boys know you're lookers."

He couldn't help the grin rising to his face, the same as he couldn't help the twang of frustration because again, she lumped him in with the rest of them. When it came to Liz, he'd been wanting solo attention for some time now. "Tell me that in private?"

She rolled her eyes and thwacked a hand against his chest. Even still, he caught her small grin. "You're insufferable. Save your ego for the stage, sweetheart. You'll be performing tonight at nine in Berkeley."

"And you'll be waiting here in the bus where it's nice and safe, right?" Kieran urged. Whoever wanted him dead wouldn't turn tail because a few cronies bit it.

Liz crossed her arms over her chest and lifted a brow. "Yeah, try and keep me in a box. See how well that goes for you. Not only do I know how to pick locks, but none of your juju works on me either. I'll be there at the show doing my job, like the rest of you."

"Hurry up, kids," Jett called from the door.

How he surpassed all of them blew Kieran's mind, but the man slunk around like no one's business. Heaving a sigh, Kieran stood from his comfy slouch beside Liz and made his way to the door. Normal nights he might sing his heart out on the stage, riding the waves of the coital energy going on all around him and maybe even taking a couple of samples home for the ride. However, tonight, his sole focus would be on Liz, because if any asshole fae paid him a visit, she'd be the most vulnerable.

And Kieran of all people knew how much monsters liked exploiting his weak spots.

Chapter Three

Liz shut and locked the bathroom door for a little privacy while she dressed for the show. Not like she applied anything too fancy, the average wingtip liner, a hint of dark shadow, and one of her dozens of lipstains. However, she lingered in here longer due to the residual jitters from last night's attack. One moment the bartender had been standing there flirting with her, and the next he became a pile of sizzling flesh on the floor.

She squeezed the porcelain sink in front of her, relieved for the alone time even if it only lasted a couple of minutes. Not like she didn't trust the boys—she did. However, no one got to see her vulnerable. Coolness seeped into her palms as she stared into the mirror.

She was a human in this fae world where she didn't belong. Not even human. With the way she saw past glamour and the occasional times she would hear buzzing, how it grew to a roar in her mind any time a foreign fae emerged—she was a grade A freak.

At one of her first homes, she'd screamed herself hoarse over the bone-thin creature that watched outside her window, the one with eyes like the moon. Within the week, she'd been back in the system, starting a trend, until she wised up enough to keep her mouth shut. She had to pretend she didn't hear the banshee's wail at night or see the minotaurs lumbering along amongst the normals. Pretend they didn't notice her in turn.

Liz pulled out the tube of Ruby Red to wear tonight and redid the lines before sucking in a deep breath. Even though those fae last night had shaken her, she was better off with the boys than wandering from town to town by her lonesome. Still, Kieran's bossier than thou demands for her to stay back in the bus tempted her. The Pay Per View porn sessions that were Discord's Desire shows left her frustrated, and ever since she'd joined, she'd been on a dry spell.

Last time she indulged in the sexual energy of their shows was on the fateful night she'd hooked up with Jett and joined them on the road. Today she'd dressed up a bit more than normal with torn fishnets, a pleated black skirt, and a silver tank top. Her trusty Doc Martens came to her knees, and she was ready to mingle. Maybe even ready to brave the audience for once. Besides, the safest place for her would be blending into the crowd. If someone came after Kieran, they'd search backstage first, not plunge straight into the horde of humans.

She slapped the porcelain sink before spinning around to unlock the door. Bright smile and a stage face. The boys weren't the only ones who could put on a performance.

When she stepped out the door, a low wolf whistle greeted her. Kieran, of course.

Where the other guys lost interest, returning to their casual flings after shows, his increased. To top it off, the steady stream of women he used to bring to the RV died down over the past month to the point where he siphoned sexual energy from onstage alone. However, passion wasn't the sole way incubi got their energy. He'd been fighting more than ever, picking them on purpose.

His wicked eyes gleamed with his grin as he scanned her up and down. "Do all that dolling up for me?" Kieran leaned against the booth beside their kitchenette.

Liz rolled her eyes, fighting hard to restrain her smile. Even though the logical part of her brain declared him off limits, one look at his teasing gaze turned her knees to jelly, and his flirting was *fun*. However, Kieran played for keeps until he got what he wanted, which in this case was her. If she were being honest, the thought sent a secret thrill through her, but she knew better than to get involved with an incubus.

"You wish this was for you," she sassed, unable to hide her smirk as she swung her hips back and forth while walking past him. She found a stretch of the black-tiled kitchen counter she liked and leaned. "I'm infiltrating the audience tonight."

"Smart," Jett agreed, tweaking the strands of his hair to make sure they were pin perfect for the show. He swerved past her to plop onto the red vinyl couch across from the kitchen. "Mingling with the crowd will keep you from becoming a target."

"Not if you're sucking face with some jackass," Kieran drawled. Even though the way he draped his arms across the length of the booth appeared nonchalant, his tone sharpened the slightest bit, and those eyes honed in on her.

"Well, lucky for me, my hook-ups aren't your problem," she shot back, her temper flaring at his assumption. "If I want to go out and suck face with a random, that's my call to make." Her gaze heated as his sparked like flame in response. If the pigheaded ass thought being part of his posse meant he could dictate her love life, he had another thing coming.

"She's right, you know." Trevor nudged Kieran in the side as he dropped beside him on the booth. "We do our own fair share of dipping into the pool. If we're allowed to then so is she."

Kieran balled his hands into fists as he turned to look at Trevor. "Did you happen to notice our kind take a keener than average interest in her? What happens when she's distracted and one of those creatures attacks? She'll be too far away to protect if we're on stage."

Liz waved her hand in front of his face. "Yeah, I'm right here. Guess what? They're after you, not me. So if anything, the other guys should be keeping tight focus on you for when the next beasties decide to pay you a visit." Even though her temper flared, Liz excelled at control. Unlike her, Kieran blazed, his emotions raging clear as day on his face. The man broadcasted such raw honesty he made the worst poker player out of the lot.

Before he said something they'd both regret, she jumped in again. "Look, I'm rolling on pure logic with this one. I'm not part of the band, and I know how to lose myself in a crowd better than most."

Renn popped up from the back of the RV while struggling to clip a dog collar around his neck. "Besides, we'll have the best view in the house keeping an eye on her from stage."

Trevor sat beside Kieran, watching him with an unreadable expression. She'd have to drill him later to figure out what the hell percolated in their frontman's brain.

Kieran heaved a sigh. "Guys, I'm sorry," he apologized. As fast as the temper arrived, it slipped away again. "I don't like my problems bringing danger on you all." Even as he spoke to the room, his eyes locked on her. That's how he always was, a bundle of emotions more raw and real than she ever hoped to possess, and seconds after the storm passed, he'd be the same charming, magnetic person as usual.

Trevor clapped a hand on his shoulder. "All the more reason to figure out who's wanting you dead. Don't sweat it, though. We all have our baggage."

"Amen to that," Liz agreed out loud, leaning against the table. "Now how about we head to this gig and you lot dazzle an audience?"

"Speaking my language." Jett wove past her, casting a wink in her direction as he made his way to the front of the bus. Even with shared tempers, sex addictions that would make normal rockstars look like prudes, and a view of humans veering toward callous at times, she'd come to trust the boys of Discord's Desire more than anyone in her life. Not like she had a breathtaking number of options for stability during her foster home hops and city jumps.

Renn followed Jett's lead, sauntering off to the front of the RV. Trevor gave Liz a nod on the way out, perfect Southern gentleman he was. Kieran hauled himself off the booth seats with a creak and gestured for her to go first.

Liz shook her head, crossing her arms in front of her chest. "I'll lock up behind us and then make my way to the normal kids' entrance." No matter how Kieran might protest, she stood knee deep in cement on this.

"Hope you enjoy the show then, darling." Heat flickered in his amber eyes, and his lowered voice made the implication quite clear. A shiver rolled down her spine, but as always she didn't betray those impulses.

"Give 'em hell, rockstar." She reached up to squeeze his shoulder. The warmth from his body emanated at the touch, and her mind traveled to the same places those wicked eyes of his did. Together, they wove their way down the aisle toward the doors. If Kieran was a normal, complication-free guy, she'd be on him in a heartbeat, but as it stood, the man camped in dangerous territory. And Liz spent her entire life running from danger—with the unique abilities she'd been born with, her survival required it.

****

She'd booked a gig in Berkeley at a college bar with a large hardwood stage and even larger viewing space for university students to flood in. Discord's Desire, while not being radio-replay material, happened to have garnered quite a name for themselves for how rowdy their live shows got. Half the time they spent on the road involved taking down their videos from YouTube since they'd alert way too much attention and get blocked from venues if folks saw what went on behind the scenes. Trevor's paranoid behavior combined with his knack for hacking meant he deleted video streams the second they entered his radar.

Still, with an underground reputation for orgies, college kids flocked to the shows looking for a good time. She walked through the swinging glass doors and showed the ID she'd clipped to her skirt—being their manager offered some perks after all.

The lights dimmed in the place, and folks bustled around her. Most were the PBR-swilling sort, while a couple of punk rock kids filtered in. A few guys along the way stopped, stared, and offered her a shit-eating grin, but after living around the guys in Discord's Desire, her standards had gone way the hell up. Starlit spotlights cascaded over the darkened room, highlighting the near hundred people crammed into this place, whether they roamed on the base floors or walked to the balcony on the second. Faint buzzing intensified in her mind as she found one of the few open stools by the bar. Liz plunked down on the worn vinyl and glanced to the bartender.

A surly guy packing more muscle than Arnold Schwarzenegger in his heyday stood behind the bar, a couple of scars marking his arms. Girth didn't intimate her, but once she got a glimpse of him, the buzzing increased to a roar, warning her away. His golden eyes flashed as he locked gazes with her. Everything about his features from his nose to his teeth appeared sharper than average, and his inhuman stare sealed the deal.

"What can I get for you, sweetheart?" he asked, his voice low and gruff. She didn't let her surprise betray her, even as fear trickled like ice down her spine.

"Glass of JD, neat," she said with a saccharine sweet smile. Years ago, Liz graduated from the pisswater beer the average venue served, and she attended enough shows to know she needed to stick to the corners to enjoy herself. The bartender's gaze lingered, but she kept her mask firm in place. The second a fae or supernatural creature knew you sensed it, you became enemy number one.

"Hefty drink for a small thing like yourself," he remarked while pouring her a glass of the amber liquid.

"I don't do anything in half measures." She kept her focus on the stage and her voice nonchalant, even though her skin prickled at this foreign fae so close to her vicinity. Sure, he might just happen to work at this bar, but the incursion last night sent her paranoia into overdrive. The place reeked of B.O. and Drakkar Noir, and the boys hadn't even stepped onstage yet. That's when the sexcapades began.

Liz accepted the drink from the bartender and took a sip. Even though her gaze slid in his direction, she kept it furtive, as she didn't want to draw attention to herself. The sweet Jack Daniels slid down her throat, sending a shudder of relief through her for one moment. One guy with a septum piercing and popped collar slid into the seat beside her. She leaned against the bar with her back turned to the bartender to remove the temptation of staring. Her back prickled at her vulnerable position— however, if the fae tried any mojo on her, his whammy wouldn't work. Newcomer kept giving her a glance as he ordered horse-swill from the bartender in the form of Coors Light.

"What's a pretty thing like you doing at a show

like this?" he said, leaning on the stool and palming the beer the bartender passed him.

Liz pursed her lips, debating what response would send him flying away the fastest. "Oh, there's a show going on? I had no idea." Her dry tone reached desert depths, but dumbass blinked and nodded at her.

"Yeah, did you miss all the signs?" At this point he'd pivoted his body in her direction. Despite the offers and interest on the table from the crowd so far, her nerves jangled at high speed after meeting the not-so-human bartender, and the specimens weren't top notch. After the thrill of flirting with Kieran day in and out, most guys didn't stack up to his level of wit and sexiness.

"Must've walked straight past 'em," she kept her voice deadpan, staring into her Jack Daniels to keep the look of annoyance off her face. Three more seconds of interacting with boy genius here would have her ready to bash her head against the wall.

To her relief, the lights dimmed even more, and the spotlights circled to the front and center stage, casting a hush through the crowd. A smile curled her lips once Kieran's sultry voice came over the speakers, the effects dropping like a pheromone bomb onto the audience. A visible ripple didn't cascade through the air, but once his voice reached a familiar intensity and the rest of the band began playing, a huge scream resounded through the crowd.

Even without the incubus abilities at work, she had to admit, the man possessed a toe-curlingly sexy voice. As she scanned over the crowd, the beginnings of the orgy broke out, where strangers locked lips and deepened their kisses. A pair in front of her started getting handsy, and all of a sudden shirts were coming off. They weren't even finished the first song, and the scent of sex laced through the room.

Liz let out a sigh. This was why she stayed backstage during the shows. Her glamour-resistance turned her into the one sober person at this lust inspired rager. Her dry spell would have to continue for now since she refused to hook up with the tool next to her and didn't mainline the swell of sexuality like everyone else. Plus, with Mr. Fae Bartender behind her, she needed to act with extra caution. Bolting from fae sent the same message as a red flag to a bull—pretty please, come chase me.

On stage, Trevor thrummed away at the guitar, his fingers plucking over the strings with the skillful focus he always employed. He leaned up to the mic in front of him to add in the background vocals, the sensual tenor blending with Ky's baritone. Renn's hair flew as he thrashed away at the drums, his hands moving lightning fast and his hooves tapping the pedals. Meanwhile Jett romanced the length of his bass, providing the deep undercurrent the siren always did as those notes came out soul-wrenching.

Kieran's voice reached a crescendo, drawing her attention front and forward. Normally when he sang, his gaze cast far and wide over the audience, as if he were romancing the crowd as a whole, but tonight, his eyes were locked on one person alone. She tried to swallow, but her throat grew dry.

Long strands of his dark hair drifted across his eyes as he clutched the microphone and rocked back and forth with it, the intensity projecting in his voice. He'd tossed his patched leather to the floor, stripped to a black wifebeater that clung to him like a second skin and revealed the intricate phoenix tattoo coiling down his arm. His hips shifted while he moved to the beat of the music, his grey jeans clinging to those powerful thighs. Yet nothing snared her as much as his amber eyes focused straight on her the entire time.

Heat flushed through her at his undivided attention, and while she'd like to blame it on all the bump and grind going on around her, Kieran got her hot and bothered. However, she wasn't one to sit back and melt. Liz met his eyes and winked with a smirk. She caught the hint of a smile by the crinkle in his eyes as he crooned away.

When he finished the song, half of the crowd screamed, while the other half tangled themselves with whatever warm body stood the closest. A couple of scantily clad girls tried to climb onto the stage, and Renn humored them with a wink and mouthed 'later.'

As they launched into another song, the guy beside her mashed face with a girl whose method of approach included fondling his balls. Liz heaved out a sigh as the band played a faster paced song, one of the fan favorite ones. She tapped her foot against the side of the stool to the beat of the music, taking another sip from her glass of JD in the process.

"Not going to join the rest of them?" a gruff voice came from behind her.

Liz almost jumped out of her seat in surprise, but keeping her composure, she instead slid around to face the bartender. Ice washed over her in a rude awakening. She'd gotten distracted by the way Kieran performed on stage and had forgotten about the not-human bartender standing behind her.

The man's gold eyes scanned her over with an overabundance of curiosity. "Ballsy for one of your kind to show up at a show frontlined by mine."

Her blood froze at the knowing in his eyes. She should run. She should run far and fast away from here. Should've bolted the second the literal warning bell in her mind buzzed away. Yet she stood there, unable to move, her nails biting into her palms, because he *knew*. To so many fae she'd been a curiosity, the butterfly whose multi-hued wings they wanted to pluck. Not him—he'd said her kind, like he'd run into them before.

Liz's throat squeezed tight, and to her surprise, her eyes burned. "What do you mean?" she asked, her voice coming out at almost a whisper. Hope twisted in her chest, thrashed in the cage where she'd stuffed it after years of waiting for an explanation to arrive. Of waiting for her parents to walk through the doors of St. Catherine's and claim her.

The bartender's thick brows lifted as he settled against the bar and crossed his arms. Fear flashed across his expression. "I'm not the only one in this place, and the others won't hesitate to kill. Scram, before I make a call you won't like."

Fear flushed through the brief second of exhilaration, scouring her system clean. Survival took over. "I'm done with my drink anyway." She finished off her glass of whisky, setting it onto the counter with a clink. Her skin prickled. The bartender made his threat clear—if she lingered, he'd bring down trouble she couldn't defend against. Time to lose herself in the crowd, and fast.

She felt the burn of his gaze as she plunged into the audience. Liz waded through the outskirts of the crowd, avoiding the thick of what devolved into an orgy. Her heart sped, a thump, thump, thump reverberating in her ears. Sweat rolled off of the half naked bodies she passed. Liz swerved to the side to avoid running into a pair of breasts that got a chance to breathe and the schlong another guy whipped out right in the middle of the arena. Onstage, the boys soaked in the sexual energy to feed.

Liz cast a glance to the bartender, but being short

had its drawbacks. Half of her wanted to damn the consequences, aim her Beretta straight to his skull, and demand the answers she longed for. But if other fae mingled through the crowd, she might not be the only one at risk.

The room exploded with heat from all the bodies pressed so close together, and already, sweat pricked her forehead. This swell of people made her goal for the backstage door even harder, and every elbow jab launched her paranoia into overdrive. Old Spice warred with Drakkar Noir as she waded her way through, trying to not choke on all the sweat-soaked perfumes.

The boys switched to a slower song by the time she waded past the crowd and reached the narrow side steps leading to the back. A big bouncer with thick-rimmed glasses stood in front of the door with his arms crossed and a scowl on his face. She waved at him.

"I'm the booking manager," she said, nodding toward the door.

He rolled his eyes. "And I'm the president. Nice try, sweetheart." Caught in the haze of the music, he eye-banged her with a lust-filled gaze. Oh hell no.

Liz clenched her jaw and lifted her chin. "Excuse me? If you think I'm some slobbering groupie, you've got another thing coming. Let me the fuck back there." She unclipped her badge and flashed it his way.

He shrugged and moved a few paces away from the door. As she stepped past him, his meaty hand inched in her direction. She was not in the mood for that bullshit, not now, not ever. Liz whirled around, grabbed his wrist, and yanked, hard. He let out a howl of pain as she dropped it and made her way up the stairs to the backstage. Of all the things she wanted to deal with tonight, mindless hornballs were the lowest on her list. The groupie assumption capped off her irritation too. If she got a nickel for every time someone made the mistake, she could open her own Five and Dime.

Their music pounded through the place, reverberating even here. The black bricked walls soaked in shadows, and dim bulbs hanging from the ceiling did little to shed more light. When she reached the landing where the boys stored their backup equipment, she stopped dead in her tracks.

Huge white letters had been spray-painted across the wall.

'Pars Virilis, Ace.'

Chapter Four

Whatever mojo Kieran filled up on throughout the night fast deflated once he stepped backstage. The scrawled note pierced straight into his heart like an arrow. Only one person called him Ace, and Pars Virilis had been repeated so often in his house he wanted to hurl.

Liz sat underneath it, a grim expression on her face and her Beretta in hand.

Despite the clear message delivered on the wall, he let out a sigh of relief as his sweaty palm pressed against the cold bricks. "So this is where you ran off to." He sidled beside her and slid to the ground.

"Luckily didn't cross paths with that fucker," Liz said, pointing to the graffiti above. "Don't think he would've been in a share and care mood."

A few girlish giggles sounded from the stage as the guys all filtered in. Along with them came three different gals of the highlighted blonde hair and stripper pumps variety, their falsies flickering and manicured nails latching onto offered arms. Kieran hadn't bothered, even though a couple of sorority girls made their way onstage after the set and tried to give him a TSA-level pat down. His brain wasn't skating anywhere near a fuel-up though, not after Liz disappeared from his sight in the crowd. He'd been performing on autopilot ever since.

Jett whisked his lady out the back door, while the other two stopped in their tracks.

Trevor squinted as he stared at the graffiti. "More shit from your secret admirer?" he asked, his voice lowering. The girl beside him tugged at his shirt and wiggled her hips, annoyed at the hold up. Trev didn't pay her any mind as seriousness emanated from him, the concern that made him such a valuable friend.

"Apparently. They made it to the show tonight but either didn't bother sticking around or are waiting to give me one hell of a surprise." Kieran's voice remained dry as his hands balled into fists by his side.

"Want me to stick around?" Renn asked, even though his arm looped around the sorority girl's waist.

"Nah, it's fine. Liz will keep me company, right?" He winked at her.

"That's what you hired me for. Eternal babysitter." She heaved a dramatic sigh and flounced her arms by her sides. Renn nodded in their direction before peace-ing out the door to get down to the nasty with his new flavor of the night.

"Are we going to head out?" the girl beside Trevor asked, her voice high and grating.

Trevor gave him a sideway glance. "Ace, eh? That a longstanding nickname?"

Kieran leveled him with a murderous look. "Not if you want your balls to remain attached."

"Touchy, touchy," Trevor said with a laugh as he swaggered out of the backstage, his girl in tow. Normal night, Kieran would've been with them, walking out with his pick from the audience as he replenished his energy. After the shake-up backstage and seeing his brother's note though, he wasn't feeling it. Though in pure honesty, he hadn't been feeling it ever since Liz came on tour with them. Ever since she strolled into their lives, the idea of other women turned him off, like artificial light when he wanted the sun.

"Want to head on back?" he asked as he pushed himself off the ground.

"If that's a sly attempt to get me into your bed, try harder, babe." Liz smirked, hopping to her feet.

"Oh, so there is hope." He grinned, his fangs brushing against his lower lip as he extended his arm.

She shook her head and looped her own through his. "Get a grip, lover boy."

"I'm told I have a pretty firm one," he retorted. Her skin against his felt like velvet seduction at its finest, and even the slight contact sent a pulse of excitement traveling straight down. The woman kept her cool at the toughest of times. She never missed a beat in their banter and rarely lost her logic, unlike Kieran, who'd been rolling on gut impulses and explosive emotion from the tender age of always.

As they stepped out of the backdoor, the crisp night breezes brought the scent of cigarette smoke and the salt-soaked air from the rolling tides along the horizon. A broad expanse of stars fought to glow against the purplish clouds congregating in the sky. They walked across the parking lot together, heading for the RV for once, rather than the nearest watering hole.

"Haven't heard the nickname in some time," Kieran muttered while they walked. It had been long ago from the bastards who'd left him behind.

"Part of your oh-so-mysterious past?" Liz teased. She nudged him in the side with her elbow as they walked along the lined concrete. "Care to explain the Latin-ish scrawl?"

"Duty to the family," Kieran said, running his fingers through his hair. "Which is bullshit, because my folks disowned me, which meant Larsen cut me out too. I don't know why they'd give a damn about me aligning to our Court after that."

"Aligning?" Liz asked, leaning against him while they walked.

"Seelie or Unseelie—growth or decay. Once you're of age, you're supposed to pledge yourself to the side you were born into and participate in the Courts. My folks were high on the food chain too, so they drilled those expectations home. Except the choice can't be coerced, and me and the guys remained unaligned. Once you've committed, you're stuck doing the bidding of the Seelie or Unseelie ruler, another chess piece on their table." He stopped with her in front of the RV. From inside, a woman's screams of ecstasy echoed throughout the place. Kieran gave her the side eye. "Might be better to stay out here for a little bit."

"Yeah, don't feel like shouting over Susie in there," Liz said before dropping to the concrete in front of the entrance. Kieran slipped down with her, disappointed she'd moved away from him. She leaned forward, wrapping her arms around her knees and pulling them tight.

"Cold?" he asked.

"I can manage," came her pert reply.

Kieran shook his head, slipping off his leather and placing it around her shoulders. "Quit being so stubborn."

"You're one to talk, rockstar," she said. Even still, she tugged his leather around her tight to his satisfaction. "So, let me guess, your family aligned with Team Bad Guy, right?"

"Not in the slightest. I come from a long lineage of Seelie incubi and succubi. And let me tell you, they're the stuffiest motherfuckers you ever did meet." He sprawled his legs out in front of him and fanned the fabric of his shirt, which stuck to his chest from sweat.

"So, what, is all this dramatic bullshit a result of your brother being unable to pick up the phone and make a call?" Liz joked, nudging his leg with her boot.

Kieran snorted. "Sadly, that sounds too much like them." He stared at the sky before them, memories floating in like the lavender clouds crowding the moon. His throat dried, causing him to swallow. He didn't want to remember the cries of the humans they'd kept in closets to feed from or the balls they'd dragged him to as a kid where he watched the true monsters hide behind masks of politeness. Years might make the memories easier to avoid, but every time he recalled the disappointment in their eyes, the phrase 'failure of the family' sliced into him fresh.

Until he'd formed Discord's Desire, he hadn't understood what being part of a real family meant. Where people gave a shit about what happened to you, not what you meant to their social currency. The guys had provided the home he'd never known.

She nudged at him with her boot again. "No getting all gloomy on me. The nickname narrows it down, so we'll hit up your brother and tell him to back the fuck off. Case closed."

A bitter smile hit his lips. "My brother will deny any accusations. My kind are talented at twisting the truth. Unless we caught him in the act with solid proof, the Courts wouldn't lift a finger. Not much different from your human law enforcement." He leaned his head against the side of the RV and stared up.

"Not my human anything," she murmured, staring at her hands. The sadness in her voice, a brief gasp of vulnerability she didn't share with any of them snared him at once. "I'm not human, I'm not fae, and my own kind—whoever they may be, haven't come to claim me." Even though bitterness edged her tone, he caught the sheer agony beneath those words and understood how it felt to always be on the outside.

"You belong here, with us," he said, his voice deepening with his conviction. Her hazel eyes softened for a moment as she looked at him, and for a moment he saw the Liz O'Brien residing behind all the snarky comments.

A loud scream from the woman inside resounded from the RV, shattering the moment between them. Liz glanced in the direction and rolled her eyes. Sure, he could've used more of an injection than the set they'd played tonight, but with the number of gigs Liz lined up for them, he didn't need to worry about going hungry any time soon. Besides, he'd rather be here beside her than off with some random broad. When he'd gotten tired of the changing faces was beyond him, but he didn't want that any more. Not when he lived with a beautiful girl whose mere presence never failed to put a smile on his face.

Leaning closer, Kieran slipped an arm around her shoulder.

She twitched in surprise at the contact. Arching an eyebrow, she met his gaze. "Slick, sweetheart, but that doesn't mean I'm slipping into the sack with you."

He heaved a sigh, ready to move his arm away as he gave her a reluctant smile. "Chill, babe. The RV's pretty occupied right now anyway." Not like he'd ever turn down a night with her, but after their talk, he simply reveled in the nearness right now.

Liz pursed her lips before grabbing his arm and scooting in tighter to him. "Fine, but only because I'm cold."

Kieran rolled his eyes. He'd take whatever excuse if it meant he got to sit there with her in his arms. She leaned in, and he pulled her tighter against him, enjoying how her body curved against his. The scent of her mint bodywash wafted his way, beyond delicious. Despite the way she curled against him, the woman remained a contradictory enigma. One moment, she'd be flirting with him, and he'd catch the spark in her eyes, feel the air shift at her arousal—an incubus could always tell. Yet a second later, she'd pull back and retreat, as if she'd stepped past a boundary line he wasn't aware of.

Right now, he'd bask in the quiet chance he'd been given.

Even though his mind reeled with memories of his family, with concerns for future shows due to the renewed interest from Larsen, and with the burning question of why, he gave up trying to figure it out. Genuine serenity didn't visit often, and he wouldn't waste it. So instead, he lost himself in the soft glow of the silver stars, of her gentle, brisk aroma, and the heat of her body curled against his.

****

Liz had passed out hours ago, but Kieran couldn't sleep. He sat at the half rectangle they called a kitchen table and scribbled lyrics on a pad of paper. After about ten attempts with most of the words scratched out, he placed the pen down.

"Care to discuss the street art left on the wall backstage, brother?" Trevor asked as he loped into the room. The man hadn't bothered to put his shirt on, wearing a pair of sweats as he snagged a folding chair and took a seat. The girls had taken leave awhile ago, so only the loud resonant sound of Renn's snoring remained.

"Narrowed it down to the dear old fam." Kieran shrugged, drawing a swirling doodle onto his notepad while they talked. "But you know how difficult they'll be to pin down. We need to find a way to trace it to my brother, not just some nickname."

"Wouldn't hold up in the slightest." Trevor nodded. The banshee would get it—he had his own battered past of dealing with the Seelie court, one that left him avoiding their kind at all cost. "We'll have to do some sleuthing on our own."

"Joy. Family reunion's the last thing I want." Kieran kicked out at the table leg, jostling the pen on the table. "Last I heard they were on the East Coast, so no chance of us running into my folks at least."

"With that out of the way, let's have some real talk now." Trevor turned to face him, those dark, wise eyes honing his way with laser precision.

Kieran quirked a brow but didn't say anything, waiting for his friend to continue.

"Though you might think we've been a mite unaware, we've all noticed. What's the deal with your current vow of chastity?"

Goddamn. Not like what he did wasn't clear as day, but he wanted to avoid this conversation. "Haven't been feeling the whole dine and dash thing lately." He shrugged, hoping Trev would drop it. Yeah right.

"Sure it doesn't have anything to do with a certain booking manager who's been touring with us?" Trevor couldn't contain his wan smile, the bastard.

Kieran restrained the urge to punch the smug grin right off his friend's face. "You'll just call me on it if I try to bullshit." He shrugged, going the honesty route. When it came to owning who he was and what he felt, Kieran rarely stuttered. "Yeah, she's stunning, but I don't think she'll be catching feelings any time soon."

"Good," Trevor replied as he leaned against the wall.

Kieran's brows knitted together at the bluntness in his friend's tone. "And what the fuck is that supposed to mean?"

"It means the lot of us have a shit track record with women, and she's been a great addition to our group. No need to muddy the waters by trying to pursue something that won't last. And she needs us. She's an anomaly amongst her own kind and in danger around ours. Be level with me, Ky. Do you think a human can keep up with your sex drive?"

Though his friend preached all sorts of logic, Trevor's words burned into his skin like a brand. Their shit track record was legendary, so why would she waste her time with someone like him, someone who his family couldn't even be bothered to keep?

"Nice to know you think so highly of me," Kieran spat back, unable to keep the venom from his voice.

"You know it's not that, Ky." Trevor clung to his irritating calm, making Kieran want to clock him in the face so much more. Though Trev meant well, he didn't need the reminder of all the complications that arose between a human and a fae. He didn't need the reminder he was sentenced to a lifetime alone, hooking up with a different girl every night to keep from turning into a husk.

"Yeah, yeah, looking out for the both of us." Kieran hopped up from his seat and snagged his notepad. Good intentions or no, he didn't want another lecture, so Trevor could keep his opinions to himself tonight. "See you in the morning." He didn't bother looking back as he walked toward his bunk at the end of the RV. Trevor would want to continue talking, and with the way his blood boiled right now, he'd be more liable to start a knock-down-drag-out brawl than have a reasonable conversation.

He hoisted himself into the top bunk—Trev would crawl into the bottom one whenever he saw fit. Even though he lay there in the darkness with his hands behind his head, sleep would be a long ways away tonight. His blood burned, his thoughts tangled into knots, and the resurgence of his family left a sour taste on his tongue. To top it all off, he couldn't get Liz off his mind, even though Trevor had been right—he should.

Yet tonight hadn't been enough, curled side by side with her. Yearning flowed through his veins like an addiction, and the more he contemplated quitting her, the more he wanted to pursue.

Failure to the family, that's what he brought to the table. A mid-tier band that satisfied his needs, a list of women he'd slept with longer than he ever wanted to count, and now his presence endangered those he cared about. Liz was a smart woman. She'd never in a million years fall for someone like him

.

Chapter Five

The hills of San Francisco loomed in the distance, accented by the fog rolling through. The tall skyscrapers of the city paled in comparison to the mark of the Golden Gate Bridge along the water, the peaks of the bridge casting sloping shadows across the highway. Asphalt zoomed by from the window. Jett drove today, so he maxed the RV speeds and raced as fast as possible down the speedway.

She stood by the coffeemaker, willing it to percolate faster. The liquid nectar plunked into the carafe at the slowest possible pace. Snores filtered from the back bunks, but mid-morning sun streamed through the windows with an agenda.

Another show tonight, and yet with Kieran's not-so-secret admirer sending cronies their way, the normal anticipation soured, turning to anxiousness. Her skin prickled as she took a seat, continuing to glare at the coffeemaker while it chugged along.

The memories of how she'd spent last night sitting with Kieran and watching the stars coursed through her, a contradiction to every logical thought warning her away from him. Instead of his normal blunt flirtatiousness, he'd been open and vulnerable as they'd talked over his family drama. And holy hell, the heady scent of sweat and spice emanating from him had been enough to send her pheromones into overdrive. The man didn't need any incubus abilities to rev her engine.

The coffeemaker spat out its last hateful drop as it finished brewing. Liz rolled up from her perch the same moment Kieran entered the room. They both stopped where they stood as a tense silence descended between them. Heat flashed in his amber eyes as he scanned her over, even though she slummed it in polka-dot pajama shorts, a battered tank top, and an off-center ponytail.

"Coffee up for grabs?" he asked, to her surprise. She'd grown so used to his flirty comments that the normalcy jarred her after his scorching look.

"Yeah, help yourself." She lifted the pot after pouring herself a cup. Steam rolled from the piping liquid. When she'd left for bed last night, he'd been calm and at peace despite the shakeup. Yet now, he brimmed with tension, and based on the circles under his eyes, he hadn't gotten much shuteye.

"Looks like you need it bad this morning," she commented. "Rough night?"

He stared into the chipped porcelain mug of coffee for a moment before responding. "You could say that."

A yawn pierced the air as Trevor ambled in, lifting his arms over his head in a slow stretch. Kieran shot him a dark look upon approach, one Liz didn't miss.

"Still grumpy?" Trevor asked, settling into a hunch at the red vinyl couch across from her.

Kieran grabbed his mug in one hand as he saluted with the other. "I'm going up front to get some air." Within moments, he stomped his way to the front of the RV.

Well, now she needed to know what happened. "Lover's quarrel?" she asked before blowing the steam off the surface of her coffee.

Trevor ran a hand through his chin-length silver strands and heaved a sigh. "You know how it goes any time you tell Kieran what to do."

Liz snorted before she stopped herself. Kieran proved as predictable as anything in that regard. The most surefire way to get him to do what you wanted was to suggest the opposite. The boy hated following orders on principle.

"He's got a lot brewing around right now. Do yourself a favor and keep your distance," he recommended, passing her a knowing look. Apart from the murmur of conversation in the front of the RV, quiet reigned here. The topic of their fight grew crystal clear.

Liz gave a slow nod in response before forcing a half-smile. "Trust me, I don't do drama. You've got nothing to worry about." She gripped her mug a little tighter, the heat from the piping hot coffee soaking into her palms.

Even as she said it, her stomach flip-flopped. Not like she didn't want to get tangled with a certain incubus, but 'want' and 'should' were two very separate things. She'd wanted someone—anyone—to acknowledge she wasn't crazy. That the mermaids lurking in the depths of the Mississippi were real. However, she learned to keep her mouth shut if she wanted a home. Foster kids who couldn't play the game got tossed into the spin cycle of a system, and she sure as hell hadn't wanted to return to St. Catherine's.

Liz lifted her mug of coffee to her lips, sipping the robust brew. She had the self-control, but Kieran was impulsive, hotheaded, and downright irresistible when he wanted to be. If he leveled his full attention her way, all the ironclad determination in the world wouldn't hold out against his storm.

The RV came to a halt with a shudder, startling Liz out of her contemplation.

"Why the sudden stop?" Renn called from the far back in the bunks. The man half hung out of the top bunk, his hairier than average leg dangling off the side. As he slipped off, his tendency to sleep in the nude sent Trevor's eyes rolling. Liz had stopped being phased by most things around this crew.

"Cover your shit up, Renn. No one wants to see it," Trevor called to him before pouring himself a cup of coffee.

"I can think of plenty who've taken an interest." Renn waggled his brows as he grinned, making his way over to his trunk of clothes. Trevor's focus returned to his overfull cup.

Liz chugged the remainder in her mug and hopped up to see what Jett messed around with, since he'd stopped drag racing them down the highway. As she made her way to the front of the bus, Kieran stalked back, passing her. He didn't look at her once while they brushed by each other, a storm cloud brewing around him. Liz gritted her teeth. Of course he'd make things as awkward as possible between them rather than slipping on his big boy panties and playing nice. She marched her way up to see Jett.

"Why're we stopping early, sweet pea?" Liz asked, leaning against the driver's seat. The worn leather crinkled as she leaned into it, warm from Jett sitting in the spot while he drove for the past hours and from the sun beaming in through the rolled-down windows. He'd cranked the music up, acid jazz no one else listened to.

"Kieran and I are making a quick stop. We're paying a friend a visit." The wicked gleam in Jett's eyes implied the person they'd be visiting was not just a woman but one he'd known or wanted to know carnally. Not like him sleeping around shocked anyone.

Liz folded her arms across her chest. "Let me guess—you're tracking intel on Ky's big brother. And you thought you'd head there without me?"

"Isn't it best for you to stay incognito in our territory? You didn't want to draw any unnecessary attention to your abilities." Jett shut off the RV and turned to face her.

She let out a sigh. He was right, except by working for the boys she'd placed herself in their world—not like she'd ever been able to escape it. "What I want isn't going to stop Ky's brother from making me a target if he figures out I'm the one human in the bunch, and an oddity at that. So right now, my survival needs include getting this mess tied up as quick as possible. Besides, the bartender at the last gig knew about the fae who spray-painted the message, and more than that, he acted like he knew *what* I was."

Jett's gaze sharpened as he swiveled around to face her. "What bartender?"

Liz winked. "You were too busy plowing whatever treasure you plundered from the audience to have this chat. The fae bartender called me ballsy for one of my kind to make a public appearance around your kind. If others know what I am, Ky might not be the only one bringing trouble to the band."

"You think he's the one who left the message on the wall?" Jett asked, resting his palms on his knees as he looked at her. "Shit, Lizzie, did he tell you what he meant by 'your kind?'"

Liz shook her head. "I asked—but he threatened me to scram before I could get answers. He worked back there before you guys went on set, and I lingered by the bar the entire time." She heaved a sigh and cast a glance to the far side of the RV. "So let me join you. I don't like being on the outs while fae are slinking around your shows."

Jett met her eyes and nodded.

Though, she didn't need to question if Jett would let her join—after all, they'd become partners in crime and fast. Kieran might put up a stink, but if he kept mouthing off like an idiot, he could go shove it.

Jett reached out and smacked her ass. "Go get ready. We're heading out in a few."

She rolled her eyes as she made sure to walk real slowly down the aisle, swinging her hips side to side. "Calm your tits, sweetheart."

Trevor and Kieran both sat in the kitchen working on their mugs of coffee and not talking to each other, drama that better solve itself fast before it infected the rest of the band. Renn walked out, a fresh pair of baggy cargoes on and a tight tee defining his abs all too well. Liz gave him a lazy salute as she made her way to her cot in the back and rummaged under for fresh clothes. They were going to need to hit a laundromat soon.

Reaching under into her suitcase, she tugged out a couple of non-crinkled items—her light green leggings and a brown tee reaching mid-thigh. It'd have to do. She slipped on her clothes and cinched a thick black belt around her waist to add some flair to the ensemble. After tossing her combat boots on, she stretched her arms over her head and walked out to join the rest of the gang.

Jett joined them at the table, and the twelve-cup coffeemaker that had been full mere minutes ago emptied out.

"Ready steady, babe?" Jett asked, looking up as she entered.

Kieran tilted his head to the side. "Thought you and I were going, Jett?"

Jett shrugged. "Nancy Drew here wanted a spin at things, since she's dealing with strange fae cropping up at our gigs." He gave her a pointed look, the 'you should have told us' payback she should've seen coming.

"What strange fae?" Kieran's voice sharpened as he focused his full attention on her.

"Bartender wasn't human," Liz said with a shrug. "He told me 'my kind' weren't welcome around so many fae. I've got the feeling wherever my abilities come from, they're about to drag me into more trouble than I'm prepared to deal with."

"Why didn't you say something?" Accusation flashed in his eyes. To be fair, they sat talking all night until she'd fallen asleep. While the other guys were out carousing, she could've told Kieran.

She scratched her nape, finding the floor fascinating. "The stuff with your brother took precedence. I didn't think it was important enough to bring up." Getting her hopes up without ever receiving answers hurt too much to mention. At least it did yesterday, when it was still so fresh.

Kieran took a deep breath in an obvious effort to control his temper, since his eyes were blazing. "Your safety takes precedence," he said, his voice low.

"Come on now, doll," Trevor said, cutting through the tension between her and Kieran. "You know you could've interrupted us at any point to share this information. If he threatened you, he could have very well been one of the assholes looking to cause problems for Ky."

Jett clapped a hand on her shoulder. "All right, enough scrutiny for the time being. The three of us are heading to Perfect Percolation."

Kieran turned to face Trevor and Renn. "You guys mind food duty?"

Renn nodded as he walked past them and hopped off the bus, his shoes slapping the pavement. "Hurry up, Trev," he called.

Trevor paused for a moment and met Kieran's eyes. "We're going to get all seafood to piss you off. You know that, right?" His lips quirked as he fought with his smile.

Letting out a snort, Kieran gave his friend a

shove. "You asshole, pick up some real food while you're out." A smile lit his face as he shook his head, and like that, their quarrel blew over. Despite Kieran's short temper, he moved past things as fast as a summer storm. And the man didn't hold grudges—when he'd gotten over whatever they squabbled about, he meant it. Liz admired the simplicity. She held onto things long past their expiration date and half the time didn't voice most of the shit that pissed her off.

Liz stretched her arms over her head as she stepped off of the bus, glad to be out of the stale scent of coffee, Axe body spray, and the remnants of cigarette smoke Kieran always tried to hide from Renn. Out here, the scent of the sea permeated the cool air, and strong breezes gusted through the city.

"So tell me why I bothered making coffee if we were going to stop at another coffee shop?" she asked, lifting a brow at Jett.

"Because one cup isn't enough," Kieran said, taking the lead as they stepped to the winding sidewalk lined by dozens of storefronts. She tossed a hand up to wave goodbye as Renn and Trevor jogged in the opposite direction, heading to the nearest grocery mart.

"Save the jingle for the commercials." Liz shook her head while they walked past the wide open windows of a brightly-lit salon, and the orange and green overhang of one of the fad vegan restaurants. The pale gray sidewalk beneath was clean from flattened gum, crumpled Burger King cups, and spent cigarettes. Despite the familiarity of the RV, Liz loved when they got a chance to stretch their legs and wander. While they'd crossed the country in the time she'd been with the boys, she'd barely gotten a chance to explore the landscape since she headed out to arrange their shows every night.

"Jessa makes a mean cappuccino," Jett said as he

shielded his eyes from how the sun refracted against the windows and parked cars. "But we're more there for the company than what she provides."

"And how do you know her?" Liz asked, half-afraid to know the answer.

"Kieran's ex-girlfriend, so she used to hang around the band a lot," Jett said, picking up the pace. "She was an absolute doll, and we were mad at him forever when they split up."

Liz's stomach squeezed, even though she had no reason for a response. Kieran dated plenty of women before and would date plenty more in the future. Just because he got a little flirty with her didn't mean she stood out from the lineup.

"Yeah, I learned the hard way incubi shouldn't date their own kind." Kieran scratched the back of his head while they walked along. "Total sweetheart, but hell, we started fighting in a fierce way."

"Someone fight with you?" Liz let out her mock surprise. "*Never.*"

He gave her the side eye before responding. "Yeah, dating someone so similar was a powder keg waiting to happen. Besides the fact we both need to feed off of others, not our kind, didn't help in the slightest. After a little while, we were both starving and surly."

"So why are we paying her a visit again?" Liz ran a hand through her tangled hair, realizing she hadn't bothered tugging a comb through it yet this morning.

"Because her place is a fae hotspot." Kieran slipped his hands into his pockets while they walked along. "If you want information or to get a pulse on the happenings in Court without attending the events, this is one of the places where all the dirty gossip flies."

"So you can get wind of what the hell your brother might be up to." Liz finished the thought. "Well then, let's get ourselves some fae-bulous coffee."

Jett stopped in his tracks and leveled a look at her. "That pun was criminal, Liz."

The grin she'd been holding out blossomed on her face at the same time Kieran busted up laughing. His shoulders shook, and as fast, the awkward tension from this morning evaporated. Liz shared a wry grin with him as their eyes locked.

"There it is," Jett called from paces ahead of them. He pointed up the block where a chalkboard sign decorated with flowers and fancy script spelling *Perfect Percolation* sat right out front of the café. Already, the buzzing in her head reached a crescendo point. Outside, a hulking minotaur hunched over a keyboard, his large figure near breaking the chair he sat in. A lamia leaned back in her seat, holding a mug of tea in both hands as her serpentine tail curled around the bottom of the table. To the average passerby, they'd see a businesswoman and a college student, nothing out of the ordinary, but the power of glamour veiled the mythical world from the modern day.

This concentration of fae almost always spelled bad news. Unlike other humans, who were food to the fae, once any monsters took notice of her unique abilities, she became a pet to be acquired and no step closer to finding others of her kind. Yet here she entered the fray on a soiree to meet with Kieran's ex. Somehow, what once seemed reasonable morphed into the worst idea ever.

"Let's get ourselves some answers," Kieran said, taking the lead as he opened the door. A tinkling bell signaled their entry. Liz swallowed hard. No time like the present. Before the door swung shut, she darted in, entering Perfect Percolation, news hub of the creatures that go bump in the night.

Chapter Six

The scent of roasted coffee hit Kieran's nose once they stepped inside the café. Behind the counter, a tall woman moved at lightning speed, pivoting around to tamp espresso and then whipping to her other side to turn off the hissing knob causing the foam to froth. She must have been a new employee of Jessa's, because he didn't recognize her. While they'd come here in search of his ex-girlfriend, he wouldn't mind if she happened to be out of town for the day—or maybe even the month. Sure, their breakup hadn't been car bomb bad, but it had also been complicated and something he wanted to leave in the past.

"Kieran, is that you?" An incredulous voice came from the swinging door leading to the café storeroom. Looked like luck wasn't on his side today.

"And me, babe," Jett said, crossing the distance between them and enclosing Jessa in a fierce embrace. His ex remained the same knockout as ever—lush black hair curling into soft waves around her shoulders, brown doe eyes, and skin skating the shade of coffee with cream. She'd lured many a man in with those looks, though attractiveness for a succubus and incubus wasn't anything shocking—a simple matter of survival.

Liz rested her elbow against the counter, processing Jessa with a cursory scan. Even in the presence of his striking ex though, Liz stole center stage, like she had since they met. The intelligence sparking behind those hazel eyes of hers was something extraordinary. Besides, with her sanguine grace and the sensuality oozing from her, she could compete with a succubus, hands down. Her lips pressed together in a firm line, and she stood a bit taller before marching up to Jessa and offering her hand.

"And who's this?" Jessa broke away from Jett, eyeing Liz's hand with disdain. "Don't tell me you brought your lunch into my café."

Kieran bristled at the accusation, on edge at the rendezvous. But before he opened his mouth, Liz took command.

"We're here to get a goddamn cup of coffee and have a quick chat. If my being a human offends you, get over it. Because I'm not leaving until I've got some answers to our current problem." Liz retracted her hand at once as it curled into a fist. Her tone remained cool and calm, but iron branded those words all the same.

Jessa blinked before bursting out into laughter. A couple of patrons maneuvered around them as they made their way to the tables in the back, since their crew stood squat in the middle of the café.

Kieran lifted a brow, surprised by the reaction.

"You've got some spunk, girlie." She reached out and grabbed Liz's fist, wrapping her palms around it. The energy shifted around there—Jessa tried to use her ability to try and make nice. She was in for a rude awakening.

"Neither the pretty appearance or any succubus voodoo will work on me, so don't waste your time." Liz yanked her hand away and gave her a look brimming with confidence.

Kieran couldn't help the amused smirk rising to his face.

Jessa stepped back a few paces, and her skin paled a shade. "What is someone like you doing with them?"

He didn't miss the fear in her eyes, or the knowing there. His ex was hiding something, and Kieran wanted to know what.

Jett reached over, squeezing Liz's shoulder. "Our manager's a couple shades different than the average human. Now let's not waste time arguing. Why don't you sit and have a cup of coffee with us?"

Kieran stepped to the counter, ordering three cappuccinos before anyone voiced an opinion. The woman behind the counter readjusted her square-rimmed glasses before diving into the fray. Scales on her arms glinted under the yellowed lighting as she set to work whipping up their beverages. Kieran didn't miss the way Jess's gaze swung his way—eye-fucking would put it lightly.

"You kept in shape," she purred, placing a hand on his arm.

Kieran heaved a sigh. He had zero interest in the woman, so he didn't bother responding. Unlike Jett and Renn, he was a shit liar and two steps worse at concealing his feelings. "How's business been?" he asked, skipping the comment altogether.

"Busy with the Mossfeather soiree on the horizon. The number of people who've swung by hoping to score an invite is embarrassing. Sometimes it pays to know the upper echelons of the Court." She grabbed a mug of green tea from behind the canisters along the counter and sashayed over to an empty table, claiming her seat. Jett jerked a head at the hand-off counter where three cappuccinos waited with perfect cream and tan swirls.

"Thanks, J," Kieran said as he snagged his cup from Jett and strode over to take a seat at the table. The other two followed seconds later. Though Liz maintained a placid mask, tension emanated off her in droves. He also didn't miss how she glanced between Jessa and him, though jealousy of any sort was wishful thinking on his part. A couple of stares lingered their way, most of them focused on Liz as the odd human out in the all-fae café. With the glamour buzzing through this place from the frequent flyer miles folks racked up, most humans got a disinclination to walk inside, a foreboding feeling that sent them traveling to some other coffee shop.

Kieran took a sip of his cappuccino, savoring the sweetness before turning his attention to Jessa. "Happen to hear if my esteemed family will be attending the event?"

"Oh, like Larsen, your heartbreaker of a brother?" She quirked an eyebrow, knowing who he angled for. While his parents had written him out, his brother maintained a healthy loathing for Kieran's choices and didn't miss an opportunity to rub in his failures. Gem of a family he came from.

"He's been leaving his calling card all around town, begging me to come play." Kieran didn't try to keep the growl out of his voice. "The usual nag, to align, align, align."

Jessa squeezed the lacquered table edge, casting a concerned look his way that pissed him off more. "I'm sure it's for your own safety," she murmured. "There have been changes at court, fae going missing, and a new enemy on the horizon. The Seelie king will only protect those in his purview." Jess had always given a damn about what all those stuffed shirts thought and had never understood why he remained on the outskirts. Yet another reason why their relationship had been doomed to crash and burn from the beginning.

"That's cute and all, but he's sending cronies to interrupt our shows. He's not only endangering our fans, but they've started picking fights with us too," Liz interjected. The flat tone in her voice and the subtle aggression meant she'd switched to manager mode, the same way she got when working out details with venues to make sure they got the best deal possible. Before her, they'd managed but not well. Miscommunications, cancelled shows, and overbooking on a venue happened far too often when they'd been in charge. Liz, on the other hand, created a circuit of shows and established a real tour.

"Darling, do you think you'd last for a hot second at a real Court function? A snack like you would get devoured in a heartbeat." Jessa grinned as condescension dripped from her words.

"You'd be surprised," Liz responded, not backing down in the slightest. "I've survived this long being able to see you crazies and haven't been offed yet."

Kieran couldn't help the pride warming his chest watching her go toe-to-toe with his ex-girlfriend. Her eyes glinted as she took a sip of coffee, projecting steel. The girl put on a tough as nails face, and even though she had her shakeups and might cry in the bathroom after a bad night when she thought no one heard, the woman was formidable. Trevor could take his advice and shove it up his ass.

"So, since we've pieced together Ky's brother is attending this soiree, how about extending us an invite to this shindig?" Jett reached over, placing his hands on Jessa's while he wheedled with her.

Jessa rolled her eyes. "Did you not hear me? It's near impossible to get an invitation if you're in good standing with the Court, and you lot are far from."

Liz pursed her lips and placed her mug on the polished table. "Not an invitation to attend. However, a premiere event such as this would want top notch music, right? What better way to make it unforgettable than having Discord's Desire play late at night once the party's reached a raucous crescendo?"

A smile rolled onto Kieran's face. They hopped

on stage, played their sets, and looked pretty, but this girl, she spun them with a brilliance few could manage.

Jessa shook her head in response, the disbelief clear. "Where the hell did you find her, and how do I get one?" She met his gaze with a rueful grin.

"Funny enough," Jett started, a telltale smirk on his face.

Kieran shot him a look at the same time Liz clapped a hand over his mouth.

"Well, I don't suppose it could hurt to ask about entertainment," Jessa said, giving Liz an arch look.

"You know we can put on a good show." Jett winked, continuing to ooze sex appeal.

"I can attest," Jessa said, honing her sensual gaze full force on Kieran. Heat burned in her dark eyes, but Kieran couldn't even muster a spark of what used to exist between them. He caught Liz's glance their way, furtive and unobtrusive, but she took notice nonetheless.

"I bet you say that to every boy in the lineup," Kieran said, his tone dry. "If you can place a good word for us as entertainment, we'll do a show at the café, free of charge." While they were a mid-tier band in the human community, they'd gained quite the reputation amongst fae. Jessa would be an idiot to reject the feeding opportunity a show at her establishment would provide many of her patrons.

She placed a finger on her lips as she pretended to mull the offer over. "Don't know, I might want an extra favor from you." He knew what she had in mind—the same thing every succubus had on the brain twenty-four/seven.

"Sorry, sweetheart, not interested." He didn't bother indulging in her games. As he spoke, his gaze roamed over to Liz. Jessa caught the changed direction as well. The woman's lips curled into a knowing smile, which sparked his shorter than ever temper.

"Well then, if you're done taking up my time with your demands, I have a business to run." Even though Jessa's response remained calm and held a seductive note, her eyes flashed irritation as they met his. The girl hated getting denied, but Kieran wasn't in the business of stroking egos, so she'd have to deal. "I'll do what I can to get you a spot at this ball."

Liz lifted her brows. "Ball? Like fancy frippery and formal dancing?"

"Poor dear," Jessa said, shaking her head. "You've never been to Court before? You'll have a delicious time." The tip of her tongue swept over her upper lip suggestively.

"She'll be more than fine." Kieran delivered her a flat stare, daring her to try and threaten Liz.

Jett leaned over and gave Jessa a peck on the cheek, all sleek sophistication. "We'll await your call, sweetheart. Good seeing you."

"Later, Jess." Kieran tossed a hand in the air after he dropped his empty mug onto the counter with a clink. Liz and Jett took the cue, doing the same before all three of them strode out of Perfect Percolation and into the gusty scorcher of a day. He cast one glance backward, but Jessa's eyes weren't probing him anymore. No, they were locked and loaded on Liz.

The second they stepped into the bright city streets and the door clicked shut, Jett passed over his pack of cigs and Kieran took one. He offered to Liz who shook her head, even though she gave it an extra-long stare. Chances were, midway through she'd steal a few drags from one of theirs. Not like he didn't enjoy the visual of her lips wrapped around the cigarette. Every time it stoked his embers to imagine those lips on him behind closed doors.

"Slick maneuvering there, sweetheart," he said as he lit the cigarette. They walked down the city street in the direction of the RV. "Jessa was ready to turn us out in the cold."

"No thanks to you." Jett shot him a glare. "Would it kill you to butter her up a little bit? She wants to jump your bones, and bad."

Kieran shrugged, trying to not pay attention to Liz's reaction. "We've been done for a long time, J. I'm not one to revisit the past."

Jett mumbled something about taking one for the team as he sucked in his cigarette, letting out a stream of smoke with his breath. Might be easier if he faked it like the other guys, but he'd always broadcasted whatever he felt. Probably why goddamn Larsen remained ten steps ahead of him.

"I'm shocked you dated her in the first place," Liz commented. "The woman's got condescension on speed dial. How ever did both of your egos fit in the same room?" Her sarcasm came off dry and disarming as always, but the edge to her words made Jett's eyes twinkle.

"Pop the claws away, Lizzie," Jett said as he chain-smoked his cig. "She's old news."

"Don't stop, darlin'. I'm loving this new jealous side to you," Kieran teased, an impish smile on his face.

Liz punched him in the arm in response. "See, rockstar? Ego. Everything has to be about you." They ambled down one of the bigger hills in the city until the lot they'd parked the RV in came into sight. The sweet scent of salt air from the sea and cinnamon from a nearby bakery mingled on the breezes, twirling strands of his hair and rippling the ends of his beat-up unbuttoned dress shirt.

Liz's laugh echoed through the air as she

responded to whatever Jett teased her about. The pair of them had grown as close as the woman let anyone in, yet last night she'd shared a closeness with him as they leaned on each other against the RV and stared at the stars. He'd give anything for more of those quiet moments with her, but seeing Jessa gave him a rude awakening. Their love had changed in a toxic way over time until Jessa had become a total stranger. A stream of smoke passed his lips as he exhaled.

A hand reached in front of him and plucked the cigarette from his fingers. This had happened so many times he didn't even need to guess the culprit anymore.

"Smoke your own cig," he muttered, giving her the side eye.

She flashed him one of those blinding grins filled with more wicked seductiveness than a succubus could muster. "Stolen smokes taste better. Besides, I'm protecting your lungs—got to keep your pipes functional, otherwise what use are you?"

Kieran snorted and reached over to pluck the smoke from her lips, his fingertips brushing across the smooth surface. The sensation sent a jolt through him, and the burning core inside him that thrived off of pleasure, pain, and passion rose to attention. "I'm fae, babe. We don't get the sniffles, lung cancer, or any other human diseases."

"If Kieran's being a jerk, I'll share, Lizzie." Jett shook his head, smiling at their bickering. "After all, keeping our cranky boss at bay seems to be the best choice after watching the tongue lashing you gave Jessa back there."

"Maybe I want a tongue lashing," Kieran teased again, pushing the line as he continued to flirt with her, all the while knowing he should stop. Knowing Trevor was right and he'd cause complications and mess her life up. Like he'd ever listened to logic though. Kieran was the king of impulse, the prince of bad decisions, and destined for a long and lonely road ahead of him.

Yet even knowing what a bad idea pursuing her was, he couldn't help how her sinful smile rolled through his veins like honey. Somewhere along the way, he'd become addicted to Liz and didn't know how to quit.

Chapter Seven

The salt spray in the air hit her senses the moment they wandered to the planks of Fisherman's Wharf. In the distance, waves came crashing to the shore with a hushed regularity, even though chatter buzzed from the surrounding crowds. Liz stretched her arms above her head as a crack rippled down her spine. The boys had finished their gig in one of the smaller venues in town, and in a few more days they would perform at one of the bigger stages in San Francisco before traveling to SoCal.

Unless Kieran's brother put a wrench in those plans. To her relief, no mystery fae loitered around this venue doling out pints, nor had any threatening messages been left. However, a moment's reprieve didn't warrant letting her guard down.

Renn stopped in front of Hangman's Bar, a place oozing slick and low key from the black fixtures to the hanging bulbs that cast a dim lighting throughout the place. Folks in here sipped at a pint or sat in close discussion along the two-seater tables lining the back wall.

Trevor raised a brow. "You sure you want to go here, Renny? I thought your style of joint had more glitter and platform heels."

He shrugged, acting cavalier. "Figured a changeup would be nice."

"Let's call it the end of the world, because for once we're not fighting over where we drink," Jett said, taking the initiative as he strolled in through the door. Kieran watched Renn, giving credence to Liz's suspicions. Renn wasn't picking this place in the lineup due to some changed desires—from a safety standpoint, the bar consisted of tight corners, making it easily observable and much tamer than their average place. With Kieran's brother after them and unknown fae popping out of the woodwork, the boys were getting more careful, meaning they also didn't bring home tail from the concert tonight.

Liz entered the bar, breathing in the balsam and cigarette smoke from the folks lighting up in the joint. Renn wrinkled his nose upon entrance—the man hated cigarette smoke, which called out the bullshit he'd been peddling seconds before.

"Sure you're digging this joint?" Kieran nudged Renn in the side and gave him a wink.

"Once I get to drinking, I won't care," Renn said as he stepped up to the bar.

"Once you get to drinking, you'll start taking people's cigarettes and stomping them to the ground," Jett argued, pulling his own pack out and lighting one. Renn shot him daggers until Trevor and Kieran did the same. At that point, Renn turned his back to them, slapping his palms on the bar and delivering his annoyance straight to the bartender.

Liz scanned the place for an open table, but a motley assortment of couples and small groups filled the two seaters. Instead, she hopped up on one of the open barstools, claiming her seat before the guys did. Seeing as the bartender wasn't a leggy female and cigarette smoke surrounded Renn, the satyr was coming across surlier than ever. The bartender switched attention off him as fast as possible.

"Pint of Guinness," Liz ordered, giving the man a slick smile and pressing the bills onto the countertop. In seconds, she had the creamy pint in front of her, and she took the first sip, not waiting for the others to join in.

The smooth jazz jingle of a ringing phone went

off, and Jett lifted his cell before receiving the call and walking out the door. Liz met Kieran's eyes as they both watched him exit, assuming he thought the same thing. After all, Jessa wouldn't be calling Liz, and she'd been rather salty with Kieran when they left. Not like she minded in the slightest. As much as she pretended the way Jessa prowled all over him didn't bother her, she'd be bullshitting herself.

Kieran pulled a seat beside her and ordered a draft IPA from one of the local breweries in the area. "So, what's to bet Jett's out talking to Jessa?"

"Guaranteed. I'm just hoping this fae shindig won't cut into your touring time at all. It'd be a bitch to reschedule all of those venues." Liz stared into the depths of her Guinness. Trevor took the other seat beside her, shooting a dark look over to Kieran in the process. Great, he'd taken to babysitting now. Renn, on the other hand, grabbed himself a gin and tonic and made his way over to a table where three ladies sat chatting, all the strappy-shoe, college-tee sort he gunned for. Not like he was too discriminating. Hell, Renn took some luscious looking boys to bed too, so where his true desires lay was anyone's guess.

"If we are invited, you should probably stay at the RV," Kieran suggested. He pounded into his ale once the bartender placed it in front of him.

Liz frowned, her temper rearing up again. "I get that surrounded by dozens of fae who think I'm a snack won't be the best position to be in, but use some logic here. You said he'd never do something public and this is going to be a spotlit affair. If he sends someone to the RV to mess up your shit, it's me and my gun against whatever monsters he's hurling my way."

"He's just afraid someone will whisk our booking manager away," Trevor said after downing his shot of fireball. "You're a hot commodity, sweetheart," he said with the sugary drawl that charmed all the women.

"Who needs a boyfriend when I've got guys like you feeding my ego," she said with a wink. With the other guys, she had no problem throwing charm their way. Flirting was compulsory for her, a fun way to slide along the surface and keep folks at a distance. However, Kieran was so blunt and direct their flirting grew incendiary, and fast. Every time she got a handle on her feelings around him, he'd spit vinegar or dive right into the subject she tried to avoid, and before long he'd gotten under her skin like no one else.

The swinging door drew her attention as Jett entered again, making a beeline for them. He lifted his phone as he approached. "We're booked for tomorrow night. That was Jessa, coming through for us." Jett placed a hand on Kieran's shoulder, a few strands of his dark hair brushing over his forehead as he leaned in closer. "Your brother's entourage will be in attendance as well, including your ex."

"Jessa?" Liz asked, curiosity getting to the better of her.

Kieran's brows furrowed at the mention of his ex. "No, my first girlfriend," he said. His tone held such vitriol she had to wonder how the hell their relationship ended.

"Well, this has been an exciting stroll down memory lane," Liz said, trying to keep the conversation light. "Asshole brother, bitchy ex-succubus, and now you're telling me you've got another nightmare in your closet?"

Kieran lifted his pint to his lips and chugged, his Adam's apple bobbing with the motion. Within seconds, foam remained in the glass, which he slammed on the counter. "Goddamnit, I need a walk. Drinks aren't cutting it tonight."

Trevor nodded even though he lifted a finger to the bartender to order another shot. "If Misandria is going to be at your brother's side, it's guaranteed to get messy. I'm shocked he keeps her around with how off-kilter she is."

"What better scapegoat?" Jett shrugged. "He can pin any of his slips on her and use her crazy as an offset to actions he might pull. Brilliant move if you ask me."

Trevor snorted. "You were made for Court bullshitting, Jett."

"And yet I chose to leave it behind for you lot. Apart from the occasional dribbles from those who deign to deal with an unaligned, I am just as cut off." Jett delivered a flourished bow from where he stood. "You're welcome."

Kieran hopped up from his seat, his fingers skating across the surface of the bar as he brimmed with tension. "I'm hitting the docks. You guys'll be here awhile, yeah?" Everyone's gaze switched over to Renn who charmed the pants off three women at the same time.

Jett gave him a level look. "Yeah, we'll be here."

"Care to join?" he made the offer to Liz, ignoring Trevor's damning looks. She prickled under the tension, knowing either way she'd be pissing someone off. While her body buzzed over the idea of getting alone with Kieran, the logical side of her knew how dangerous indulging would be. As wild and intense as the waves crashing to the shore.

"I've got a drink to finish," she said, lifting her Guinness. Even though she went with the safe option, tightness squeezed her chest, the impulse begging her to ditch responsibility for once and indulge.

His expression darkened, but he turned around on

his heel and threw a hand up as he headed for the door. "See you folks later."

Jett hopped into his seat. "He's got it bad for you, girlie," he commented, flagging the bartender.

"How the hell does everyone know besides me?" Liz asked, irritation crawling through her so strong even Guinness couldn't cure it.

Jett lifted a brow, his pale blues seeing straight through her shit, same as he always did. "You've known from the get go, honey. No one as perceptive as you wouldn't have figured it out by now."

"I talked it over with him." Trevor let out a sigh. "You can guess how well that went."

"Why?" Jett argued. "As long as Liz isn't protesting, who cares what they choose to do?"

She tilted her head in surprise at her best friend's defense. While Trevor's argument mirrored the logical one in her head, as always, Jett spoke to her heart in a way no one else did. They both knew when the other needed to play superficial, when real talk cut too deep. Even though he sometimes thrashed in his bed at night trapped in old memories and his eyes would dull at the mention of certain subjects, she never pushed. Same as he never pressed with her.

"Because we both know Kieran gets fixated when he's locked onto someone or something. Makes him a fantastic band leader, because hell, I couldn't imagine any of us throwing the passion he does into spearheading this thing. But it's hell on wheels if either of you catch feelings." Trevor's gaze skated to Liz.

Liz hunched forward, pressing her crossed forearms on the cool porcelain. "You must be thinking of some other girl—this model wasn't equipped with feelings," she snarked, all the while staring at the black tile of the bar.

"Maybe I'm not worried about yours." Trevor's knowing glance infuriated her even more.

Jett wrapped an arm around her shoulders. "Well, I care about your lack of feelings, unlike the man from the Heartless South over there. And I say, follow your impulse with this one. If you hadn't tangled in a back alley with me, we might've never gotten such a fantastic asset to the band. Besides, you've been shouldering way too much responsibility, and your dry spell has lasted ages. Being around your aura is like getting sucked into the Sahara."

Liz fought to restrain her smile as she smacked a hand against Jett's chest. "Thanks, jackass. You know how to lift a girl up." Except, he did. He ignored the arguments she'd been making and spoke a different logic, the sort her heart understood bright and clear. Tipping her glass back, she sucked down the rest of her pint to the dregs. The thick foam coated the sides, but she placed the glass on the counter and wiped her hand across her mouth to get rid of the residue around her lips.

Trevor let out a sigh and tossed up his arms. "I guess someone needs to go check and make sure Kieran hasn't gotten lost in the ocean or picked a fight with the first person to bump into him." He gave Liz a sidelong glance, the implication loud and clear.

Liz saluted as she strolled toward the door. "I get it, Trev. Trying to get me to clean up the mess this time." She appreciated the two of them for their subtlety, because if she voiced anything out loud, common sense would kick her ass, and she'd plunk herself down in her barstool. However, right now the urge to smooth the bumpy edges between Kieran and her tugged stronger than the tide rolling to the sea.

Stepping outside of the bar, Liz pinched at the hood of her hoodie as if the flimsy fabric would shield her from the cool air that descended with the night. For some, the temperate climate was paradise, but Liz liked to dance in the flames, to bask in the burning heat of summer and a swampy night, like her childhood home, Louisiana. Not like she'd been back there for a long time, nor would she want to. Soiled memories were best left buried.

The weight of the gun she carried underneath her oversized tee pressed into her side. Though she'd always kept mace on standby, pepper spray paled in comparison to her shiny new Beretta 92-FS. With fae on the prowl and looking to cause problems, she wouldn't even consider going unprepared, and after all the long hours she'd put in at the range, her marksmanship ranked top notch.

She wandered along Fisherman's Wharf, basking in the flashing lights from the candy shacks and t-shirt shops open this late. Throngs of visor wearing tourists who soaked in the sights passed by, as well as the platform-heel undergrads who stumbled drunk along the boardwalk.

Farther along the wharf, Ghirardelli Square lit up, beckoning wanderers over to the grassy knolls, which led to a strip of ocean kissed sand, glowing a silver hue under the moonlight. If Kieran planned on clearing his head, he wouldn't be diving into a bar or storefront. He'd head to a section with more space. Liz cast a glance around her before breaking into a jog, eager to cut through the crowds herself.

As much as she loved her life on the road with the boys, she'd be the first to admit she got claustrophobic. Between the crowded gigs, the crowded RV, and the crowded pubs they packed into at night, alone time and personal space reached a coveted minimum. The strong winds picked up strands from her ponytail and tossed them around behind her, and her hood flew back from her head as she picked up speed.

A couple of folks stopped and stared as she jogged past them, but she couldn't care less if they gawked at her. Right now, the freedom surged through her veins, and her heart soared while she made her way to the shore. As soon as she crested those hills, a lone figure stood out, the waves lapping to his feet as he wandered toward the ocean.

She slowed to a walk once she bypassed the strip of grass and reached the soft sand that sprayed under her footsteps. Even though she approached with quiet thumps, as she closed the distance between them, Kieran turned to face her.

Moonlight turned his pale skin shades paler and enhanced the liquid amber of his eyes. His tall, lean form cast an elongated shadow along the slumps of sand as he walked toward her, hands in his pockets. He leaned down to pick up his leather jacket, which he'd left in a crumpled pile away from the ebb and flow of the tides. She couldn't help but admire the lithe muscles on full display with his wifebeater and low-riding jeans.

"Trev send you to fetch me?" he asked, slinging his jacket over his shoulder as the distance closed between them. Even when Liz slowed, her heartbeat continued its marching speed, and heat flushed through her.

"Wanted a breather too. Renn has shit taste in bars." She flashed him a grin as she continued walking by, angling toward the ocean. Liz didn't bother checking to see if Kieran followed—he would. The murmur of the tides cast a heady lullaby through the air between them, thickening the tension that descended when their eyes met. She kicked off her Keds and let her toes sink into the cooled sand before making her way to where the water imprinted on the beach.

"So how many other ex-girlfriends do you have hiding in the woodwork," Liz asked the moment Kieran stepped beside her, his shadow mingling with the water's stain on the sand.

"More than I'd like," he answered, raking a hand through his tousled strands. "But Misandra was a sadistic bitch in the worst way. Not only does she top the list of people I don't want to deal with, but I sure as hell don't want her anywhere near you."

"I'll make sure to spray on an extra coating of fae-repellant before hitting the ball." Liz crouched to run her fingertips through the water, the icy kiss sending shivers down her spine.

His hand rested on her shoulder, warmth soaking straight through her hoodie. Liz glanced at him. He reached down with his other hand to help her stand again. As she rose, the tension between them caused her breath to hitch.

"Those assholes will find any vulnerable point they can and exploit it. Whether I like it or not, you're a weakness of mine." His voice hardened with a steel edge.

"Gee, Romeo, I love it when you call me weak," she said, even though she got the gist of what he said. However, the intensity in his eyes glowed fierce enough to bowl her over. Jett missed the mark on that one. Her entanglement with the siren had been a wham, bam, thank you ma'am back alley fuck. Kieran, however, he delivered soul-branding passion that would mark her for an eternity, for good or for bad.

"You're the strongest person I've ever met, Elizabeth O'Brien. If I could muster a mask like you or the others do and hide from the world, maybe these bastards couldn't sink their teeth into me so easily, but hell, I've never been able to hide a damn thing."

If only she didn't find his raw honesty so damn attractive. His palm slid around her arm, and once their eyes locked, they'd reached the point of no return. The second their mouths met, she'd dive full force into the fury of the storm. His tongue slipped out to wet his full lips, sending a thrill through her. She lifted her chin to meet his eyes, intoxicated by the lust descending between them and the heat connecting in their gaze.

A muffled noise pricked her attention, but she shut it out, focusing on the moment between them.

Until Kieran's grip tightened around her arm and his gaze broke, locking in on something behind her.

The seduction of the sea-drenched air shattered once the word 'run' passed his lips.

Chapter Eight

For a moment, Kieran thought the shadows were playing tricks or a massive wave crashed to shore. Except, his instincts were too honed over the years to ignore the tugging in his gut that spelled bad news. And the creature who rose from the frothy seafoam, dripping with kelp and cloaked in the shadows, confirmed his gut call.

Of course, this would happen when he stood inches away from Liz, ready to dive in, damn the consequences.

Kieran's hands balled into fists. "Run, he barked.

A growl ripped from his throat as he whipped around to face the creature, ignoring his own advice. The beast fast approached and, from the looks of it, not to offer a casual chat about the weather. The pale light of the moon glinted off the razor points of defined fins rippling down the thickly muscled back of what had to be one of the Finfolk of Orkney. Scales coated it from head to toe, and as their eyes met, he got a full-on glimpse of the gray opalescent orbs staring at him.

"What the fuck is that?" Liz piped up behind him. Kieran's hand clenched and unclenched at the sound of her voice.

"What part of run don't you understand?" he hissed out, not daring to look away from the creature kicking up sand as it fast closed the distance between them.

"The part where I'm running and you're not." The heat in her voice came through loud and clear with the same intensity it did every time they clashed. From behind, a safety clicked off, and he gritted his teeth, reminding himself to clock Jett for taking her gun shopping in the first place. The sheer amount she'd brandished her Beretta since she'd picked one up was staggering.

"At least follow my lead," he said as he rolled his shoulders back, standing a little taller. "Maybe it hasn't been sent to fuck my day up."

Liz snorted as she stepped next to him. "Right, and I'm Little Bo Peep."

"So that's who the bonnet in the RV belonged to—I thought Jett developed a new fetish." Kieran strode toward the creature, the urge to fight pounding through him with the regularity of his heightened heartbeat.

This close, the stench of the finfolk rolled his way, like walking through the fish market in Chinatown combined with a metallic odor that made him wrinkle his nose. The creature began to speak, but the words were garbled by thick rubbery lips revealing a pair of shark sharp teeth that would hurt like a bitch.

"If my brother sent you, why don't you turn back and tell him to come out and play himself. I'm tired of cronies," Kieran complained, his voice echoing along the empty shoreline.

"Come to take you to the depths," the creature managed to hiss out, the last word drawn out on a rasp. A slow blink somehow made it creepier in this dark night. The tides rolled up to wrap those chilling tendrils around his ankles.

"Like hell. Didn't you hear? I've got an appearance to make tomorrow night. You wouldn't want to deprive the Mossfeathers of their entertainment." Kieran reached for the knife handle he kept tucked in his waistband. In one quick motion, the blade freed, the silver surface drinking in the moonbeams.

"Return empty handed and I don't get paid." The

creature's words elongated, and those webbed hands lifted, revealing nasty claws at the tips.

"Wouldn't want that, would we," Liz muttered, annoyance in her tone. "Maybe your big bro's feeding your fighting fetish, babe. He seems to be tossing a buffet at you."

A wide grin crawled on Kieran's face as he wielded the blade. "How considerate." He hunched, ready to charge. The air between them thickened, tensing for violence as the creature steadied into stance. Even though he should keep the defensive, right now, his blood boiled, adrenaline gushed through him, and damn, he wanted to tear into the creature who dared disturb those precious moments with Liz.

His muscles coiled, and at once, he sprang forward.

The blade in his hand rose as he closed the feet between the finfolk and him.

The moment he arced down with the knife, a length snapped around his wrist, a tendril searing his skin. He'd thought kelp hung off the creature, but the tendrils were a part of it, adding a cherry on top of this hellish sundae. The tendril tightened around his wrist, causing him to grit his teeth. His skin throbbed from the contact. Except he was an incubus with the inherent abilities.

He reached forward with his unencumbered hand and grabbed the creature by the misshapen throat. Leaning in, he drew the chi toward him, the energy so thick in the air he could taste it, the near translucent sheen of it like an oil slick in his visual.

Pain radiated from his wrist, but when the finfolk figured what game he played, it released him, backing away. If he let the distance grow, he'd be fucked. Those tendrils gave the creature a step up he didn't have.

"Move out of the way," Liz called out. "I can't get a good shot."

"I've got this," he shouted through gritted teeth. Before the creature dodged, he plunged the knife down, sinking into the finfolk's lumpy, muscular arm. Blackish blood spurted, the hot liquid spraying across his arm and imprinting on his shirt. The creature let out a garbled sound as it whipped around, another of those tendrils snapping against his side. It sizzled the thin fabric of his shirt, searing through it.

"Stop. Being. Stubborn," Liz said, her voice terse.

He yanked the dagger back before lunging forward and plunging with the tip of his blade again. The knife snagged against the cluster of scales, sliding down before it sank into the deeper flesh beneath. Another shout pierced the air, but Kieran wouldn't spin around and run the other way. If his brother was going to send the denizens of the supernatural community to attack him, he would sure as hell deliver a don't-fuck-with-me message home.

His side stung, residual from the touch of the tendrils. Those things were turning into a problem, and fast. Kieran pivoted to the side before those kelp-like things launched at him again, and the creature crouched, narrowing its filmy eyes as it readied to charge forward. The second he caught the push-off from the webbed foot, Kieran side-stepped. As the creature flashed by him, he sliced again with the knife, this time aiming for those damned tendrils. One flopped onto the sand, right as the waves came to steal it away.

The creature's filmy eyes widened, and it let out a howl, much louder than when he'd tried to fillet into the fish.

The bark of gunfire split the air a second later.

A bullet burst through the creature's scales, but

even with the spray of blood, the finfolk brute didn't react as strongly as it did to the severed tendrils. Every fae and mythological creature possessed different vulnerabilities, so sometimes figuring out weaknesses and abilities turned into a game of roulette. Time to play pluck the tendril from the finfolk.

Before he struck out again, the creature surged past him toward his new threat—Liz.

"Fuck," Kieran spat out as he broke into a flat out run to intercept. If those tendrils were hell on his resilient skin, he imagined how they'd flay a human's. Liz honed her Beretta on the moving target, and her eyes narrowed as she tried to aim.

"Run, damnit," he called out, his voice hoarse with concern.

Her lips pursed as she focused on the target, ignoring him. "Hell no," she shouted as she pulled the trigger. Another bullet burrowed into the charging finfolk, but apart from the spurt of blood that lit the air, it didn't stop the momentum in the slightest.

"Asshole, I'm the one you want," Kieran called, trying to sway the creature's fixation on Liz. He spurted ahead, his limbs burning from where the tendrils stung, his muscles straining from the reserves he pulled to lunge forward. Even though his knife made a shit projectile, he needed to try something. He lifted his dagger as his legs pumped underneath him, and he loosed the blade.

The handle dragged it down, but the knife sailed through the air faster than he could cross the distance. The tip burrowed right into the creature's side, an inch or two away from missing entirely. Another of those gurgles rippled through the briny air as the finfolk whirled around, stopping in its tread.

Kieran didn't slow for a heartbeat. His knife clattered to the ground. As he hurtled toward the creature, wind tugging strands of his hair back, he lunged down to grab for the handle. Those tendrils sought to strike home, but at least he'd pulled the heat off Liz.

One of the tendrils stung his shoulder again, but now he knew the creature's weak points. Rather than seizing an attempt to slice and dice those fins or aim for the eyes, he lopped off the offending tentacle. Another garbled howl broke through the air, the irritation clear in those milky, luminous eyes. Liz circled around from the other side, wielding her pistol and refusing to run like he'd asked. Stubborn, infuriating woman.

Before the creature moved away, he struck in an arc, wheeling around to catch a couple more of those tendrils under the snicksnack of his knife. The bright blade sliced through them with ease, and each time another flopped onto the ground, the creature's body convulsed more and more. The creature's claws reached out for him, seeking purchase in his vitals. Except the finfolk revved him past the boiling point, and he was ready to explode.

The second those claws swiped for him, Kieran dove in, slicing down the sides for every spare tendril his knife touched. Right as he ducked in, the claws sank into flesh, sending a searing pain wracking through him. However, once those remaining tendrils dropped with a wet slap to the ground, the creature's grip faltered, and it trembled where it stood. He didn't waste any time. Up close and personal, he took advantage and plunged the knife right through the scaled ribcage, slipping straight through to pierce the creature's insides.

With a howl, it leapt away from him, but rather than heading in Liz's direction, it took off at a dead run toward the sea. Before Kieran followed it, the finfolk disappeared into the froth and pulse of the tides as they swelled toward the shore.

His hand balled into a fist as he slammed the tip of his knife into the soaked sand. The swirl of the tides came to wrap around his legs, and he ran the blade through the saline water before jamming it into its sheath. Footsteps pounded behind him followed by her soft scent of citrus mingling with the breeze. Liz's hand rested on his shoulder, a slight motion that tightened when he didn't jump in surprise.

"Hey." Her voice broke through the static of the rolling tides. "We should head to the RV."

Kieran heaved a sigh, knowing she was right. Even though he healed faster than a human, he'd sustained enough wounds to keep him from being tip top until his next show. Sure, if he found a human to sleep with, he could heal up tonight, but he wouldn't risk the powerful tension between him and Liz over a little pain.

"Unless you need to go trolling for some tail," Liz said, letting go of his shoulder as she straightened beside him. He swore she read minds. "That's how your kind heals, right?"

"Doesn't hurt much." Kieran shrugged, hiding his wince as the tattered fabric of his shirt brushed against the raw wound. "Let's head back to the RV anyway—it couldn't hurt to throw some disinfectant on these burns." When he glanced over to Liz, her arms were crossed and one brow quirked as if she saw right through his bullshit, but she didn't push. If the guys were around, they wouldn't take no for an answer, throwing some girl at him who's name he'd forget once he heard it.

He grabbed his leather, which he'd tossed to the ground the moment the battle began. By some miracle, the poison hadn't eaten through the fabric. The worn jacket saw him through countless bar brawls, and he would've been pissed if one of his brother's cronies messed it up. Even though he longed to return to the moment before the finfolk approached from the depths of the sea, the subtle magic that had threaded through the air dissipated, and Liz donned her mask again. The woman avoided vulnerability like a diabetic dodged sugar.

"Are you sure we can't send your brother a sternly worded letter about keeping his henchmen in check?" Liz joked while they walked toward the boardwalk. The second they neared the weathered planks, streetlights came into view. The dim lights cast a stale yellow hue onto the path they walked along, and the remaining crowds lingered by open doors at bars. Loud vocals with some preening guitar strains blared as they passed by live cover bands, while other places set their radios to top volume.

"Either my brother's bored, or he's jealous. The man has two settings when it comes to me, and so my choices narrow to finding a better diversion for him. Nothing is more dangerous than a bored fae." Kieran ran a hand through his tangled hair, trying not to grit his teeth when his injured shoulder muscles bunched together and delivered raw prickles of pain.

"What about taking the other route?" Liz asked. He glanced her way, waiting for her to continue. "You know," she said, "shaming him so totally in his social circle he won't have these cronies to throw your way. Revenge is a package best delivered with a live grenade."

He snorted, shaking his head. "Otherworld be damned, you're a vicious little thing."

"Folks don't underestimate me twice." She shrugged, though her lips curled in one seductive grin. They veered away from the bars and the lights, heading along a darker stretch of boardwalk toward the parking lots where they'd stationed the RV. With the night in full fervor, the rest of the band would be back at the bar watching Renn try to simultaneously hook up with the three ladies he'd been chatting up. Not like Kieran minded—he'd take any time alone he got with Liz.

She scampered ahead of him, her stride fast as her Keds slammed against the pavement. The number of cars died down from the full flush inhabiting the parking lot earlier, casting their dingy tan home on wheels in a lonelier light. Her keys jangled from the lanyard she kept tucked into her pocket as she flung open the door to the bus.

Liz glanced at Kieran. "Let's get you cleaned up," she said, crooking her finger toward him. The motion went straight south, and he let out a low groan as his erection sprung to attention. Not just her husky voice, but the leonine grace to her every move pushed him to the brink. He'd roped off in the shower more times than he wanted to count, and he wasn't sure how much more of this torment he could take.

The steps creaked as he sank hard into them. Once he closed the door behind him and bypassed the driver's seat, he tossed his leather onto one of the seats bolted to the wall. Liz made her way straight to the bathroom, and after a couple of rattling noises came from inside, she emerged holding a roll of gauze and a bottle of antiseptic promising to sting like hell.

"Never knew you were into the sadomasochistic stuff, sweetheart." Kieran winked at her as he reached out for the gauze in her hands. She pulled it back, away from him, and tilted her head towards the empty seat he'd thrown his leather on.

"Sit," she directed, in a tone brooking no arguments.

Kieran slumped into the seat, barely aware of the way his injuries stung—his focus remained on her. "I like it when you boss me around." He smirked, leaning back in the seat while his legs opened wide. His erection strained the fabric of his jeans, but he left enough room to keep it from being too obvious. Life as an incubus taught him real fast the optimal way to manage those sorts of things.

"Yeah, we'll see how much you like it once we get started." She kept the same matter of fact tone even though she fought with a smile. After she cut off a piece of gauze and doused it in rubbing alcohol, her eyes skimmed over his shirt. She heaved a weary sigh. "Do I need to ask?"

"Not in the slightest." Kieran couldn't keep the heat out of his voice as he slipped off his shirt in one liquid motion. She leaned in with the soaked gauze, close enough to touch, to kiss. Her clean citrus scent wrapped around him, setting his veins on fire.

A second later, excruciating pain followed. He gritted his teeth as she pressed the swab into the first graze, saturating the wound in disinfectant. Those hazel eyes of hers darkened in intensity while she worked on cleaning his wounds with a perfunctory readiness. Not like he'd expected flinching from the steel woman.

"You're awfully quiet." Her voice broke through after a few minutes of silence. "Don't tell me a couple of scratches have you down and out?" she teased him.

"Oh, the pain. The agony." Kieran delivered in a monotone.

"Good," she said, not looking up from the imprint along his abs as she dabbed it down. "Serves you right for being stubborn and hurling yourself into danger."

Kieran's brows lifted. "Are you kidding me? Who's the one who wouldn't run the hell away like she was asked? The creature showed up for me, and you put yourself into harm's way." Heat rushed through him right as the pins and needles from the disinfectant sizzled against his raw skin.

"Yeah, but you're the one who'd be missed, rockstar. I'm some human nobody." Even though she smirked, her words rang hollow, and his stomach twisted something fierce. Those words repeated too many times in his own head. Bypassing the pain of his wounds, Kieran reached out, closing the distance between them as he placed his fingers under her chin to direct her eyes to him. His blood blazed at the hint of vulnerability she blinked away as her gaze turned to steel.

"Don't you *ever* say that," he hissed, heat flooding into his words. "You're one of the most remarkable women I've ever met, and you can guarantee your absence would be missed. You belong here, Liz, and I'll always do anything in my power to make sure that doesn't change."

She blinked for a moment as if stunned by the strength of his reaction.

Kieran didn't regret a moment of it though. The woman might keep a level head to her, and her control over her emotions put his to shame any day, but he'd watched her enough to realize when truth and fears ringed her words. He'd seen the sharpening in her eyes and heard the hitch in her breath. He would do anything to stave away the same loneliness that sliced into him year after year.

The tension between them grew like it had before, and as she pulled the gauze away from him, her wrist went limp. He caught her gaze on him and didn't look away, meeting the challenge. The tip of her tongue darted to trace her rose lips, the mere sight enough to make him pant. He leaned forward, hell bent on making his own claim.

The RV door slammed open with a bang.

"Ky, you get back here?" Jett's louder than average voice echoed through the place.

Like a startled deer, Liz stepped away at once, and the moment shattered.

Kieran rifled a hand through his hair, letting out a low groan. "I'm here, you asshole," he shouted.

Liz made quick work of tossing the used bandage into the trash, and she headed toward the bathroom with the remaining gauze. As she walked away, the swing of her hips in those tight jeans dosed him with desire. Tonight, taming his beast would be hell.

Chapter Nine

As the sunset dimmed to night outside the RV window, instead of getting ready for another of Discord's Desire's gigs in San Fran, Liz tugged on a rented dress and dolled herself up for the Cinderella ball of her nightmares. Not only did she feel ridiculous shuffling through the matted carpeting of the RV in this floor length champagne sheath dress, but her stomach twisted at the thought of the hordes of fae swarming around this soiree. A girl didn't spend her years avoiding danger to all of a sudden thrust herself in the middle of shark infested waters.

Yet that's what she would be doing tonight.

After applying another wave of mascara with her magic wand and wiping away a few flecks staining her cheeks, she slunk out of the bathroom, not ready to put on the cruel heel contraptions the dress place suggested. A few stray strands of hair tickled her nape, but she'd managed to tame most of her chestnut hair into a loose chignon tucked to the side. Rustles and slams sounded from the guys attempting to get dressed, as if a fight club had broken out in the middle of the RV.

She stepped out of the bathroom to dodge Jett skidding back with a wide grin on his face as Kieran lobbed a fist in his direction. Which placed her right in the line of fire.

His fist stopped a whisper away from her face, and he froze in place with his gaze locked on her. "Damn, girl," he murmured, lowering his hand as his eyes smoldered. "You look edible."

"Can I go a minute without babysitting?" Liz folded her arms over her chest, choosing to ignore the silent thrill his flattery sent through her. Kieran flashed her one of those megawatt grins that made women swoon, though she'd become immune to the charm early on. Unlike her, the boys got to wear their ripped-up jeans, leather jackets, and ten-hole stompers. Even at a swanky affair, they were hired as Discord's Desire, which entailed a certain image.

Jett wove an arm around her shoulders, pulling her in tight, and the scent of whatever expensive cologne he wore wrapped around her. He donned an open black button-down and wifebeater, and he'd run product to spike the shorter strands of his ebony hair, adding to the jaded mystique that worked for him on stage. "Didn't you see babysitter in the fine print of your contract when we hired you?" he teased, all cheekiness.

Trevor leaned against the window, his thick forearms tensing as he crossed them in front of him, and his demeanor was more distant than normal. His easy smiles vanished as he stared out the window, utter seriousness in his gaze. Folks walked along the street toward a big lit up house with the clay tile roof trademark of this coast. Out of anyone, her nerves should be on edge about stepping into the pocket of the Otherworld, a land where fae reigned supreme and humans rarely entered unless bewitched. Before Liz could ask what bothered him, Renn came over and shoved his hair in front of Trevor, putting the unruly mop in full focus.

"Pull some of your voodoo on this mess, Trev," Renn demanded, headbanging in front of him as if he stood front stage at an Iron Maiden show.

Trevor shook his head, trying to mask the faint smile at the way Renn thrashed about in front of him, making his thick black hair ten times messier. "Stop twitching like an electrocuted tentacle. I'll tame your nightmare if you've got some gel."

"Thanks, ass." Kieran shot Trev a look at the mention of tentacles. If they saw another of the finfolk in the next century it'd be too soon. His gaze slipped to her and lingered. Her mind drifted to those moments before the creature had arrived, of the heady scent of brine and sandalwood from his close proximity and the storm-thick attraction broiling in the air between them. She passed him a wink, not missing the opportunity to stay focused on the here and now.

After rummaging around the bathroom for a heartbeat, Trevor emerged with one of their many bottles of product and ran it through his bandmate's hair.

Liz barely restrained the laugh bubbling inside her at the sight. "You lot are worse than a bunch of girls getting ready for prom," she teased, taking a careful seat on the booth bolted to the wall. After all, she didn't want any stains on this thing since she'd be returning it tomorrow, and she'd seen more spills than she could count in this RV. Trevor smirked while he continued to tame Renn's hair until the mop turned into messy slick strands that screamed sex. Renn wore a loose white tank he'd rip off mid set. The drummer had a nudity problem that wouldn't quit, and the fans over-encouraged him.

"Nah," Kieran piped up. "Once you see the penguins in their suits and tails throughout this shindig, we'll look like the scruffiest nerfherders there. I'd never be caught dead in a suit—all the fancy attire's for Court people like my folks and Lars."

Jett elbowed him in the side. "Come on, I think you'd look dashing in a suit. Our too-pretty front man could pull it, right Liz?" His eyes glittered with mischief as he glanced her way, being a pain in her ass on purpose. No wonder Kieran tried to slug him.

Liz refused to fall for the bait. "You boys don suits and I'm pretty sure the women in the audiences would faint straight away." To be honest, the idea of Kieran in a suit revved her engine in the right way, but no way in hell would she toss gasoline to his blazing ego.

"We should get a move on," Trevor said, nodding toward the door. "The sooner we're prepped the better."

Kieran turned to her with seriousness in his eyes spelling a bossy tirade to follow. "Don't eat anything there," he said. "Or accept any gifts. No favors, nothing. Suspect every nice turn someone tries to do for you, because being a human in this setting, they'll all be making an attempt to sink their claws into you. Any promises made amongst fae have a way of binding—we are under the subjugation too."

"You're forgetting—I'm not quite human. If your mojo doesn't work on me, I doubt enchanted food or drink will. But, better to play safe." Liz rolled her shoulders back, feeling the stress settle into them at the prospect of the night ahead. When the boys started their set, she'd be alone in a room full of people who'd want her as a pet or a tasty snack. "You're making baby steps," she said with a smile. "I'm shocked there aren't threats to lock me up in the RV during all of this."

"Like you'd listen." He shot her a look, probably remembering the dismal result when he tried to boss her around the other night. She grinned wide before pushing herself off the seat and slipping into the strappy four-inch heels that were going to be hell to walk around in all night.

Trevor stood by the door, tapping his fingers along the frame as if he were sounding out a melody on his guitar. Even though his nerves marched on full display for whatever reason, when he sank into the music onstage, he'd be fine.

Jett gave Renn a shove forward. "Come on, beauty queen. Time to go."

Renn returned the favor with an elbow to the side, making Jett glare at him. "Try and keep up, asshole."

Liz heaved a sigh as she maneuvered past the lot of them. If Jett and Renn fought any more, she'd ship them to couple's counseling.

The second she stepped off the RV and caught the full view of the mansion in front of them, the sight dosed her with adrenaline. A foster kid who spent most of her life downing instant mac and cheese and patching holes in her Goodwill buys didn't fit in amidst flash and cash.

The tan exterior glowed with a rosy hue due to the miniature lanterns lining the walkway, marked by conical shrubs carved with precision. Intricate black metal railings tipped in gold decorated the balconies, long ones adorning each of the three floors and backlit by the amber light gleaming out from the long rectangular windows. She didn't know whether to expect some portal to step through leading to this section of the fae realms, but up ahead looked like a regular mansion.

A group of men strolled by, the glint of their Rolex and diamond studded cuff links marking them as money. While most humans passing by this place on the outskirts of the city would see the rich and elite congregating, Liz bypassed the veil of glamour. The group of men might not be short on cash, but she noticed the curl of the one guy's ears and how his veiny muscles almost burst out of his tux. Another of the men reached close to seven feet tall and had a gaunt, skeletal frame with red eyes and ashy skin, clearly not human. Her tongue dried as they neared the entrance of the building.

The atrium held several more potted plants flush with crimson orchids and the burble of a fountain spurting into a wide-rimmed marble bowl. The patterned glass entrance let the light spill out onto the tan tiles in shards. Even though she walked forward with the boys, her tread slowed as she clicked along, and she couldn't help soaking in her surroundings. Why on earth had she thought playing a gig in the middle of Fae Fest was a good idea? Oh, right, because a crazy, half-suicidal part of her wanted answers. Not only of why Larsen sent cronies after them, but the long-held one of who the rest of her kind was. Where she belonged.

The closer they got to the door, the more her stomach flip-flopped with anticipation, even though she kept her mask in place.

A hand rested on her shoulder, almost causing her to whirl around. She glanced to see Kieran behind her. Even though the smiles were gone in the wake of entering into his least favorite place, the warmth in his eyes and palm made a dent in dousing her nerves.

"Don't tell me big, bad Liz O'Brien has a case of the jitters," Kieran murmured in her ear, a teasing note in his voice. Without any instruction manual, the man figured out how to press her buttons.

She forced a calm smile, meeting his eyes with a boldness she sure as hell didn't feel. "Hoping I'd be some fainting flower falling into your arms?"

"Where's the fun in that?" He stepped to her side, linking his arm through hers as the butler by the door nodded in recognition, allowing them into the threshold. Once they stepped inside, her skin prickled like she walked through a spiderweb. She'd been expecting some big flash-bang of an explosion but felt underwhelmed—until she stared at her surroundings.

They stood in the mansion, yet apart from it at the same time. The vaulted ceilings stretched higher, and the effervescent glow of fairy lights danced across the expanse, held by no strings, no attachments—pure magic. The walls which had subtle gilt decorations before now gleamed with trails of molten metal that dripped and yet never fell, a slow mutation as it formed whorls and patterns across the surfaces. Hibiscus and gardenia wove along railings, and fuchsia dangled from any hanging lights, the vines and blooms twining around everything imaginable.

The whole experience swirled her mind like too much whisky, the infusion of sights, foreign scents, and the colors and light that sparkled and danced in her peripheral threatening to overwhelm. How the fae managed to slum through the human realms was beyond her—returning to regular San Francisco, the colors would be muted, the senses dulled.

Renn swaggered past them with his confident, nothing-to-lose stance, and Jett slunk after him, lifting his hand in greeting to one of the groups congregated in the foyer. Out of all of them, only Jett had the social graces to mingle here. Liz cast a glance behind where Trevor brought up the rear, each step begrudging as he fidgeted with the silver buttons on the sleeve of his leather.

"Trev, why don't you take care of setup," Kieran called to him. "I know you'll miss all the socializing before we're on set, but someone's got to do it."

Liz pursed her lips, ready to argue if he wanted it done so badly he could do it himself, when Trevor sped ahead of them.

"See you in the back, brother." The gratitude in his eyes when he looked over to Kieran was tangible, and at once, she knew their lead singer gave Trevor the out to deal with whatever bugged him in private. Trev gunned it for one of the decorative side doors on the opposite end of the foyer.

They made it a couple of steps in before a satyr with gypsum horns and a frame the size of Renn's stepped in their way. His burgundy uniform marked him out as help.

"Would you like a drink, sweetheart?" His eyes glimmered as he zoned straight in on Liz. So this was what Kieran meant.

Liz shook her head. "Thanks, but I'll pass." Kieran's grip tightened around her as the satyr darted to the next group, offering libations to them as well.

Throughout the foyer, all types of fae and mythical creatures wandered through. She caught the glow of amber eyes from a shifter or the serpentine scales and forked tongue of a naga woman slithering through the place. To her surprise, she noticed several humans wandering in the midst as well, made clear not just by the lack of horns and fangs but also by the glazed expressions on their faces in thrall of whoever worked their mojo on them. She'd seen it often enough with the women who hurled themselves at the boys after Discord's Desire shows to recognize the signs.

A woman stepped in front of them, her ebony skin contrasting with the patterned leaves that molded into a dress, tapering from her ample breasts to trail along the floor like forest bedding. She wore a crown of thatched twigs twined together with exquisite precision. Her long black curls tapered down her shoulders and back with a wildness reserved for the woods.

"Kieran, don't you know it's rude to bring a snack to a gathering like this?" The woman's tone emanated cold even though she gave him a gracious smile, not even regarding Liz with a glance.

His grip tightened to a steel clamp around her arm. If she didn't know how on edge he was, she might complain, but she noticed the flare in his eyes, and standing so close to him, she felt his muscles tense.

"I'm not a snack, just their booking manager," Liz said, not caring if the bitch considered her rude. The way these Court types treated humans like cattle pissed her off already.

"Misandra, I see they let you out of your cage. What a pity," Kieran snarled, swinging from calm and suave to feral in the span of a second.

Liz's eyes widened with recognition of the name. So this had been Kieran's first love, one of the many in his younger years who fucked him up. Cold steel coursed through her as her glare on the woman hardened.

"Please, if anyone appears an animal, you're doing quite the job already." The woman's silk tone remained unruffled even though the malevolent glint in her eyes gave her away.

"I enjoy breaking my mother's heart. She always wished I'd strut around like a stuffed peacock and waste my years engaging in pointless arguments in Court," Kieran shot back with venom in his voice, although he'd eased off of the tight grip on Liz's arm. She'd seen him angry before, and she'd seen him fight, but she'd never seen the bitterness gripping him fierce like it did now. She understood the stir of those tired embers all too well. How the cold ache threatened to shatter you over the years until it claimed you too.

"Funny, because he was the one invited here to entertain," Liz jumped in, unable to help herself. "I'm not sure what you're contributing to the party besides a nasty tongue and an appalling lack of taste."

Misandra's head whipped in her direction, her wild curls sliding around her shoulders. Those dark eyes that seemed so distant and hadn't regarded her once turned their full focus on her. And with the concentration emanating from them, Liz could guarantee the woman attempted to whammy her with whatever fae abilities were in her wheelhouse. It took every ounce of willpower to not stick her tongue out in defiance and follow up with a 'suck it, bitch.'

"You little whore," Misandra hissed out, after a few minutes of focus which availed nothing.

Liz continued staring at her with a flat-lidded gaze, refusing to back down. One of the branches that coiled down the woman's dress in what Liz thought was decoration began to move, the tendril rising into the air.

"Don't you dare." Kieran stepped between the two of them, putting his hands out. His voice, a silken purr, grew hard and heated. "She belongs to me." He stared at Misandra until the tendril lowered, returning to casual decoration on her dress.

Even though Liz opened her mouth to protest—she belonged to no one—common sense kicked her in the rear. Fae had queer notions about everything, especially humans, and until she talked with Kieran about what the hell he meant, she would go along with it.

With those words spoken, the imminent violence shattered with a sharp laugh from Misandra who pulled away from them. "You should've told me you'd acquired a new pet, Kieran, darling. Seems like she's got more use than the average human as well. Well, ta, love. I must make my rounds with people of actual consequence."

Liz's blood burned at the woman's words even though she hid her reaction, keeping her chin lifted and her eyes on the mark.

Kieran growled, not restraining his rage in the slightest. "Speak to Liz again, and I'll gut you right on the floor here, laws be damned." His voice purred low and as deadly as the viciousness flashing in his eyes.

"Wouldn't waste my time on an owned human." She gave a shrug as she wandered away from them, her leafy dress trailing along the polished cherrywood floor.

Liz crossed her arms over her chest. Her hip jutted to the side as she glanced over to Kieran, waiting for an explanation.

Once the bitch shuffled far enough away, he took the lead, guiding them toward the wall. "So, I'm guessing you'll want to know what that was about," he said, his gaze skating the wooden planks. Liz pursed her lips, not saying anything as she tapped her finger against her arm. With the way he oozed raw and realness right now, letting him stew was a little too fun. "I'm sure you've noticed how humans are regarded amongst my kind. Not exactly championing their rights or anything," he started.

She fought her smirk, but it won out.

As he lifted his head to look at her, the realization crystallized in his eyes. "Winter's breath, woman. You're too damn intelligent."

"Figured it was one of your kind's inane rules. Look, bucko. I'm my own woman, but I'm not an idiot. We're in your kind's territory right now, and I'm all about surviving. My pride can take a little bruising if it means coming out of this alive."

He shook his head, a smile growing on his face and the tension that bunched his muscles tight leaking away. "You're a perfect package, O'Brien."

She couldn't help the self-satisfied smirk in return. "Like you're one to talk, rockstar."

He opened his mouth, about to respond, when a tall man with ladykiller looks stepped in front of them. The amber eyes, the thick black hair, and the angled jaw were all dead giveaways. Even though this man wore a tailored Armani like he came out of the womb in it and slicked his dark hair into a contained coif, he wielded sexuality the same way Kieran did.

"My, my, little brother. You've managed to snag yourself an invite to this? Who did you have to whore yourself out to? Jessa?" The man spoke with a sneer once he stepped into their vicinity.

Yep, couldn't be anyone but Kieran's asshole brother, Larsen.

Chapter Ten

Kieran's fighting instincts rocketed into overdrive once Larsen stepped into view. And when the bastard opened his mouth, no power in the universe could stop him from tearing the man's throat out.

Until Liz stepped between them, placing her hand on his arm while she glared at Larsen. A better sedative couldn't have been found. Even though his blood raged at the sight of his brother, her calm strength gave him the control he needed. After all, if he went apeshit here, he'd be dead in minutes with all the enemies he'd stacked up over the years. And once they tore into him, those vultures wouldn't hesitate to take out the other guys, or Liz.

"Why don't you go bother some other folks?" Liz suggested, meeting Larsen's gaze straight on.

Kieran had hoped they could wander through the place unobtrusively, gathering information as they went, but from the moment they stepped through the door, it was bad news bears.

"You'd deprive me of time with my kin?" Larsen placed a hand over his chest, his voice a mockery of concern.

"Shove it, asshole. When Mom and Dad signed the writ, I ceased to be a blood relative."

Larsen made a demure clucking noise, so reminiscent of the one Mom used to when he'd stirred up trouble but she didn't want to raise her voice in polite company.

Kieran's hand balled into a fist before he even realized it. Larsen had sought him out the second Discord's Desire arrived. Except unlike the gigs they played in the human realm, here among the fae in a Court function, his brother's hands would be tied. No fae on fae fighting would break out in public unless sanctioned by the host.

Larsen's gaze flickered to Liz with a deadly curiosity. Kieran's blood turned to ice. If his brother hadn't figured out his weak spot for her, he would after tonight. Without asking, Larsen reached over to grab Liz's wrist, running his fingers along her pulse in a seductive way to turn any normal human to putty.

Liz's lip curled in disgust, and she yanked her hand back.

Though Kieran couldn't quash the internal triumph in his chest at watching her reject the man who'd stolen everything from him, dread followed.

Larsen's eyes narrowed. "Rather dangerous to show up in the Otherworld after declaring war." He stepped a pace away from Liz, as if he'd touched something poisonous. Her brows rose, and even though she kept a level expression, Kieran caught the glimmer of hope in those hazel eyes.

"Who's declaring war, brother?' Kieran asked, hoping maybe Larsen would have answers as to who her kind were.

"The hunters," he said, his voice dark with disgust. "More than ever, you need to align. Fae are going missing, and the only way you'll fall under Seelie protection is if you swear your allegiance. As for your girl, she's walking around with a huge target painted on her forehead. There are many, many of us who wouldn't mind draining her dry."

Liz folded her arms over her chest. "I belong to Kieran, sweetheart, which means something in these circles."

A look of surprise followed by loathing flashed

across Larsen's face. "You absolute idiot," he said, fixing his gaze on Kieran. "You've brought the enemy right into your home."

Kieran placed his arm around Liz's shoulder. "Back off, Lars. She's not my enemy—she's our booking manager and my friend. Like I've said before—I don't care what politics you're involved in. I'm not going to align." His muscles tensed as he pulled her tight to him. Even knowing his brother wouldn't act in public didn't help the surge of fear flushing through him with the way Lars dissected her with his eyes.

"Best get rid of her before you end up dead like the others," Larsen responded, his voice cold as ice. "If you want to survive, you'd better choose a side, brother." The hard glint in his eyes suggested he'd found a target. Even though Kieran wanted to throat punch his brother here and now, Court functions worked differently. Best to get the hell away for the time being.

"Alignment can't be coerced. May as well give up while you're ahead." Kieran met his gaze. *Yeah, asshole, message received clear as day.*

Larsen smiled, but he didn't bother with any more small talk as he caught the eye of a curvy siren who'd wandered in.

"What the hell is a hunter?" Liz asked, her voice sharp with curiosity and her gaze glued to Larsen's retreating figure. He hadn't let her go, even after his brother strolled away in those pretty little Gucci loafers. Truth be told, he didn't want to. His brother scrambled his head in such a bad way he didn't trust her an inch from his side around these sharks. Whatever war loomed between the Seelie and these hunters, he wanted no involvement.

"I haven't the slightest clue," he muttered as he stomped his way across the polished floor, the soles of his combats leaving smudges. He took the small victories where he got them.

Past the foyer, the first room they entered had a bar in the corner. The surly sprite bartender's palms pricked with condensation, leaving imprints on the glasses. The red and orange flecked marble of the countertop offset the cherrywood, and a myriad of folks loitered around the tall high-tops in this room due to the close proximity to libations.

"Should've snuck in a bottle of hooch if all food and drink is off limits for me," Liz complained while they stepped up to the bar.

"Two glasses of scotch. Neat," he ordered. The sprite blinked her lazy eyes at him. She gave a quick scan over his attire before she whipped up the glasses and handed them over. Kieran turned toward Liz and handed her one. "You can have drink I've offered you, because it comes with no tricks," he said as they strolled away from the bar.

In another room, strings started up, followed by a sweet chorus of what had to be sirens, their enchanting voices twining together in pristine perfection. Nothing like the raucous shows he and his provided.

"And here I was thinking you were leaving me parched." She swirled the amber liquid around the cup before taking the first sip. Together they strolled through the room, heading toward the one with the crooning sirens. After all, they'd be stepping onto the stage later in the night. Eyes glided over them from all directions, but Kieran welcomed their derision. He didn't duck his head or try to hide, and instead, met their stares head-on with a scorching one of his own.

"Sweetheart, I never leave a girl wanting," he murmured in Liz's ear as they found a wall to lean against in the entertainment room. The sirens reached a beautiful crescendo, holding several humans and some fae spellbound while others swayed or tapped their feet to the music. Of course, Liz remained unaffected, her complete immunity unique.

She lifted the drink to her mouth and took a sip, her onyx bracelet jangling with the motion. He followed suite. Despite the way she hid her motions behind a mask, he'd grown to recognize her tells—how her eyes hardened on the defense rather than the slips of warmth he'd been privileged to see. At the moment, her lips pressed tight together as she tracked over the room—he didn't have to be a psychic to tell that Larsen's accusations rattled her. Liz needed more information, and bad.

"I see you've made your way to the bar," a voice purred upon approach. Jett, of course, with his slick socializing smile in place. Kieran's shoulders relaxed at the sight of his friend rather than another asshole arriving to give him lip and stir up the past.

"There was reason to drink," Kieran mumbled, letting the refined tingle of the scotch glide down his throat. "Plenty of reason."

"Family reunions and ex-girlfriends," Liz placed her hands on her hips, a move that didn't fit the demure dress she wore, and one he adored her for. "Oh, and apparently I'm owned by Kieran for the party?" She pursed her lips and leveled him with a gaze.

Kieran ducked his head to avoid Jett's stare. "Before you say anything, Misandra and my brother were both ready to lunge in for the kill due to certain complications. I had to step in. This way, anyone who wants at her has to fight me first."

"So there's more to this?" Liz asked, her voice bristling on edge.

Jett folded his arms in front of his chest. "Not like

I disagree with your choice, Ky, but there's more to claiming ownership than he's letting on. It's not a temporary thing—by making the declaration, he's accepting responsibility for your safety from here until eternity in the fae community or until someone challenges and kills him."

Liz's lips thinned.

Fuck. The impulsive move seemed natural in the moment, a surefire way to keep her safe. Jett was right though, he hadn't thought the repercussions through. Still, even if she wanted nothing to do with him down the road, and even if she broke his heart, he couldn't imagine a day he wouldn't want to keep her safe. She wasn't a fling or some pretty face to him. Liz O'Brien had become a vital person in his life, one whose presence grounded him, and being around her soothed the bitterness and rage that burned in him for so many years.

"Jett, care to take a walk?" Her voice turned to ice as she turned away from him.

Jett winced, tipping two fingers in Kieran's direction with a salute. He mouthed a 'sorry' as he walked off with Liz.

This party proved to be a veritable nightmare from the moment he stepped in. He lifted the glass to his lips and chugged the scotch in one gulp, needing the blaze more than anything right now. The ache in his chest burned something fierce, and here amidst all the finery, Court manners, and people who despised his existence, he'd never felt lonelier.

He plunked his empty glass on the bar and circled around to the foyer they'd entered through, his stompers slapping against the tile. Misandra's gaze lingered on him while he strode through the room, but he didn't bother looking up as he found the side door Trevor had entered, leading to the back rooms behind the stage. A couple of women slunk up to him while he dodged past butlers carrying trays laden with everything from small spoons of caviar to spongy treats dripping with the pink nectar from the Summerlands in the fae realms. Kieran bypassed it all as he slammed the door behind him.

Shadows filtered over him, and a couple of boggans shifted farther into the corner. Clanks sounded ahead, combating with the muted performance of those sirens. He followed the noise, turning a corner to stumble onto Trevor hard at work assembling their equipment. They had plenty of time to get ready, and the four of them prepped fast, but he'd sent Trevor for the sole purpose of getting out of the limelight. After the mess that occurred at the party so far, Kieran wished he had joined him from the outset.

"Didn't expect you here so early." Trevor straightened, dusting off his pants in the process.

Kieran didn't miss the glance behind him as if he expected Liz to come slinking up at any moment. His chest tightened. She'd walked off with Jett with a coldness that froze him to the core. Liz might not forgive him for this one. "You had the right idea from the get-go hiding out back here." Kieran leaned down to grab the stand, extending it to full length and pulling the cording out to plug in his gorgeous dynamic mic, all glossy chrome.

"Love the dose of paranoia these sorts of functions inject me with. Don't suppose you happened to catch if Tymarch Alberich was in the crowd?" Trevor's voice remained light with his Southern lilt, but Kieran caught the trepidation there.

"No, but the day I meet him, he's a dead man. No way I'd let him take away my best guitar player." Kieran growled, his voice low and serious as hell.

"Property doesn't get a say in the equation,"

Trevor plucked at a couple of strings to test his guitar, his fingers spitefully finding the strands and echoing the bitterness in his tone. His eyes darkened as he refused to look up, caught in a spin cycle of bad memories.

"None of that nonsense." Kieran met his gaze, heat blazing in his own. "You're my friend, my brother. *Never* property."

Trevor set the guitar down with gentle movements belying the intensity emanating from him. He began walking as if he'd stroll right past Kieran, but instead, he stopped in front of him and clapped a hand on his shoulder. "I'd follow you anywhere, brother."

Kieran nodded and pulled his best friend in tight. He remembered those early years after he'd met Trevor, the cold loner who wanted to start a band to stay on the run. The man he'd first encountered would've never been honest about his fears and would've never disclosed his past. The man he'd first met was ice, but over time, Kieran wore him down. Amongst the humans, Trevor wouldn't need to worry about his former owner coming for him—in the Summerlands and pockets of fae territory in the Otherworld he could be tracked and retrieved.

"Care to share why the hell you're retreating back here so fast?" Trevor pulled away, working on his guitar set up as if he'd never left it.

"First people I run into on the floor are Misandra and Larsen. And I may have claimed ownership over Liz." Kieran mumbled those last words, because he was in for one hell of a reaction.

Instead, Trevor shook his head and smiled. "You didn't think it over for a damn second, did you?"

"Not in the slightest." He gave him a sheepish smile. The guys knew what a hothead he was and anticipated it from him the moment they signed on to this gig.

"Rockstars coming through," Renn shouted as he strolled through the side door, startling the group of boggans who'd about given up on privacy. The huge grin on Renn's face spelled cocky, and the way he swaggered in like he owned the place provided a sheer contrast to all this stuffy Court formality.

Jett entered in with him, hands in his pockets as he leveled their drummer with the utmost disdain.

Kieran kept his eyes glued to the door, waiting for Liz to trail in behind them, but no such luck.

Jett stepped beside him and lifted a hand in the air before he spoke. "Before you ask, she's in the entertainment room and will be waiting in the audience. That way we can keep an eye on her while we play and no one can get away with any foul play. But it's time to prep for the show since the siren serenade is coming to a close."

Kieran pressed his lips together, the burning pit in his stomach begging him to press for more information.

Jett's eyes glimmered with knowing. "Yeah, she's seething, Ky. Let her stew for the time being. Our girl's reasonable."

Though Jett was right, Kieran couldn't help the urge riding through him to ditch the gig, track her down, and make sure things were okay between them. He didn't like the icy way they'd left things, and regret burned through him with an urgency demanding resolve. After all, Kieran didn't do regret.

"Take the advice for once," Trevor suggested, cutting through his thoughts. "Besides, we've got a show to play."

Kieran exhaled as he grabbed his mic stand, prepping to drag it out onto the stage. He might be amidst the Court he hated with all their stuffy rules and regulations, but his band never conformed to their schtick. And those poor miserable bastards had invited Discord's Desire to play a gig at their hoity toity soiree. A grin spread on his face. "Let's go inject some life into this cemetery parade, boys."

Chapter Eleven

Jett plied her with three scotch and sodas, and her temper hadn't fizzled. The second they stepped out of this onerous party, she would tear Kieran a new one. Of all the stupid, impulsive things he could've done—her grip tightened around her glass, close to the breaking point. She sucked in a deep breath, forcing a slower exhale as she leaned against the back wall of the entertainment room.

Once the sirens stepped off stage a lot of the crowd cleared, since most folks were dipping out for a snack and a top off of snake venom or whatever the hell these creatures drank. However, once the boys stepped on stage, the crowds would return. They always did. No matter how infuriating a certain front man could be, the guys had an unparalleled charisma they channeled into their live shows, and all of their sexy fae mojo didn't hurt.

Liz scanned the room, not wanting to admit she searched for Larsen. The hope he had the answers she searched for hurt too much to bear. Besides, if she truly was one of the hunters at war with the fae, the sole thing keeping them from murdering her on sight was Kieran's stupid claim. If they'd have let her slip her Beretta into her dress, she might feel safer, but according to their Court laws, bringing weaponry to one of these shindigs equated to walking in with a live grenade.

"You came with the band, yes?" a voice drew her attention.

Liz blinked for a moment before she realized the question was directed at her. A woman approached, and to her relief, not of the scowling Kieran's exes variety.

At least, not one he'd mentioned. This tall, lithe beauty radiated elegance to the point Liz felt like she fumbled around in Keds. Her cerulean dress shifted into lighter and darker shades as she moved, wrapping around her with a mermaid flare. Those inquisitive dark eyes held the fae wildness she expected, but unlike many of the others, this woman appeared more human. Apart from her tipped ears and the mischief in her gaze, the lady didn't need much glamour to pass.

"Yeah, I'm their booking manager," Liz said, lifting the scotch and soda to her lips. Kieran's rules ran through her head again—don't accept a favor, drink, or food. Unlike their brilliant band leader, she wasn't the sort to blurt out whatever came into her head.

"I've wanted to see them play for a while. They've been stepping into my territory," she said, tapping one manicured finger against her full plum lips. However, based on the amusement dancing in her gaze, she didn't mind the competition.

"As the odd human out, I'll give full disclosure— I've got no clue whose territory we step into, unless you're talking state border lines." Liz kept her focus on the woman beside her, even while the guys dragged equipment on stage. Her nerves skated on edge in this place, and though Kieran did the fool job of claiming ownership over her, she didn't trust the fae here for a heartbeat. "Name's Liz O'Brien by the way."

"Danica Maslanka, and I mean the entertainment side of the street. I'm a leannan sidhe, Lizzie O'B, one of the tastemakers of our kind." Despite the woman's elegant attire and stance, once she opened her mouth, her tone emanated playfulness, and her eyes glinted with amusement.

"Lizzie O'B's a new one. Hope it doesn't stick," she teased. Even though her guard remained up, she'd rather deal with slick talking gals like this one than all the clipped words and polite roundabouts she'd encountered thus far. Besides, Liz couldn't help the curiosity bubbling inside, that maybe, maybe this woman knew a hint of what Larsen mentioned earlier.

"I'm surprised they're playing here." Danica cast a glance her way, intelligence lighting those deep chocolate eyes. "Those boys are as far away from an uptight Seelie shindig as they come, especially being neutral."

Liz eyed her back. Of course, the woman fished for information, but Liz wasn't born yesterday.

Danica pursed her lips as if she chewed on her thoughts. "Ah, fuck it," the woman said, with none of the delicacy Liz expected. "Blink twice if Larsen's stirring up shit for your boys again." The side of her mouth quirked into a smirk. Liz blinked twice out of sheer surprise.

"What have you heard?" Liz asked, her voice sharpening.

Danica scanned the entertainment room, watching all manner of gilt and polished fae filtering in. Discord's Desire had assembled on stage, and Ren tapped his drumsticks to a light beat as they prepared to play. She didn't miss how Kieran's eyes locked on her when he gripped the microphone.

"Not here," Danica murmured, crossing her arms. Her focus lasered ahead. "Too many listening ears."

Liz frowned, mulling over the idea. She wasn't asking a favor or offering food, and the woman wouldn't harm her since Kieran claimed her based on their weird societal rules. As Kieran's possessive gaze burned into her, the anger from moments before returned, that the ass would dare jump into something like declaring ownership without asking her first. If he planned to keep her locked in a cage for safety, he had another thing coming.

"Then let's find somewhere we can talk," Liz said. Even though her nerves thrummed from the idea of walking anywhere alone with a strange fae, her irritation marched in louder. Unlike the other fae she'd encountered, Danica didn't come off as plastic, cold, or dismissive, and Liz needed answers.

The melody began as Trevor plucked the strings, transfixing the audience. Jett's low bass notes wove in, and the percussion and bass beat of Renn's drumming followed as the song's pace picked up tempo. When Kieran's velvet voice penetrated the air, a hush slid over the crowd. His gaze marked her like a brand, so Liz took the opportunity to lock eyes with him, flash a big smile, and wave before she slunk out of the room after Danica. Let him stew on her disappearance for awhile.

Danica loped through the crowd with a gazelle's stride, but Liz followed just as fast, swerving past a group of satyrs who were beginning to leer at the crowd. Their kind were raring to go at a moment's notice, and with Discord's Desire's pheromone charged performance, they were straining the seams of their tailored dress pants. Liz gave herself a mental pat on the back—another good reason to get the hell out of this room. She dealt with enough randy fae in the RV and didn't need the extra trouble.

The cool breezes from outside filtered into the next room. The open doors led to an atrium lit by torches, hanging bulb lights strung around the vicinity, and illuminated bowls of water rippling with the breezes. An ornate fountain bowl of carved marble fishes dominated the center, and the burbling sound echoed in the quiet of the near-abandoned area. With all the flash and noise coming from Discord's Desire, the couple of wooden benches out there lay empty.

They found a bench far enough away that light from the open glass doors didn't spill onto the pavers, and the shadows devoured the thatched surface. Liz's bare arms prickled with goosebumps as she took a seat beside, Danica whose focus never rested one place for long. This wasn't a woman of patience but a veritable firestorm full of sparrow curiosity and lit sparks.

"Care to share why you're not running circles around our conversation like the rest of the people in this joint?" Liz broke the silence between them.

"Only if you want to explain what one of your kind is doing in a shindig like this. From what I've heard, hunters would rather see the lot of us slaughtered and yet here you are, living with Discord's Desire." Her eyes danced, and her mouth quirked in a small grin.

"Touché," she replied with a wan smile. She stretched her arms over her head, despite the strain of the stiff champagne dress she wore.

While she was desperate for answers, she'd been around the block long enough to know demanding them wouldn't get her anywhere. Desperation never played a winning hand in negotiations. For the first time since she arrived into this building, she took a deep breath, and her nerves settled to a simmer. The soft moonlight filtered in through the glass ceiling, creating patterns onto the slate flooring, and the hint of salt in the air added to the crispness.

"So I'm guessing you're not part of the Larsen fan club," Liz said, pressing her palms into the overlaid crosshatched wicker. "Just a stab in the dark here." She took care not to ask direct questions, because based on the way these folks operated, they'd lawyer their way into construing answers as favors.

Danica kicked her feet back and forth along the

bench, more energetic and youthful than the elegant image the woman cast inside. Her cerulean dress fluffed with the motions, the ethereal fabric floating feather light for a moment before it descended.

"The asshole thought it would be fun to take my little sister for a spin and leave her in the dirt. No one fucks with my little sister." Her voice grew tempered with cool conviction. "So, needless to say, I've been keeping my ear to the ground for a bit when it comes to his goings on. Hence why I knew he ordered a hit on his own brother." Her gaze flicked to the atrium entryway, and her hands balled into fists.

The silhouette was unmistakable, even though Liz had just met him. Larsen Blackmore stepped into view, the shadows and icy light turning his features to perfection. The man possessed a cold, coiled beauty, so different from Kieran's ripped-jeans raw heat. Liz preferred to dance in the flames.

"What are you lovely ladies doing out here unaccompanied?" Larsen's voice came out a low purr while he prowled over to them as slick as a panther. Knowing the ugly man behind the beautiful face though, the package didn't deliver.

"I'm pretty sure I'm accompanied," Liz said, turning her head to look at Danica, sarcasm dripping from her voice. "Didn't we come out here together?"

Danica's smile grew. "Larsen, in case you didn't take the hint, your company's unwanted."

His smile didn't falter, but his eyes sharpened. The man perfected his mask in a way that made Liz's attempts look like child's play. "I wanted to inquire as to how my dear brother's doing. You seem to know him well." Those shark-like eyes slid her way, pinning her with his predator intensity. Not for the first time this night, she wished she'd ignored the rules and brought her

Beretta.

"Just peachy. Now that they've got a proper manager, we're doing tours all over the place." Liz delivered a sugar smile with her words, because she sure as hell wouldn't admit they'd been struggling with the henchmen he kept sending their way.

"How are the senior Blackmores doing?" Danica met his gaze, knowing in her own. The woman kept a pulse on all the goings-on around here. For her to bring it up in the first place must've meant troubles brewed amongst the family.

"We're advancing, as always," he demurred, fixing her with an acidic stare. "How's Lenora doing?"

"Better since she's away from you, bastard." Danica's light tone didn't drop for a heartbeat, but the menace crept into her voice nonetheless. Liz pursed her lips together to hide her grin as Larsen blinked, affronted by the woman's lack of social pirouetting.

"Good to hear." His voice came off pinched as he zoned his attention on Liz. She gazed back coolly. With a shark like him, she couldn't let him see how much the man set her nerves on edge. "How did my brother end up procuring a hunter to his side? If you're willing to betray your own, there are better opportunities than traveling with unaligned fae. If you were looking for employ, I could offer to pay you more than most of your kind would see in a lifetime."

She'd been waiting for him to try and spring some ploy. Based on the sadistic relationship Kieran and his brother had, it was only a matter of time before Larsen tried to take his 'toy.'

"Oh honey, you don't know the slightest thing about me." Liz smirked, crossing her arms in front of her chest. "It's cute you think I'd go scurrying once you flash some cash, but I'm not interested. If you haven't taken note, your company's not in high demand right here." The words spilled out of her mouth before she helped it, but as Danica's smile widened and Larsen's gaze darkened, satisfaction welled in her chest.

"Claimed or not, you're the enemy, sweetheart," he responded in an acid tone. "You'll only ever bring him trouble." Without another word, Larsen turned in his Gucci loafers and strode toward the open doors.

Liz's heart pumped fast. Even though she kept a confident smile on her face, the sinking in her chest arrived with the realization she'd painted a big bullseye on her forehead for whatever cronies he would send after them. And unlike the rest of the boys, she didn't have fast healing abilities or acid-resistant skin. All she had was a Beretta, a mile wide stubborn streak, and a mean mouth.

"I *like* you, girlie." Danica's chocolate eyes gleamed as she clapped her hands together.

Liz controlled the worry flushing through her. The brief conversation with Larsen revealed one thing: Danica had told the truth about her sister. "If you're looking to take the asshole down a peg, I want in."

"We're drawing straws at this point." Liz shrugged, pressing her palms on the bench. "The boys are playing this gig so we can try and find out why the hell Lars has taken an interest in Kieran now."

"I can hazard a guess at the cause of the stir-up, just not why he's honing in on his brother," Danica baited as her plum lips curled into a mischievous grin. Liz tilted her head to the side, careful not to ask. Even though the woman appeared trustworthy, as the one human in the swimming pool, she needed to keep her wits about her. "The Blackmore family's taken a social dive as of late. His father got involved in a failed plot against one of the Seelie leaders, so they're on the shit list."

"That sort of thing common?" Liz raised a brow.

Danica shrugged. "Our kind have long lives and get bored easily. You do the math."

"Fair enough." Liz smoothed her voluminous skirts, watching the sheen of the fabric ripple in the soft light of the atrium. The acoustics from Discord's Desire's show filtered in from a few rooms over, and Kieran's silken voice carried with the breeze. Of course, upon glance in past the glass doors, a horned fae pinned a nymph against a wall with their lips locked, and a satyr engaged in the bump and grind with two eager participants. She squeezed her thighs together at the mere memory of the other night and how close she and Kieran came to diving off that ledge.

"Will you be in San Fran for a bit?" Danica asked, rising from the bench before she shimmied to smooth out her lengthy dress.

"Yeah, we're playing a couple of shows in the area this week." Liz followed suit and hopped up from her seat, not comfortable hanging out here by her lonesome after the way Larsen stormed off. The song finished with a crescendo, and Kieran's shout into the microphone echoed to where they stood.

"Thank you, folks, we are Discord's Desire!" It was the phrase they always used to sound off the end of their set. Which meant she better get her ass in there so Kieran didn't storm through the place on a murderous rampage to find where she'd disappeared to.

"Here," Danica said, slipping a business card into her hand. "If you want to swap dirt in a more private place, then you and the boys can come hit me up. I might even have some intel on all this hunter business. Don't think I didn't notice the thirsty look crossing your face at the mention."

Liz nodded, not glancing to the card as she slipped it into her bodice. Without pausing for a heartbeat, the two of them strolled toward the glass doors, heading for the now crowded entertainment room. She lifted her chin as she returned to the lascivious environment, the stench of sex thickening the air, remainders of their performance. Her stomach flip-flopped once she walked into the room. Even though the boys had exited the stage, she knew what would come the moment she stepped to the back.

She and Kieran headed for a collision, but time or fate would tell if she awaited a sweat-slicked back alley entanglement or an inevitable implosion.

Chapter Twelve

The walk to the RV was agonizing.

The second he stepped offstage, Kieran beelined for the crowd, searching for where Liz had wandered off to. She appeared almost as soon as he dove into the crowd, but instead of talking to him, she brushed by on her way to the back with the others, her glacial gaze piercing him through. He quickened his pace to walk in line with her, but she just murmured 'Once we're out of here.'

Jett hung back to spend more time socializing while Renn and Trevor gave one glance in Liz's direction and decided to find somewhere to slam a few pints in town. Which left him alone with Liz at last as they returned to the RV. He dreaded and craved this conversation, which based on the arctic way she regarded him could go horribly wrong. However, given time to simmer, his own defenses were riding in on horseback, and he didn't believe he made the wrong call on the situation.

"Where did you dart off to?" He shattered the silence between them, curiosity getting the better of him. The air froze in response. His temper stirred in the interim, because when it came to her, he'd fight for a resolution. "Fine. Be pissed off. I did what was necessary given the situation. Maybe I should've conferred with you, but we didn't have the time for a discussion on the floor of the shitty ass party, and I made a gut call. I'd do it again, too." His gaze heated as they reached the RV, and both of them came to a halt.

Liz met his eyes, her hands on her hips. "Do you think I'm so fucking weak?" Her voice came out low with restrained anger waiting in the wings. "I get you're impulsive. I get you made a gut decision, but this one doesn't just affect you. It's about me. You can't have a hold over me for the rest of my life. What if I leave? What if I fall for a guy on the road and end up retiring my constant travels to build a life with him?" Those words sliced into Kieran with an intensity that twisted and burned.

"Then we'll go our separate ways. I didn't make the call because I'm binding you to my side from here to forever, babe. I claimed you because I will always care about you, come what may." Even though his insides seared and he struggled to see a future without her in his life, he'd hold by his promise. He didn't want a world without Liz O'Brien in it.

She opened her mouth as if she were about to argue but closed it again. Her brows furrowed together as she processed his words, and pensiveness settled over her. Even standing in front of him with her fists balled, her lips pressed all serious-like, and ruffled in a flowing dress that made her skin glow, she looked radiant. The tension stretched between them to the point he could burst.

Liz let out a sigh and uncurled her fists.

"You're an idiot," she said, shaking her head. The pressure deflated from the room, and relief saturated his chest. A weary smile played on her lips, one he latched onto. He'd believed she might cut him out for good then and there.

"Not arguing in the slightest." He leaned against the RV and lit a cigarette. The smoke unfurled as the sweet hit of nicotine flooded him. Tonight stirred up too many turbulent emotions between encountering Misandra and Larsen and then the goddamned tension between him and Liz.

"Look, I get your brother is a psychotic freak." Liz sidled next to him and pressed against the RV. "He approached me while you were onstage."

Kieran's insides plummeted. Not again. Not this nightmare parade all over again. Any time he'd come close to happiness, his brother found a way to intervene. And who wouldn't go for Larsen? The man was loaded, high up on the Court food chain, and the slick sort of handsome women lost their shit over. Just once he wished he'd be the one chosen in the end.

"What did he offer you?" Kieran's tone grew bitter. "Money? Protection? A one night stand you'd never forget?"

Liz's eyes narrowed. "Do you think I gave his proposal a moment's consideration? Fuck you."

He let out a cloud of smoke with another exhale to keep from responding at once. Already he'd jumped to incorrect conclusions. His stomach tightened. "Sorry," he bit out. "To say it's happened before would put it mildly."

"You're never going to escape the past if you've entrenched yourself in it," she muttered before stealing the cigarette from his fingers and sucking in deep. A vicious trail of smoke bloomed from her mouth a moment later. She exhaled before passing it back. "I get it—this is the back and forth you and your brother have had from the beginning of time. But why not break the trend? If the Court and his standing is the most important thing to him, then steal your power back."

"You think I haven't tried?" Kieran tapped ash onto the concrete. "He's got enough resources and connections to keep him a step ahead. Most times I'd ride out the wave until he got distracted."

Liz's mouth curved in a sharp smile, her eyes hard. "Yeah well. See if he's got so many connections while your father's disgraced."

His head snapped up so fast he near gave himself whiplash. "Where did you hear that?" Kieran wouldn't have been on the news chain since he'd been cut out of the family. Smug satisfaction welled inside him that the man who valued his status and position more than his own flesh and blood would fall. The entire Blackmore family consisted of self-serving vipers with Court addictions on power trips the size of Mars.

Liz shrugged, opening the door to the RV. "Hey, I wasn't wasting my time at the ball. We went for a reason." He followed her up the steps and shut the door behind him, curiosity pulsing through his veins like a second heartbeat. She hustled toward the back of the bus, pausing to kick her heels to the far corner of the RV, and then she tested her zipper. Her fingers snagged it, but she lost the grip a second later.

"Need help?" Kieran offered, his gaze lingering on the creamy slip of skin exposed by the low backline.

She gave him the side-eye. "That's not an invitation to strip me."

"Who me? I'm a perfect gentleman," Kieran responding with mock indignation as he slunk up beside her. This close, her clean citrus scent lingered, and when he grabbed the zipper of her dress, his knuckles brushed against her warm, yielding skin. The temptation to taste surged through him so strong and fast his erection near popped the fly of his jeans. He took his time unzipping her dress, watching the way her breath hitched as his knuckles trailed down her back.

And with her, the attraction was all real, unlike with the humans and fae who reacted to his incubus abilities. Every gasp, the taut muscles of her neck, and how her chest swelled belonged to Liz. Her neck lay a whisper away, and it took all of his control to not lean down and press his lips against the slope. Before he gave in to temptation, she whirled around, clutching the front of her dress against her breasts.

"Thanks," she murmured, a breathy quality to her voice that shot straight through to his painful erection. Winter's breath, he'd have to spend some quality time in the shower after this. She took two steps toward her bed in the back but paused. One of her straps slipped down her shoulder as she spun around to face him again.

"Kieran," the words barely left her before he closed the gap between them.

No more hesitation. No more waiting.

He dipped down, claiming her mouth. The air between them grew syrup thick, and her sweet taste flooded his mouth, a delicious, ripe nectar. Sparks ignited when their lips touched as he let the electric waves roll through him. If the sight of her sinful body made him hard before, it was nothing compared to having those lush lips on his. He wanted more. His hands grabbed her waist as she deepened the kiss between them. When she opened her mouth for him, he plunged his tongue inside, caressing hers. Her hands latched onto his shoulders with a possessiveness that ratcheted his need.

Kieran had his fair share of kisses in the past to the point where they all blended together over time in an endless blurred parade. Several stuck out in his mind, like the beauty of a pristine summer night, but once his lips crashed against hers, he knew this would be one for the books. If he thought one taste would be enough, he was damned wrong. The woman demanded his attention like an addiction, and as he met her mouth again and again he couldn't get enough.

She grazed his lower lip with a nibble, a continual tease. She would deepen her kiss a heartbeat later to playfully tug away again in a moment. He had enough of patience, and each time she led him around, he'd devour her anew.

Her nails dug into his shoulders, sending a thrill through him that left aftershocks and testing his restraint. Renewed energy flooded through him, sending him diving back for more. The low moan slipping from her throat rocked him to the core. Her other sleeve slipped down her shoulder, and his fingers latched onto the sleek fabric, ready to dash it to the floor.

Drunk on lust, he traced her lower lip with the tip of his tongue before diving in again. Her thighs pressed against his with a demand he would gladly acquiesce to.

A clash sounded from the door of the RV.

Adrenaline pierced through the haze as the warning bells went off in his head. In the same moment, Liz surged away from him on the alert. Kieran whipped around to face the intruder, his shoulders tensing and his hand groping for the knife at the table.

"Well, wasn't that a waste," Jett called as he creaked up the stairs. By the time Jett headed toward them, Liz had vanished. Kieran stood there, his heartbeat racing and heat pumping through his body. His second-in-command strained the seams of his jeans. In the matter of seconds, all the fire igniting between them vanished with the interruption, and agitation flooded through in the wake. Letting out a hiss, he reached into his pocket for another cigarette and lit it on instinct.

"Come on, man, do you want Renn up our asses all night?" Jett complained as he reached past him to yank the window open.

Kieran sucked in a drag as if his life depended on it, resisting the urge to deck his siren brother for terrible timing. His body hummed like a guitar string begging to be plucked, but based on the way Liz hurtled to the back, it didn't look like those desires were getting fulfilled any time soon. The irritation tapping at his veins soured his mood at once.

"Well, I wouldn't be getting much intel anyway with Larsen getting in my way half the night," Kieran muttered between drags.

"Jessa says hi, by the way. She's got it bad for you, bro." Jett popped into the booth. Based on the eye scan Jett gave him, Kieran's state of pissed off broadcasted clear, but Jett ignored it anyway.

"Like I give a fuck." Kieran ashed in the glass cup lying around much to Jett's apparent disdain.

A slight rustle drew his attention coming from the back of the RV. Liz emerged in a long olive tank top and tight shorts he wanted to rip off the second she entered the room.

"Lizzie, maybe you can soften Ky's mood. He'd make a kitten cry with one look from his surly mug." Jett joked, clasping his hands behind his head as he leaned into the booth.

As fast as Kieran's lust departed, it returned the moment their eyes met. He shifted, trying to keep his hormones on lockdown as she wrapped those long legs around a chair, bracing herself on the back. She would've been twined around him if they hadn't been interrupted.

Funny first for him, because he never used to care about privacy with any of the other women he'd dragged into his bed. The guys had caught him nailing former conquests against the side of the RV, backstage, or even in the bathroom at a bar with no shame. Whether due to Liz's elusiveness or because he'd felt mighty possessive as of late, he didn't want what emerged between them to be shared around the RV. He wanted something unique, for him alone.

Her gaze snared his, and her lips curved in a feline grin that got his heart marching in double time.

Ever able to keep her cool, she responded to Jett. "Maybe he just needs to let off some steam." Even though her tone didn't hint it at all, the wicked ways her eyes gleamed set his libido on fire. He sure as hell could think of a few ways to blow off steam, all of which involved her in his bed.

"Want to hit a bar? It's not too late," Jett offered, tapping his fingers along the surface of the hardwood table in front of him.

Liz shook her head as she settled into the chair. "I've got some discussing to do with both of you." She flipped a business card between her fingers, too fast for him to catch the words.

Kieran quirked a brow. They'd gotten so caught up in the moment he'd forgotten their discussion from before and the information about his family she'd been about to disclose. He settled into the booth, wishing his erection would vanish.

"Either of you ever met a leannan sidhe named Danica before?" she asked, squeezing her bare thighs against the sides of the chair.

Kieran fought to pay attention to what she said, distracted by the way her body moved. He'd been an idiot to think one taste might be enough.

"Heard the name but never exchanged digits or anything." Jett glanced between the two of them with an annoying know-it-all look reaching his face. He drummed his fingers on the surface of the table, the man unable to stay still for the life of him.

"God forbid you meet a woman and not sleep with her." Liz placed a hand against her forehead in mock agony.

"And deprive my gifts to the world? It'd be cruel." Jett winked. "How does this Danica have the inside scoop on Ky's family though?"

Liz's grin widened. "That's where this gets good. She searched for us because she's got her own vendetta against Larsen for how he treated her sister. You wanted an ally? You've got one."

Kieran couldn't help the burn of pride in his chest at how out of the whole bunch of them, Liz had navigated her way through a Court function and obtained the very information they'd been searching for. Not everyone possessed her focus or savvy. His brother had acted like having a hunter in their midst would bring down a world of trouble, but for Liz? He'd brave it.

"Larsen's enough of a cad I'd half-buy it." Jett continued his incessant tap-tapping on the hardwood. "But what's to say she's not manipulating us for her own gain? Deceit is instinctual in Court functions."

She reached forward to tap Jett on the nose. "Come on Nellie Naysayer. Trust me on this one. Larsen came out to proposition me, and he stormed off in a hissy after the tongue-lashing he recieved."

A tightness in Kieran's chest unfurled. She sat there clutching the chair and talking about tossing out his brother, the one who'd stolen woman after woman he cared about in the past. How she didn't hesitate to give Lars the middle finger when he sprung his offer, one that tempted so many before. Of all the women he'd dated, dined, and fucked, he'd never met one more resilient. More remarkable.

And he knew right then and there, even if whatever flared between them immolated, if it all crashed and burned, he'd remember Liz O'Brien for a lifetime.

Chapter Thirteen

Renn and Trevor were hungover as shit in the morning since they'd stayed out until dawn. Liz heard them groaning in the kitchen all the way to the driver's seat, which she'd settled into. Meanwhile, over at the big kid's club, she planned their next step against Larsen.

Even still, she couldn't help the accelerated heartbeat at the mere thought of getting any answers today. She'd gone years begging for even a hint of what she might be, and the first tastes were a tease. She needed to know if others existed out there, others between the human and the fae.

Liz veered into the right-hand lane, squeezing the behemoth of an RV into the slight gap between a Prius and a VW Beetle it shouldn't have fit into. After the way Kieran kissed her last night, she didn't sleep a wink, but with Jett up her butt sideways for company hours afterwards, she and Kieran never got the chance to pick up where they left off. She squeezed her thighs together as heat pooled there from the mere memory of how his touch ignited desires that hadn't sparked in a long time.

And holy hell, the incubus could kiss. She'd never felt so swept away by locking lips with someone, and if they hadn't been interrupted, their entanglement had been heading in one direction. Despite the way she'd fought the idea for so long, after tasting the smoke and whiskey on his lips, and after the breathless thrill of their crash together rocked her as strong as a tide to shore, she didn't know how to turn back now. Even if she warred between wanting to fight him and fuck him on a daily basis.

Liz let out a sigh, wishing the tension inside her

would uncoil with the breath. It didn't.

"Are we there yet?" His silken voice came from behind, almost causing her to veer off the road. Instead, she kept her grip tight on the wheel and her eyes focused on treading the asphalt ahead of her. The second she locked gazes with the infuriating incubus, she'd want to jump his bones all over again. God knows she barely restrained herself last night while she'd been laying down Danica's proposal to Jett and Kieran. She'd wedged the business card on the dashboard, an address right outside of central San Francisco, so Liz made the judgment call to take a little detour while last night remained fresh.

"Cool your jets, rockstar. We just got rolling today," she said, trying with all her might to ignore how her body heated at his scent, or how his voice made her heart beat in double time.

He wasn't making it easy as he leaned against her seat, inches away from her, so near his breath tickled her ear. "Hard to cool down when you're so damn close," he murmured, the words shooting a thrill straight through her core. Her mind traveled to his hands on her hips, their clothes on the floor, and all the things his talented mouth could be doing.

Bad Liz. Stay. Focused.

"Well, unless you're planning on boning the information out of Danica, I'd take the aforementioned advice, since we're almost there." Liz kept her cool, even though she'd give anything to pull the RV in park, throw caution and responsibility to the breeze, and pick up where they left off last night.

Kieran snorted. "Nice evasion, sweetheart. But you can't keep dodging around me forever."

"Don't know, I've been told I'm pretty boss at pirouettes." Liz maneuvered the gigantic RV onto the turning lane toward a more residential neighborhood. The streets grew broader with some fringes of trees, and the folks milling about the sidewalks lessened the farther out of the city they got. High up where they were, San Francisco Bay twinkled in the distance, a glittering cerulean gem. She made the right-hand turn onto another street, this one leading to a tan office complex, much shorter than the soaring heights in the city proper.

However, the sign on the offices listed spelled out Maslanka Talent Agency, same as the film reel logo on the card, so she pulled into the narrow lane lined with shrubs that led to a parking lot around back. While the parking lot wasn't a full house to her relief, enough cars crowded it to make navigating a tricky process, one not helped by a certain incubus who refused to clear out.

"Time to go woo ourselves a leannan sidhe," Jett announced, marching up to the too crowded front of the bus.

"Guys, the plan isn't sleeping with her," Liz argued, rolling her eyes. "We're looking for help trying to figure out how offing Kieran would help Larsen elevate the family name in the slightest."

"Ugh." Renn groaned, joining them up front while he pawed at the side of his head. She cast a quick glance to where the three men squished themselves in the front of the RV, a big bucket of testosterone. Making a point to ignore them, she focused on putting this beast into a couple of parking spots without clipping mirrors in the process.

"Clean yourself up, Renn. You're a mess." Jett began laying into him, because the two of them couldn't go five minutes without bickering.

"Whatever. The woman works with musicians all day long—I'm sure she's not going to faint from a little chaos." Renn shoved his way to the steps before she'd parked as if he planned on tuck and rolling out the doors. The man's hair was disheveled, and he reeked of last night's Jager, but altogether he didn't look too off with the smudged eyeliner around his eyes and the ripped jeans he wore.

"A little chaos is one thing. You smell like you showered in spunk," Jett said as he joined Renn on the steps. Unlike the drummer, Jett wore a clean gray button-down, pressed with the edges sharp, a contrast to the glint of his piercings. The two were night and day different.

"Yo, keep your nastiness to yourself, brother." Kieran jumped into the fray, even though he leaned against the driver's seat, the heat in his gaze as they locked eyes making it clear he crowded her on purpose. Of course he did.

Liz put the RV into park and turned off the behemoth. "All right, guys, have at it." She let out a sigh as Renn near tumbled out the door. All three of them exited with the speed of puppies ready for a walk, and by the time she unbuckled her seatbelt and stood, they waited outside.

"Reckon they're all a bit antsy." Trevor winked at her as he approached from the back. She stretched her arms over her head, listening to the rippling crack of her spine.

"Yeah, well they can wait, because Danica's my contact, not theirs." She shot a glare to the guys who had ceased paying attention to her and instead started roughhousing while standing in the middle of the parking lot. Renn lobbed a punch toward Kieran who whirled around, diving in for a headlock. The drummer's ragged strands waved wildly around as his laughs pealed through the air. Jett crossed his arms over his chest, pinning them both with a judgmental stare. Not bothering to join in the fray, Trevor slipped his hands into his pockets and trekked across the parking lot toward the door.

Liz shook her head and locked up the RV before following Trevor's cue, letting the other guys figure out they'd been left in the dust. Her nerves jangled with the insistence of a ringing phone for the answers she'd been promised last night. Even if Danica knew a hint more, Liz would take it. The leannan sidhe had been right—she was thirsty for any ounce of knowledge regarding the hunters.

When she stepped into the foyer of the building, goosebumps prickled her arms from the stale air conditioning flooding the place. The anticipation soured her stomach. Places like these always reminded her of Dynamic Foster Care's office, the stench of cleaning fluids competing with those butterscotch hard candies that filled every crystal candy tray on the desks. After her first few home switches, those candies came to taste like disappointment. She hunched forward with her arms crossed as she followed Trevor down the hall.

An arm slipped around her shoulders, flooding her with warmth. Before she glanced over, she knew Kieran had approached.

"We're here to befriend Danica, not fight her, right?" he asked with his voice light but those amber eyes burning with seriousness. "Because you look like you're ready to tear into someone, not make nice."

Liz shook his arm off her shoulders as she straightened her stance. Even though she liked the feel of his touch more than she wanted to admit, he was right on one front—she needed to present her best foot forward here. She offered him a strained smile. "Offices don't sit well with me. Too many shitty memories." He'd shared his own bullshit, so it couldn't hurt to give him the heads up on hers.

He nodded, keeping pace with her as they crunched along the stiff gray carpeting together. She lifted her chin and sucked in a deep breath, even if the musty air stifled her.

"Don't worry, doll, she won't steal your job, even if I do end up sleeping with her." Jett walked past her, a grin sliding to his face. As always, Jett rerouted conversation with skill and knew how to distract. She shook her head, grateful to both boys. She didn't often set off a mine in her field of memories, but she'd take a life on the road with questionable finances over a stable nine to five in one of those prisons for more reasons than her uncanny ability to see past glamour.

"You try and find someone else willing to deal with Discord's Desire's bullshit. Babysitting, dodging horny motherfuckers, and fighting for my life were never part of the contract I signed." She grinned as she picked up her pace to a march. The glass doors at the end of the hallway were printed with the Maslanka logo and neared by the second.

Trevor beat her to the doors, but he opened them for her like a gentleman rather than tuck and rolling through like Renn would. Liz walked in, hoping last night hadn't been some fluke or trick. The moment she stepped in, her fae-senses started tingling.

The scent of jasmine wafted in here through the laden air, and based on the lack of flowers decorating the place, blooms didn't cause the fragrance. While this office had the clean white lines of the others with a flawless desk in the front and inkspill black carpeting, the babbling of a fountain that spilled down the back wall in a bronzed off section offered a soundtrack unlike the static silence of the hallways. The receptionist's sharp gaze flicked their way at once, and a too-sweet smile plastered onto the woman's face as she stood from her seat.

"Are you here on an appointment?" she asked. Her green tinged skin and wild curls hinted nymph heritage, and upon closer observation, small plants blossomed in bowls all across her desk.

"Yeah, Liz O'Brien, here with Discord's Desire. Danica should be expecting us." She conveyed confidence she didn't feel, because with the way the woman eyeballed her, the nymph gunned for a reason to toss the lot of them out. After picking up the phone and mumbling into it, the woman let out a sigh and pointed toward the corridor to the right, leading to a bunch of closed black doors. "Far one on the left. Don't waste her time."

"A plus on customer service, sweetheart," Trevor drawled on their way by, earning him a dirty look.

Liz led the charge toward the door marked with Danica's name on it. Her hand latched onto the knob, and she turned, pausing for a second before opening the door. She hoped this woman wouldn't be turning some trick on them. After dealing with a taste of Court life last night, she understood why the boys wanted no part of their poisonous politeness. But Larsen's agenda pushed them to take the leap. She opened the door, stepping inside.

Danica's office stretched far longer than the closet it appeared, a spacious suite with a massive mahogany desk in the back and bookshelves that spanned ceiling high. A bar resided along one of the side walls, a myriad of half-filled, multicolored bottles crowding the surface.

"Come on in, Obiwan," Danica called out, waving them forward. Her friendliness coasted in like the other night.

Liz slipped her hands into her pockets and

approached with a smile. "Got tired of the old nickname?"

Danica stood from behind her desk, wearing a tailored gray pantsuit that screamed business, but the bright blue pumps, chunky blue bracelets, as well as the thick-rimmed glasses she wore added a layer of personality. Within seconds, she walked over to the bar, beckoning them to come join her by the obsidian surface.

"Nickname got passé—this one's better, timeless." Danica winked as she poured herself a glass of whiskey. "Anyone care for a drink?" she asked, glancing around the room and lifting the handle. Like she needed to ask. Within seconds, all four of the guys crowded around the bar, ready to imbibe, even though Renn and Trevor were nursing wicked hangovers for that reason.

Liz stepped in, ready to pour herself a glass when Kieran's warnings returned to her—never accept food or drink from a fae, at least, she amended, one she didn't know and trust. While she'd like to believe in Danica, she'd been around the block enough times to not trust anyone until they'd earned it.

Danica's sharp eyes scanned over her, and without asking, she placed the extra glass under the bar. Renn and Jett were giving the woman a once over, which meant by the time they left, they'd be making a pass to sleep with her. Trevor seemed consumed in his own thoughts, so he leaned against the wall with a glass of whiskey in hand. Kieran, on the other hand, cut straight to the point like Liz expected.

"So how the hell do you know so much about my family?" Kieran confronted her, his tone edged with accusation.

Danica didn't blink at the bluntness but instead hopped up to sit on her desk, letting her heels dangle over the sides. "Because your brother hurt my sister. And no one fucks with my family. So I've made it my business, and as you can see, I've got more connections than most would dream of. Some might scoff at all the business I do with humans, but I find it exhilarating and useful. Better than mucking around at Court in the same circles for a half century."

"Ignore him, he's got his panties in a twist." Liz gave Kieran a flat-lidded look as she strolled over to the desk by Danica's side. "You want Larsen taken down a peg, and we want to help. However, we've got no leads and no direction to even start in, so if you're such a study on the Blackmores, anything you might've heard would help."

"You're an absolute darling, you know that?" Danica slapped the surface of her table. "If all the clients I dealt with were peaches and cream like you, my job would be the easiest thing on the planet."

"You haven't struck her bad side yet," Jett said, joining them where they stood. "Kitten's got claws."

Renn stayed by the bar, making some mottled concoction of liquors in his cup that couldn't taste good. Trevor continued his scan of the room as he observed from a distance.

"I've got your lead," Danica said, pressing her palms on her knees and hunching forward. Her eyes danced with mischief, which seemed to define this woman. "He's been seen habiting a certain place that isn't well known apart from folks in this area, and if there's anywhere to dig up dirt, it's at the Lotus Garden in Chinatown."

Jett's gaze darkened. "That place is ripe with Unseelie."

"Why do you think I haven't gone traipsing down there myself?" She pursed her lips, fixing him with a look. "But if I had others to watch my back, we could start figuring out why the hell Kieran's brother's been visiting on a regular basis. I can almost guarantee he's finding his hitmen there. After the Blackmore's fall from grace, they aren't rolling in cronies."

"And how do we know you're not another hired gun trying to drag us to the most dangerous place possible?" Trevor spoke at last, placing his glass of untouched whiskey on the counter.

Danica shrugged. "You don't know that. But hell, I think if anyone's more at risk it'd be me—going into an Unseelie heavy casino with five folks who could turn around and ditch me at the slightest hint of trouble."

Liz nodded. The woman spoke a whole lot of logic right now, which she latched onto. She met Kieran's gaze, trying to gauge what he thought of this whole deal. After all, if anyone would be transparent, it'd be him. He gave her a nod in response.

"We'll go." Liz stepped up to Danica, extending her hand. "Partners?"

A soft smile spread across Danica's face, none of the dancing wildness she expected from a fae. This was something real. Genuine. The woman placed her hand in Liz's and shook.

"Partners. Now let's go mingle with the nastiest fae on this side of the West Coast." Even though a smile lit her face, gravity descended with her words. "Now, I'm assuming you'll want to discuss a certain topic in private?" Danica asked, arching a brow.

Liz shook her head. "The boys can hear it too. I'm living with them after all, and if my kind are a threat to theirs, they deserve to know what trouble they're getting into." She stepped a few paces away, crossing her arms over her chest and wishing she had something in her immediate vicinity to lean on. The vicious swirl of hope and anticipation threatened to consume. She took another step back to steady herself and smacked straight into a solidness behind her.

Kieran wrapped an arm around her shoulder, offering the support she'd been craving. "Lay it on us. We're not willing to risk our booking manager. I've been told they're tough to come by."

Danica tapped her heel against the desk she sat upon. "There have been fae going missing for years, and whispers of hunters—humans able to resist the fae and ones who've made it their sworn mission to destroy them. Think like ... Buffy the Vampire Slayer for our kind. Except, Jolly Old King Tiberius just got a signed declaration of open war—meaning the hunters are tired of hiding in the shadows—they'll be searching for blood."

"Don't suppose they have a headquarters I can crash?" Liz joked, barely daring to believe what Danica said. That she had a purpose, a reason for these abilities. Her heart squeezed tight in her chest as she leaned into Kieran's hold, her lifeline at the moment. While there were fae she'd love to take down, the boys of Discord's Desire were ones she would protect with her life.

Danica grabbed a thick steno pad and one of the six dozen neon green pens scattered across her desk and scribbled something. She ripped off the paper and thrust it forward. "Here's an address. It's not headquarters, and it's hearsay, but it's worth a shot. Though I'd recommend going by your lonesome."

Liz stepped forward, her legs trembling from excitement as she grabbed the piece of paper from Danica and stuffed it in her pocket. Their eyes met.

"Thank you," Liz said, her throat squeezing tight. She'd been an outcast her entire life—a freak amongst the humans, an outsider amongst the fae. Yet for the first time she had the chance to find others like her out there.

Liz just needed to tackle a minefield of Unseelie at the Lotus Garden first.

Chapter Fourteen

The preparation for the ball had been all glitz and no teeth, but for the Lotus Garden tonight, Kieran took the opposite approach. He didn't bother with handguns, but they kept their own storage of weapons—anyone outside of the Court did. Tonight, he busted out his nastiest pair of black jeans, a wifebeater, and his leather jacket. Simple was best.

"Otherworld be damned, need any more needles, porcupine?" Renn mouthed off while Jett slipped knife after knife into the utility vest he donned.

"Sorry, my plan consists of a little more than stumbling in and trying to fuck my way out of the situation," Jett said, ignoring Renn while he placed a bigger dagger inside his boot, this one copper. Most of them packed at least one copper-lined weapon in case this night devolved into a fight with the Unseelie. The metal would scald anyone from that court.

Trevor's fingers twitched while he sat at the booth, staring at the window, like his smoker's urges ramped up to overdrive. His nerves must be riding him hard. Any fae-governed locales spelled bad news bears for Trevor on the off chance he'd run into his old captor.

Liz buzzed with silence as well. She slipped her Beretta into the waistband of her baggy cargoes and popped brass knuckles on the inside liner of her black hoodie. Given the current climate toward hunters, taking her into a place like the Lotus Garden begged for trouble, but both sides had to respect she belonged to him. While the poaching penalty on a claimed human was death, some fae—especially Unseelie—liked living on the wild side and wouldn't mind the risk. His stomach tightened, and he fought the protestations rising within him about her coming. He would only get attitude in response, and worse, she'd sneak out and follow, which would leave her unguarded.

All of this tension raced through him, setting his nerves on fire. "You lot look like you're preparing for a funeral," he said, his voice echoing around the weighty silence of the bus. "We're taking a sweet tour of San Fran's underground. I bet we'll make tons of friends. The guys at the Lotus Garden are known for being cheery bastards, right?"

Trevor snorted. "Yeah, butterflies and sunshine that lot."

"Let's see how cheerful they are with my Beretta up their asses. We're going for information, and we're rolling out right after," Liz said, her hand slipping to her waist.

"Elizabeth," Jett said in mock surprise as he placed his hand over his mouth. "Who put that foul mouth on you? It's like I don't even know you anymore."

"Save the shock and horror for the gonorrhea you're going to get when you try to bone one of the ladies strutting her stuff around the place. Can almost guarantee Lotus Garden will be overflowing with prostitutes," Liz muttered.

"You promise?" Renn grinned as he slipped his pipes into his pocket. For anyone else, it'd be a mere instrument. For a satyr, pipes were an instrument for destruction.

A knock shook the door of the RV, drawing everyone's attention that way. Kieran took the initiative and strode toward the front of the bus, brimming with unspent energy.

Danica stood outside, arms crossed and looking nothing like the business professional they'd encountered this morning. She'd donned black leggings, black stompers, and an oversized purple jacket with plenty of pockets. Even still, the easy smile she flashed upon entering the RV provided a direct contrast to the doom and gloom crowding out the air in here.

"Did someone die?" Danica wrinkled her nose once she stepped into the bus and peered at the rest of them.

Kieran snorted. "You'd think with the way these bastards are brooding."

"This is my face for everything," Trevor commented, standing from his seat, which caused a jangling in his pockets to tip off the sheer amount he'd packed away for this excursion. "I mean, we're going to a puppy parade, right?"

"Oh yeah," Danica responded, rolling on pure sarcasm. "That's the main event of the Lotus Garden, followed by a kitten dance party."

"Plus, strippers," Renn said. "A bunch of walking, talking Five Hour Energy shots."

"And we'll never get to any of them if we don't get a move on." Kieran took the reins like always, heading for the front of the bus. Even though his adrenaline kicked into high gear, guilt flooded through his veins like a numbing poison. No one would be dealing with this mess or heading into danger if his brother hadn't made him a target. Hell, Liz had enough problems to deal with after finding out who her people were without needing his bullshit. The nagging fear descended that she would run off with the first hunter she found, her time as their booking manager a mere pit stop on the road.

They'd parked in one of the nearby city lots, yet another fee he'd swindle his way out of—incubus charms had their perks. This time of night, the neons glowed on every corner, and the slope leading to Chinatown was bedecked with busy storefronts with silk purses and brassy ornaments cluttering the windowsills. The giant red arch adorned the entrance with gilt statues on either side. Even though the salt-water breeze spanned most of San Fran, here, the outdoor produce vendors and fish purveyors who hadn't packed up yet gave the air in this area a flavorful and sometimes terrible odor.

Jett locked the doors tight as the last to spill out of the RV, and together, their group took off, heading toward the Chinatown entryway. Average humans near jumped out of the way to make space, not wanting to try and navigate their way through a group of thugged-up folks in black leather. Not like he blamed them—they weren't projecting tourist-friendly in any sense. A group of girls stumbled out from one of the dimly lit sushi restaurants, their laughs pealing in the air as they made their way to the sidewalks. One look at the crew approaching, and even the drunk girls veered out of the way.

"Well, that's a first," Jett said. "I'm used to women throwing themselves at me, not heading the other way."

"Poor baby, dealing with rejection like the rest of us average folk." Liz patted Jett's shoulder, a grin rising to her face.

"How do you deal with their constant whoring?" Danica wrinkled her nose, with a bluntness he hadn't expected from one of his kind. Kieran's brows lifted in surprise. No wonder Liz liked her.

"A good pair of earplugs and the ability to nap through anything." She flashed the other woman a broad smile. Even though Liz put on her best show face—they all did—Kieran knew her well enough to notice her tells. The way her hand rested on the hip her Beretta hid beneath, the sharper edge to her words, and the quick way her smiles disappeared after each quip signaled she skated on adrenaline.

Farther into Chinatown, fewer folks wandered these streets, and many of the storefronts shut down for the night, leaving gaping black holes along the main section. Kieran wandered closer to Liz on instinct. He didn't trust what might slink in the alleys.

"Didn't know I ranked high enough on the VIP list to get a bodyguard," she murmured to him as he slid beside her.

"Top of my list any day," Kieran said without thinking, the intensity clear in his voice. Her eyes flashed with surprise at the admission, and he cursed himself. Before he bungled it further by saying something he regretted, Renn's loud mouth gave the timely intercept.

"Who wants to call this shit off and go get dumplings?" He complained while they passed yet another restaurant, the open doors greeting them with the drool-inducing scent of spiced meat.

"Dumplings are for closers," Danica responded. A building came into view in the distance, framed by rose-colored bulbs blinking on and off in regular intervals. A rinky-dink sign with bent neons spelled out Lotus Garden.

Trevor brimmed so full of nerves he pulled out a cigarette and began smoking, even with Renn in their midst. Clouds streamed from his lips as he took the lead, gunning toward the building.

"Don't leave my side," Kieran said, leaning to whisper in Liz's ear. "This isn't a place to mess around." The nerves in his chest reached a drumline beat, and every step closer, more fears blossomed—not for his own safety, but if anything happened to Liz, he'd lose it.

Liz lifted a brow at him, crossing her arms over

her chest. "Whatever you say, Your Royal Bossiness. I'm just a dim-witted doll about to toddle into traffic."

"Cute," he shot back. "The Unseelie around here'll make those ones with the acid spit look like bunnies. My mojo works on some of them though, so sticking with me might mean less necessary brawls."

Liz placed a hand over her chest in mock surprise. "Actual logic, coming from you? I may faint."

Trevor reached the exterior of the Lotus Garden first, and he leaned against the plaster wall, ripping through his cigarette until ash tumbled to the ground. The rose-bulbs cast patterns on the banshee's silver hair, deepening the shadows under his eyes. Trev wouldn't be feeling better until this whole jaunt was over.

Danica stepped up next, casting a glance at the clear display of nerves. "What's got you in a tizzy?"

Jett clapped a hand on Trevor's shoulder while Renn beelined for the door. "My brother here has some fae friends he's avoiding."

Danica nodded, smart enough to let the matter drop rather than pressing on.

Liz rolled up to the door, following Renn's busting on in approach, while Kieran tailed her. He hadn't been kidding about sticking to her side. When they entered, the smell of tobacco and spilled beer greeted his inhale in a powerful way. The seething darkness of the corridor ahead guaranteed no casual passersby would venture in, and even Renn slowed his pace to approach with caution. A gray door greeted them at the end of the hall, visible due to one dim light shining overhead.

"Can't we save ourselves the trouble and cap your brother?" Trevor mumbled, stopping a hair away from bumping into Kieran's back as they came to a sudden halt.

"I wish," Kieran said, running a hand through his hair. A slight sweat broke out along his arms, and he couldn't shake the foreboding while they stared at the door ahead of them.

An elbow hit his side as Danica muscled to the front. "Out of the way, bucko. This isn't a place they let anyone into."

She stepped into view and knocked three times at the door. It creaked open for a moment, even though no one stepped into sight.

"What has an eye but cannot see?" a gruff voice came from behind the door.

Kieran rolled his eyes. Of course, the place would involve some sort of riddling.

"A needle," Danica said with a surprising quickness. Either she'd studied up beforehand, or she'd been lying about her worries of coming to this place by her lonesome. For their sakes, he hoped it was the former not the latter. She stepped back, and the door banged open as the handle slammed against the dark wall.

"Come on in." A gruff minotaur hulked in front of the entryway, leaving them a mere gap to enter.

Kieran's back scraped against the doorframe as he pushed his way through, brushing against the creature's thick fur. He tried to ignore the overwhelming stench of wet dog. The minotaur cast a sullen glare even as he delivered a charming smile in response. The moment they stepped by, his arms prickled with the familiar shift into fae territory. Stepping into the pockets of the Otherworld was like entering a whole different country.

Lanterns hung from the ceilings, strung in wide arcs and twinkling with a cold metallic glow reminiscent of stars. The walls were a deep carmine, blending with the stretching shadows that covered the tables in the corners of the room. This casino didn't roll in machines, but instead big tables dominated the center of the place, turning the gamblers into a spectator sport as different fae sat around playing blackjack and roulette.

On the far side of the place, a small stage elevated from the rest of the casino with a spotlight cast down on a sultry succubus who oozed sensuality onto the crowd in waves. The woman's slinky black dress exposed plenty of skin, and her pouty mouth was the exact sort the rough and tumble folks down here would start slinging fists over.

Kieran shook his head, immune to those charms. Not like he hadn't taken a spin in the sack over a sweet pair of legs in the past, but none of those women seared his very soul like Liz did.

The working girls wore bright red cheongsams exposing plenty of thigh, marking them out from the other ladies who happened to be in attendance. Some sat on laps at the tables, their high, fake laughs crystallizing in the air, while others were leading men to back booths with long crimson curtains for privacy.

Renn lit up like Christmas at the buffet of women wandering through the place.

"Stay on task, jackass." Jett elbowed Renn in the side, beating Kieran to the punch.

While the glitz of the place bedazzled, as quick the seediness surfaced. Kieran led the way to one of the round bar tables in the shadows, carving his way past the grizzled bastards who made mobsters look like schoolgirls. The Unseelie were an ugly bunch, the monsters that came crawling straight out of your worst nightmares. A wispy creature half his size glared at him from another table, red eyes glowing from the face enshrouded in shadow.

Liz brushed by his arm in an effort to veer as far

away from it as possible.

Danica swerved past to claim the nearest seat at the empty table, quiet for the first time since he'd met her. After a clatter of chairs, everyone snagged a seat at the perfect vantage point to survey the whole arena, which brimmed with all different shapes and sizes of fae.

"I could use a drink," Liz muttered by his side.

Trevor grunted in agreement while his nails threatened to burrow into the surface of the table.

As if by magic, a goblin approached, a slide to his step and a hunch in his shoulder. "Does the lady want a beverage?" he asked, a twinkle in his eye.

Kieran glowered. "No, but I want two pints. In fact, a round for the table would be a good start."

The goblin nodded even as he scowled, his leathery skin crinkling with every movement. As fast as he appeared, the creature stepped away, vanishing from view. The slipstreams in the Otherworld were effortless, and here into Winter's realm meant wandering farther outside these gates in the opposite direction would place them into the dangerous Arctic territories.

"We're not going to get anywhere unless we mingle," Danica complained, smacking a palm on the table. Her voice reached a level of whine competing with Renn as those bright, curious eyes scoped out the arena.

"Any suggestions who to fraternize with?" Jett asked. He played with the buttons of his sleeves while casting the occasional distasteful glance to the surrounding crowd.

"Why don't we hit a table?" she suggested, looking over to Trevor who shook his head with his lips forming a flat line.

"I'll go," Kieran intercepted, knowing his friend would prefer sticking to the shadows or even better, getting the hell out. He glanced to Liz next to him. "Only if you'll be my good luck charm." He winked, hoping she'd humor him.

"Fine, since I'm sure as hell not blowing any money here." Liz shrugged. Her boots thumped onto the smooth tile as she hopped up from her seat. "What about the pints?"

"He'll find us," Danica said, leading the way over to the roulette table with a couple of empty seats. Five players crowded the table: two severe, but stunning pixies who buzzed around rather than using the seats, a spriggan whose long oaken tendrils brushed against the rim of the table, a troll who took up more space than reasonable and whose long scraggly body hair brushed anyone nearby, and a white lady whose opacity flickered every so often.

Kieran sank into the nearest available seat even though the goblin dealer didn't even pause to look at him. He glanced to Liz and gestured to his lap. "Want a seat?"

As expected, she crossed her arms over her chest and delivered one hell of a look in response.

Danica slipped into the space next to him, taking her place at the table with the ease of familiarity.

The white lady flickered beside her while the pixies zoned in on them the second they stepped to plate.

"Let's hope some of this Blackmore luck helps me tonight," Kieran said, making sure his voice projected. The dealer glanced up for the first time at that. "My brother's a big spender here. You might know Lars already," Kieran said to him, even though the dealer looked away.

Liz leaned in beside him, her lips so close they brushed his ear. "Great job at subtlety, sweetheart. You're a real pro."

Her lip quirked with a smile while she teased

him. The heat of her breath tickled his skin, revving his engines into overdrive. He wanted nothing more than to carry her over to one of those booths in the back and have his way with her. However, tonight they had this task ahead of them, and without a performance to recharge, he'd have to wait until tomorrow's show. Unless he picked a fight down here. Wouldn't be too hard with the cabals of nasties congregating in the Lotus Garden, but he'd have to face the wrath of everyone he'd dragged with him.

"Place your bets," the dealer intoned, his voice rasping low, similar to many of his race.

Before Kieran spoke, the goblin server stepped up, placing a cloudy looking pint of something that should've been ale in front of him. "House special." The goblin grinned, delivering all three to the table before vanishing in thin air again.

Kieran lifted the liquid to his nose, taking a whiff of what smelled like bog water and mud. Danica hadn't tried the exploratory route and tipped back a sip to splutter and spit into her glass.

Liz pursed her lips and pushed the drink over in his direction. "You're the one who ordered it," she said with a smart ass grin.

"Your bets?" the dealer repeated, fixing them with a glare from night dark eyes.

"Black," Kieran said on impulse, even with the low payout.

"Weaksauce," Danica said, placing her chip on the red three. "Going for a single, myself."

Before he responded, the wheel began to spin, clicking away. The pixies let out giggles, their voices tinkling in a high, irritating tone. The troll hunched forward so his shadow spilled over the entire table. The ball stopped right on the red seven. Danica kicked the table in frustration while the pixies let out high pitched squeals that might've been cheers. However, he'd lost, so he tossed his chips in. Right now, he didn't want to throw more money at this shitty place, he wanted to corner the dealer and shake some information out of him.

"Will you be adding this onto your brother's tab?" the dealer asked, his gaze sharpening on him. Fuck it. Kieran leaned forward, placing his fingers on the goblin's hand to try and get his mojo working.

"How much is racked up?" Kieran asked, even though he noticed the white lady staring at him something fierce in his peripheral. He shouldn't be using his powers open and blatantly on other fae like this, but unless they were going to speak up or challenge him, he would risk it.

"32,451 as of the Rembrandt Company's payment last month." The goblin spouted out, his ornery gaze focused on Kieran. Well, well, his brother had been a busy boy. If this dealer had intel, he'd squeeze him for all he was worth. After all the roundabouts they dealt with at the Mossfeather Court function, he chomped at the bit for some front forward dealings.

"No cheating at the table," the troll boomed, slamming his fist down and shaking the chips in the process.

"We should scram, rockstar." Liz tapped his shoulder, urgency in her voice.

"One more minute," Kieran said, focused on maintaining touch with the goblin. "I've got a few more questions."

A shout echoed through the chill house music of the bar.

"We need to get the hell out." Her voice sharpened. "Trev's in trouble."

Chapter Fifteen

"Get the fuck away from him," Jett bellowed in a deep, dark, and dangerous voice Liz had never heard before. As expected, things tumbled into powder keg territory and fast. When the shouts sounded, Liz's attention strayed from the table as she hoped beyond hope the ruckus stirred up was some random barfight. Well, it was a barfight, sure, but not random.

Two gargantuan trolls circled around Trevor who crouched in a fighter's stance with the silver glint of knives in his palms as he watched them. His dark eyes hardened with more venom than she'd ever seen from the laid-back man, and his big frame and bunched muscles coiled with violence he begged to unleash. Her heart squeezed with fear at the sight. As much as Trevor could handle himself in a brawl, those trolls meant business.

She scanned the crowd for Renn—the satyr ditched the working girl he'd been talking to and strode in Trev's direction. Her legs tensed as she prepared to bolt that way too, even though she wouldn't stand much of a chance against these heavyweights.

However, Jett hadn't been shouting warnings at the trolls. A gentleman wearing a white suit with a salmon button-up strode to Trevor's side, the yellow sheen of his skin and bloodred eyes hinting less than human. The man's slicked hair and glinting cufflinks signaled him as sleazeball in Liz's books even though she hadn't a clue what hold this man had on Trevor. However, the second this guy entered the ring, Trevor turned feral.

His mocha complexion grayed to ash, and the circles under his eyes grew deep and charcoal, enhancing the difference between Trevor and a normal human in a big way now. The calm air about him and the wan look in his eyes vanished, and his features grew gaunter while the air around him turned darker, as if he were sucking the life from it. Those brown eyes of his glowed pure silver, and he'd grown a foot in mere seconds, since the trolls didn't tower over him anymore.

"Oh, shit," Kieran cursed next to her, his face paling. He grabbed her hand and together they sprung into a dead run toward the blooming chaos in the center of the place. A set of footsteps pounded beside her as Danica kept pace without question.

"I'm collecting the merchandise that belongs to me," the gentleman in the white suit said. Everything from how his hands remained in his pockets to the way his shoulders leaned back suggesting he couldn't care less.

Jett on the other hand slipped out his knives in broad sight.

Even as Kieran tugged her forward across the room, she dipped down with her other hand to slide her Beretta from her waistband. With the shitstorm of a fight brewing, she wouldn't enter unprepared.

"I don't belong to you." Trevor's voice took on a glacial chill matching the flare in his eyes.

Liz's skin prickled with goosebumps, his intensity conveying all she needed to know. Bile rose in her throat as so many minor instances clicked into place. The way he'd get twitchy around too many of his kind. How he disclosed little about his past. And she'd seen him more than once hit panic attack mode in confined places. Kieran's grip tightened around her hand with a fierce protectiveness as she stumbled. The thoughts of what Trev must've been through made her want to heave.

They skidded to a halt in front of Jett and the man

in the white suit, and Kieran let her hand drop before he marched up to the guy.

"Walk. Away." Kieran's voice came across quiet as if he were having a level conversation. However, Liz knew him better than that. If this man didn't acquiesce and fast, he'd never survive the hurricane their front man prepared to unleash. Because simmering behind his quiet tone came a fierce and righteous temper. Liz and the others never questioned Kieran as the band leader for this reason. Out of all of them, he stood unshakeable against any opposition, and he'd never back down against those who threatened the people he cared about.

"Be reasonable," the man continued. "We've been searching for our pet for a long time now, and if you don't hand it over, I'll be demanding recompense next."

Liz's eyes burned at how Trevor flinched as the man called him an 'it.' As this bastard devalued her dear friend, someone who in the span of months had come to mean the world to her.

Wrong words to say in front of Kieran Blackmore.

The gentleman couldn't move fast enough to dodge as Kieran's fist flew.

A loud smack echoed through the Lotus Garden, which had quieted. Fights shouldn't have been shocking to the thugs crowded around these tables, so the reason for the hush must've been the status of the guy Kieran nailed.

Liz lifted her pistol, aiming the muzzle straight for the bastard.

The gentleman in white staggered back a few paces, wiping his hand over his mouth to clear away the trickle of blood that stained his pristine suit.

"We're leaving, with our *friend*." Kieran stared at

him with malevolence.

Seizing the distraction, Trevor spun around to lob a kick at the nearest troll to catch them off guard. The creature whipped around right as Trevor's kick collided with its spine, and it let out a grunt. The air tensed in the Lotus Garden, even though the goblin dealers operated their tables with the keen disinterest of business professionals at work. The patrons didn't hide their curiosity though, and folks tilted back their pints at their seats, watching with keen fascination.

"You can try." The gentleman straightened as if he'd never been punched, his slick salesperson mask returning to place. He sneered at Trevor. "You're not worth muddying my hands over. I'll leave my boys to bring you in." The man glanced over to the two trolls in his employ. "I've got somewhere I need to be, but make things unpleasant for this lot. The Alberich family isn't one to cross."

Kieran lunged forward to grab the man by the collar, but before his fingers latched, one of the taller, ganglier goblins on the staff intercepted, catching his wrist. Bad move, because the incubus rared to bust in heads. His amber eyes flashed like the stone, his jaw formed a hard line, and his neck corded from how hard he tensed. Kieran whipped around, lobbing a punch straight for the goblin's jaw.

The man in white turned around to cross his arms over his chest, brows high as if surprised by Kieran's audacity, like no one dared to spit in his pudding before. His eyes roamed the crowded place, and Liz's stomach squeezed with foreboding.

"One time offer. My name is Tymarch Alberich, and I'll award a hefty sum to whoever can return my property to me before the end of the night." His voice rang out through the casino, carrying over to the tables where all shapes and sizes of Unseelie fae sat and watched. Tymarch paused to shoot a gruesome smile in Trevor's direction before he turned on his heel and strode out the door with a clipped, perfunctory tread.

In one proclamation, he'd turned this entire joint against them.

"Run." Kieran gave the command, his voice low as urgency spread through them. Except he wouldn't be following his own orders, not while those two trolls loomed over Trevor with intent to maim. Liz didn't budge an inch, instead aiming her Beretta straight for the troll hulking over Trevor. He'd taken the other one out in the seconds of distraction, but this big, brawny creature hulked over him, ready to make a grab.

Pulling the trigger, she fired.

Once the bark of gunfire exploded in the air, chaos ignited throughout Lotus Garden. Kieran hurtled toward Trevor at a breakneck pace while Jett whipped around, his mouth opening as he unleashed his own form of deadly weapon—his voice. Renn pulled out his pipes as he raced across the room toward them, the first sweet strains of his melody inciting any passersby to distraction, targets forgotten. Danica, the smartest person in the room, began gunning it for the door.

The troll's yellowed eyes flashed in Liz's direction once the bullet burrowed into his shoulder. Shit. She'd been aiming for the skull. Those bushy brows furrowed, and a feral growl ripped through the air, almost squashed by the cacophony coming from a table of boggarts who tossed their seats back with echoing clatters. Some patrons remained by their seats at the tables continuing to gamble their coin while the dealers paid them due diligence, but the rest of the goblin staff assembled en masse, and it rested on a coin toss whether they marched their way to toss them out or try their hand at collecting a reward.

The moment the troll caught sight of her standing there, pistol in hand, Liz took off. A keening shriek followed, Jett's sonic blast burrowing into the beast. No way she'd stick around to get obliterated. Her Keds squealed against the slick tile as she headed in the same direction as Danica, making a beeline for the door.

Kieran reached Trevor, shoving him forward and latching onto his sleeve as the two of them scrambled to follow suit. Jett and Renn approached from opposite sides, working on crowd control in their own ways. Since most of the thugs in here wouldn't be after those two, Jett tripped a pixie along the way while Renn's piping stirred up infighting with every step.

Her hair streamed behind her with how fast she careened through the Lotus Garden, yet when the stomps of the troll shook the floor behind her, she couldn't go fast enough.

Liz veered up beside Trevor and Kieran who ran neck and neck while Danica waited for them by the open door, arms crossed and combat boot a' tapping.

"Leave it to you rockstars, unleashing chaos every place you go," Liz teased between sharp breaths, her heart pounding a demanding beat in her chest all the while.

"We're walking, talking destruction bombs." Kieran flashed a grin as they raced along, ignoring the shouts and screams behind them. A lob of spit sailed through the air overhead, and Liz almost collided into Kieran to get out of the way.

Heat exploded behind Liz, licking against her back so fiercely she thought her jacket sprouted flame. She spun around. The tiles behind her had been reduced to a smoking spot, and her back stung from the blast of accompanying heat. The culprit stood in the distance, a sprite whose arms were licked with fire. Trevor stopped and whipped around, his hands balling into fists.

"Go. They're here for me." He let out the command, his dark eyes burning with conviction.

Jett caught up, sliding to a halt beside them. His shoulders heaved, but he palmed a knife in one hand, ready to attack. "What are we waiting for? Get the fuck out of here, man."

"Don't be a martyr, Trev," Kieran said, his voice low and resolute. "You know I won't let that shit slide."

Renn rushed up, barreling into the lot of them like a juggernaut as he gunned it for the door. "Stop waiting around, assholes," he called out before he hip checked her.

Kieran stepped beside Trev, clapping a hand on his shoulder. "You don't leave, I don't leave, brother. So this is your call."

The troll still raced after them. Jett's sonic shriek might've blasted it back a little, but those creatures were built like concrete walls, so the second she lined up another shot, her bullet flew through the air. This time she didn't miss. The shot burrowed through the creature's skull, exploding fluids out behind him as he teetered from the force of impact.

Trevor let out a low curse, because Kieran leveraged the one thing he wouldn't risk—the lives of his friends. Liz didn't wait for the command as she followed Renn to the door. Danica disappeared down the corridor, and the minotaur bouncer had bounced himself at the start of the chaos, apparently deciding this mess was better left sorted out by itself.

Another spurt of flame hailed overhead, this one coming to crash a foot in front of her. She skidded before veering around the charred tile, not fast enough to escape the chunks of debris to go flying past. One sliced into her arm, searing and stinging at the same time. Jett reached out, slinging an arm around her shoulders as they hurtled toward the door.

A too-familiar shout sounded behind her, but before she could turn back, Jett tightened his grip and shoved her forward into the corridor. She fought to stop, but her best friend gripped her with a desperation in his hold that refused to give. Her heart seized tight in her chest, but together they booked it down the corridor at top speed, not stopping to look back. Not stopping to check, even though Trevor and Kieran lagged behind them.

And the shout had come from Kieran.

The second they exploded out into the brisk night air, their feet smacking against the pavement, Jett's grip loosened. Liz whirled around, scanning behind with fear that made her stomach lurch. They had to be there. They needed to be behind her.

Trevor leapt through the entryway, tugging Kieran with him, and once they burst through, Renn slammed the door shut. The closed entrance would give them a matter of seconds before folks smashed it open and continued pursuit.

Kieran took a hit. Claws had plunged through his chest, the long and sharp sort she would've expected from the crowd of monsters who congregated in there, and blood leaked all over the front of his chest, soaking his shirt. Each step forward he took, he heaved ragged breaths, and his muscles contracted in spasms, signaling he'd been hit worse than it looked, and it looked bad. Real bad. Liz's throat dried, her mind jumping to hospitals.

But hospitals wouldn't help a fae like him. Incubi healed through a different means.

Liz sucked in a deep breath, resolve settling over

her like a metal coating. She knew what she needed to do.

"Jett," she commanded, her voice strong despite the way her insides shredded as Kieran glanced to her. "Get Trev out of here, fast. Renn, lead them on a goose chase through the city." Trev shook his head, clinging tight to Kieran who breathed too unevenly to argue. She fixed the banshee with a don't-fuck-with-me stare before continuing, "I'll take care of Ky. He'll be safer if the heat's not on him, and tonight, it's you they're after."

Jett stepped to Trevor, jerking a thumb at the sidewalk. "Let's get out of here, fast."

"I'll go with," Danica volunteered, her gaze sharp on the door, ready for the burst of monsters they'd left behind.

Liz grabbed Kieran's arm and tossed it around her shoulder, picking up the slack from where Trevor held him up. The guy was all muscle, and she staggered for a second under his weight, but a moment later he steeled his legs to help her.

His amber eyes met hers, understanding lit there. "You don't have to do this, Liz," he murmured, an honest sincerity in his voice that broke her heart.

Right now, they didn't have any time to argue. She didn't have time to hide behind the walls she'd built after a lifetime of loneliness. Only the earnest truth would convince him to go, because the stubborn ass would sacrifice himself rather than pushing her toward anything she didn't want.

"I want to." The words came out in a quiet murmur, but his eyes widened. At that, arguments dried, and she tightened her grip on him as they cut a path away from the Lotus Garden.

Chapter Sixteen

Fuck. Kieran's chest squeezed with pain at every breath, and as the spins hit him again, his foot rolled to the side, causing another halt in their progress. Liz didn't complain once, just readjusted their stance as they staggered down another alley farther away from the casino. He tried to steer his focus ahead, but with the way he leaked blood, he barely noticed where he stepped let alone what street they might be on.

The boggart had leapt in, hell bent on sinking those claws into Trevor, but his best friend had been through far too much. Kieran didn't hesitate to jump in the way. His throat tightened, his body screaming out in pain. The stark vulnerability in her words struck him speechless, something he'd never expected from Liz. Not from the woman who never let those iron gates fall.

With the way the world spun around him, it took several seconds to realize they'd stopped. Before he asked, Liz lowered to the ground and took him with her. He stared at the night sky, seeing the glistening stars through the slit between buildings, which made it clear they'd slipped into an alley. His back scraped against the bricks of the wall behind him, even though he barely felt the sensation compared to the mixture of numb and raw emanating from his shoulder. He winced, because every motion sent another agonizing sweep of pain shuddering through him.

Until her lips pressed on his.

He leaned into the kiss, tasting the nectar sweetness as it rolled through him like a balm. Despite the way his shoulder pulsed and leaked more dampness, the tentative scrape of her lips scourged his mind of everything but her nearness and the sharp citrus scent coiling around him. The heat surging through him every time their gazes met returned full force, as if he hadn't been wounded in the middle of a fight. Because right now, his world consisted of Liz O'Brien kissing him in this alley, and he wouldn't trade that for anything.

Her thighs pressed against his on either side as she crouched on her knees in front of him, so close he couldn't stop his length from turning rock hard. She braced one of her hands against the wall while she tilted his chin up with the other to direct him. As much as he wanted to sweep her off her feet and slam her into the wall, right now he had a hard time getting his legs to cooperate. Yet as she swept the hot tip of her tongue in to explore his mouth further, tingling returned to his limbs while her chi flooded through him, healing him.

He leaned into the kiss as he began to regain strength, urged by the strokes of her tongue against his and how heat bloomed in the air between them. Despite the metallic stench of his blood and the cool mildew of the surrounding alley, Liz's clean citrus scent ignited his veins. She was steel tempered in fire, unafraid to lend her strength. As much as Kieran wanted to be unique to her and wanted to share the intense pull of admiration and awe that swept through him any time they neared, if this was the closest he got, he'd take the memory. He'd treasure it.

She continued kissing him until she broke away to press those swollen lips against his jaw, then his neck, the subtle sweeps making him strain his jeans. All those careful movements to make sure she didn't hurt him further after the number those claws had done. Screw that. He wanted her unrestrained and wild.

His hands circled around her waist, finding her waistband as he slipped his thumbs between the elastic of her panties, skating along her smooth as sin skin. She let out a low moan against his lips at the sensation, which encouraged him to go further. Her hoodie curved around those full breasts so perfectly he couldn't wait to peel it off her body. If he had his way, she'd be panting and undone in a matter of minutes. At least if his damned shoulder would cooperate.

The more energy flowed between them, the more the blood stopped pouring out and the wound began to knit up and heal. He drew in the thick, oil-slick sheen as the chi between them multiplied by the second. Every time her lips touched his, the numbness and pain faded away until he became present in each time their skin grazed. Heat pooled between her legs as she pressed her body against his. He placed a hand on her shoulder to brace himself before tugging his shredded shirt up. She yanked it the rest of the way, tossing it onto the ground beside them.

He reached down to pop the button on her cargoes, enjoying the way black lace peeked out as the pants slipped down her hips. She kicked them off behind her, baring the silken skin of her legs apart from her Keds. His balls ached over how many times he'd gotten off to the sight of her in those tight shorts she wore around the RV and how his temperature spiked every time she flirted with him.

"God you're gorgeous," he purred in her ear, loving how she shivered against him.

"No need to sweet talk me, rockstar, I'm already there," she murmured, thrusting her lace-clad core against him.

He swept his thumb over her sweet spot, feeling her wetness soak through her panties. "Well maybe I want you begging," he whispered in her ear, leaning in to bite the lobe.

"Fat chance." Her gaze glinted with wicked promises as she teased him.

In retaliation, Kieran dipped his fingers past her panties and found her tender clit. The smooth, steady strokes he applied had her breaths hot and heavy against his cheek until she plunged her tongue into his mouth to muffle the sound of her moans. He increased the tempo as she squirmed on top of him, arching her back. Wild strands of hair tumbled past her shoulders.

He'd forgotten all the pain from moments before at this point, focusing on the sheen of her lips, the flush of pleasure in her cheeks, and the way her body responded to his touch.

"You've got the control here, babe. I'll stop as soon as you beg for it." His grin widened, knowing the exact response he'd get. His girl was a fighter.

"Fuck off," she ground out. Her words were cut off by her sharp moan as he plunged his fingers inside of her. Her body bucked against him, making his balls tighter and his dick harder. The urge to claim her rose with every heartbeat, but he fought it down. He wanted this time between them to be as unforgettable for her as it would be for him.

"I can go at this for hours," he teased, moving his fingers in her faster as he began stroking her clit with his thumb. She shot him a glare as she fought the moans slipping past her and arched her back in response. Her slick pussy tightened around his fingers, signaling she was close to spilling over the edge. Her hands wandered down until she fumbled with the zipper of his pants, determination in her hot gaze.

In response, Kieran worked her faster, disrupting her focus. She managed to pull the zipper, shifting down his jeans, but once his erection popped free, a low groan slipped from her lips. Her breaths hitched, and her nails dug into his shoulders as she came, her pussy tightening around his fingers with her climax. The glow of her hazel eyes as she looked at him and the way her cheeks were flush with pleasure branded into his mind, amplifying the desire to bury into her.

Her lips descended on his with a languid enjoyment as she radiated from her orgasm. He removed his fingers to grab the zipper on her hoodie, tugging down. She shrugged it off her shoulders as his hands went for the tank she wore, doing away with that and snapping her bra open next. Rather than helping him, she went straight for his jeans, tugging them farther down his legs. The moment she pressed her hot, wet core against his shaft, his balls squeezed tight, and he needed to restrain himself.

"Sorry, rockstar, this girl doesn't beg." She'd tossed the kid gloves away, not afraid of him teetering on the edge anymore. Her eyes glinted with ferocity, one strengthening his need for her. Her hands clapped on his shoulders, and without hesitation, she lowered herself onto him.

He plunged into the hot heat of her with a slick glide. He'd fantasized over this for so long, and yet none of those imaginings came close to the real thing. To the sweat rolling down his arms as he thrusted into her, to the thick tension in the air between them, and even to the harsh scrape of the asphalt and brick behind him, keeping him present. Liz's breasts bounced with the movement, the creamy skin so enticing. Kieran leaned up, cupping one and squeezing tight before grazing the pebbled tip of her nipple with his teeth.

Another moan slipped past her lips, the bliss clear on her face as she closed her eyes and sank into the undulating motion of their bodies crashing together. His energy returned to him in a fierce way, flooding through with renewed intensity. He slid his hands along her hourglass waist, gripping her hips before he cupped her ass. Her eyes fluttered open in surprise as he clenched her tight to him while buried into her and lifted them both off the ground, rising to his feet.

She twined her legs around his waist once he lifted them off the ground, her heels digging into his ass. Kieran spun her around to slam her against the brick wall before thrusting into her all over again. She let out a surprised squeak that elicited a smile from Kieran. The wildness she stirred in him unleashed as he plunged into her, again, and again, and again. Liz leaned up, her lips meeting his in desperation as she clenched tighter around his length. The way she squeezed around him drove him crazy, closer to the brink.

She scored his back with her nails and scraped his lower lip with teeth as she bit down, the gleam in her eyes playful and fierce. He could do this dance with her forever. He got drunk on the heady air between them and the ecstasy that surged through his body every time he crashed into her. She stirred an intoxicating frenzy of emotions inside him. He cupped her ass, gripping onto her as he quickened his pace. Her pussy pulsed as she neared her climax, and his balls tightened again so close to spilling into her.

Her lips grazed his neck while his buried into her glossy chestnut locks. Sweat rolled down his back, drops prickling along his arms. She tilted her hips up as a scream ripped from her throat—her pussy squeezing his length when she climaxed again. The sound of her calling out his name pushed him over. The hot stream spurted from him with an urgency he couldn't halt as he emptied into her. After the first wave, several aftershocks rocked through him to the point his nails dug into her ass while he leaned against her body, keeping them upright.

Liz twined her arms around his neck, and she sank against him to deliver a long, lingering kiss while they both shuddered in the aftermath, sweat slicked and messy. He sank into the kiss, savoring the honey of her lips and the slight metallic tinge from where she'd drawn blood. Pressed against her like this in the softness of what culminated between them, Kieran didn't want to pull away. Didn't want the moment to break.

Liz slid out of his grip first, landing on her feet with the thud of her Keds he'd never removed. She sagged against the brick wall with a small smile as she tugged her panties up and began zipping her cargoes back on. Kieran ran a hand through his hair, because it was either that or run his hands along her exposed breasts to her hips and take her all over again. And Winter's breath, he wanted to. The way her hazel eyes glowed with satisfaction set his chest thrumming with pride and revved his engine in the perfect way.

Except this hadn't been about the dawning of something breathtaking between them. He'd gotten fucked up by a boggart at the club, and Liz bit the bullet to heal him. Nothing like a pity fuck to throw a bucket of ice on the afterglow.

"How're you feeling?" Liz asked as she zipped her hoodie up. "Is your wound all healed now?"

Yeah, that sliced straight into the ego. This back alley heat had been a quick-fix, nothing more. When it came to Liz, he did the chasing and always would. No matter how much he fabricated something real and lasting, they had a lot of lust percolating, and she'd thrown him a bone.

"Just dandy." He slipped his bloodied shirt on and wrinkled his nose at the mess the asshole boggart made of his favorite leather. "Thanks for your civic duty, Florence Nightingale."

Her eyes narrowed as she slipped her hands into her pockets, the hunch to her shoulders signaling her defenses were back in place. "You know I wouldn't let anything happen to you. Besides, we were both overdue for a bit of fun." Liz's voice took on the too calm tone she got when she glided in superficial mode, where she shielded herself from the rest of the world, which happened to be most cases. And right now, it set his blood boiling.

"Can't have anyone thinking you've got real emotions, can you." He regretted the words once they came out, but he couldn't help himself. Right now, he wanted to cross the space between them, throw his arms around her, and kiss her senseless, but even he felt the distance she'd placed between them the second they finished. Every time he got a glimpse of the real girl behind all the calm coolness, she locked her doors tight.

"Fuck you," she said, her gaze flashing as she stormed out of the alley.

"Goddamnit." Kieran trailed off, leaning against the brick wall they'd been slamming against moments before in the exact passion he'd longed for. Well, he'd wanted an emotional response—he'd gotten it.

Chapter Seventeen

The mood at the RV was dismal.

Liz didn't contribute much to the atmosphere either. After the break in her dry spell and the unforgettable orgasms she had with Kieran, she should've been riding the high. However, the moment she'd asked about his wound he'd gotten edgy, and not until after he'd pissed her off to kingdom come did she figure why her inquiry might've landed the wrong way. Still, the man ran off at the mouth like such an asshole she wanted to punch him in the face. Even if she figured why he'd gotten pissy, the damage was done, and she'd closed up shop.

Because she didn't have 'real emotions.' Yeah, she kept her shit on lockdown. Yeah, she didn't air her vulnerabilities to the world. But the bastard didn't understand how much she'd given to him, those soft moments between them she didn't offer to anyone. So if he couldn't take her like this, he could go fall in a ditch.

Kieran hadn't returned yet, and she and Jett sat on the asphalt of the parking lot in silence while they both sorted out the tangle in their heads, avoiding the obvious emotional minefields of the night. Trevor stormed to his bunk in the back, and no one had the balls to go and drag him out. Even though her insides tingled in the wake of the way she'd crashed together with Kieran, the thought of him made her temper flare all over again. Jett took one look at the storm cloud expression on her face and knew better than to ask, one of the many reasons he was her best friend.

"So Danica headed home?" Liz asked, trying to regain some normalcy as they sat leaning against the huge tires of the RV.

Jett nodded. "And Renn's out getting a nightcap while he stays visible around Chinatown. He's been sending me updates." He rolled his eyes, lifting his phone to pictures of some girl's tits. "Generous, isn't he."

Liz snorted, glad for the distraction from the turmoil brewing inside her. She and Jett were both aboard the Closed Off Express heading to Avoidance Station. Kieran was nothing like them. He epitomized everything she avoided, all his raw, clear emotion exploding out into the stratosphere. And yet, she couldn't get enough of him. Even as he enraged her, he pushed her past the coolness she'd erected, forcing her to reckon with things out in the open, and after years of stifling and suppressing her feelings, holy hell it was delicious.

"Renn's not here, pass a cigarette," Liz said, opening her palm in front of Jett.

He shook his head, a smile on his lips. "Buy a pack of your own for once." Still, he plucked one from his pack and passed it over, pulling one for himself too. In minutes, embers blazed on the ends of their smokes, and the rush of nicotine hit her system.

"Can't buy a pack, I'm quitting." She smirked, knowing with the way she bummed smokes from the boys she'd fail at the endeavor for the thousandth time. Her gaze traveled the length of the lot, anticipation building in her chest. As much as she didn't want to admit, she waited for Kieran to come into view, gearing up for the second they'd clash again. She craved his passion as much as these smokes.

After tonight though, she didn't know where their future lay. All the tension between them, the constant flirting, led to their clashing together in the back alley. If he'd been pursuing her for the thrill of the chase, the fire would soon turn cold and die out. She'd seen the tail end of these sorts of things before and understood the allure of the unobtainable. However, the reverse would prove a hell of a lot deadlier. Because she'd also witnessed the depths of his courage and ferocity toward protecting his friends, and if what blossomed between them warranted even a fraction of that, she was in trouble.

She let out a slow exhale of smoke, watching as it drifted to the skies.

"Did you at least manage to get some information from anyone there?" Jett asked. "We've been pulling nothing but dead ends with this mess."

Liz sucked in another drag from the cigarette to curb her bitterness. "Nada. We'd started talking with the dealer when the fight broke out. And you can sure as hell guarantee we won't be welcomed back there any time soon."

"Joy." Jett slammed his fist to thump against the RV. "How're you and Ky?" he asked, keeping his focus on the parking lot ahead of them since he knew the territory he skated.

"How are we ever?" Liz let out a sharp laugh. "At each other's throats one way or another."

"Speak of the devil." Jett tilted his head to the left toward the parking lot in front of them. Kieran stalked their way with his hands in his pockets, tangled dark strands slicked back, and a scowl on his face.

Liz couldn't help how her insides twisted at the sight of him. Her body begged for the sinful way he'd stroked her to completion and the tenderness in his amber eyes. The intense desire there made her half-believe the girl who'd wandered her entire life could stick around forever.

Jett waved him over, and Liz offered a small wave, trying to play cool despite the jagged way things had been left between them. He gave her a look that slammed her to the core, coldness she'd never seen from him in the past. Fine, if he was going to be an ass, two could play at his game.

"Hey, hey, Ace," Jett teased, doing his damndest to ease the approaching storm cloud. The childhood nickname from the brother he hated didn't add anything good to the pot.

"Trev safe?" he asked, jamming his hands into the pockets of his shredded leather as he focused on Jett, point blank ignoring her.

"Yeah, he's holed up inside." Jett jerked a thumb toward the RV. "Not sure if he wants visitors, but you can always try."

Kieran let out a slow exhale, like he tried to rein in his temper. "Someone has to. Besides, I'd best change out of these duds." He plucked his shredded wifebeater, covered in dried blood.

Jett clapped a hand on his shoulder. "Glad you're okay, brother."

"Yeah," Kieran said, chewing on his lip before he glanced toward Liz and gave her a nod. His amber eyes flashed, but right now she couldn't read anything from him apart from pissed the hell off. The angry words she'd reserved for him dried on her tongue in lieu of the cold shoulder she'd been given. Without another word to either of them, he strode up the steps into the RV.

Jett glanced her way, brows raised. "I'd say that's a bit more than the average fight. Don't tell me you cut his dick off as a trophy afterward or something."

Liz let out a bitter snort, his acerbic humor fitting her mood. "Your guess is as good as mine. Might have had to do with calling it a bit of fun, but you know me. I'm down for a no-strings back alley tangle."

Jett winked. "You and I have always been on the same page." He let out a slow exhale of smoke, and his gaze hardened a bit. "Though maybe I underestimated Kieran's fixation with you. I thought the boy set his mind on you, and a quick fuck would sort you both out proper."

Liz shook her head, ashing on the ground. Deep in her gut, she knew Kieran played for keeps. In the vault she kept her heart, she understood the precipice she dove off once they'd locked lips. He might think he saw forever in her, but Liz had long given up on the concept with anyone.

Broken homes made for a broken girl, and no matter how much she wanted to glue her pieces together, cracks reappeared, and she shattered anew. She tossed the butt of her cigarette to the pavement and ground it out under her heel. Tonight, sleep would be hard to come by.

****

The knocks on the door of the RV splintered the silence at once, and Liz almost tumbled out of her bunk in surprise. After last night, everyone slept in. Even though she'd blinked awake with the morning light, once she got a taste of the oppressive silence weaving through the place, she pulled the blanket over her head and returned to sleep. Rustling came from the other bunks as the persistent knocking continued.

Liz tugged her messy hair into a ponytail and straightened her navy-blue shorts and the long gray tee she'd worn to bed. Whoever the hell decided to disturb them right now would deal with her pre-coffee. After all, any bastard trying to threaten their lives wasn't going to knock. She strode down the corridor, almost colliding with Kieran as he hopped off the bed. Neither of them said a word to each other, the awkwardness from last night continuing to her chagrin.

She sure as hell wouldn't volunteer emotions, and for the first time since she'd met him, he shut off. Which left them in the best standoff ever.

Liz blinked hard, trying to get the sleep out of her eyes as she pounded down the RV's steps to open the door.

Danica stood on the other side of the glass with her long hair pulled back in an elegant chignon, and the matching green manicure and jewelry offsetting her cream blouse and tailored black flare skirt. Altogether the woman came off way too put together after the hellish time in the Lotus Garden the night before.

"Hey, Obiwan." Danica waved, a huge grin on her face as if they hadn't been chased out of a casino the last time she saw her. Before Liz said anything, Danica hopped up the steps and slid past her to wander toward their makeshift kitchen.

All four guys stumbled out from their beds in different shades of ragged. Jett, as usual, appeared the least unkempt of the crew, even though his button-down was rumpled and he fixed strands of his hair. Renn slumped into the nearest chair, clutching his forehead, shirtless of course. Trevor and Kieran competed for surliest as both of them formed a black hole on the booth no one else wanted to approach with a ten-foot pole.

"You lot look miserable," Danica said, crossing her legs in her seat. "What's wrong? Last night we came, we saw, we kicked its ass. No one's dead, so I don't see reason for the funereal air percolating around here." She paused for a second, eyeing the coffeemaker. "Speaking of percolating…"

Liz shook her head, grateful for the woman's hyper rambling, even if she didn't reciprocate. "Like you need more coffee. How deep in are you, six cups?" She pulled out their metal can of coffee and prepped a batch.

"Four cups barely scratches a dent in the morning anymore." Danica flashed her a grin, her smile infectious.

Jett crossed his arms in front of his chest. "Unless you got some new intel you're bursting at the seams about, I can't see last night as anything but an abysmal failure. Our one lead and we're guaranteed banned from the place."

Danica slapped her suitcase on the table in front of her, the sharp sound causing Kieran and Trevor to snap out of their stupors. She unhooked the latches, flipping it open to a stack of papers. "Here's all the information I managed to rummage up about the Rembrandt company. Or weren't you paying attention last night?"

Kieran leaned forward, his excitement at the lead trumping the funk he'd been clinging to. "They'd been paying off my brother's debt. I do remember—we'd been right in the middle of questioning the dealer."

"Bingo." She stabbed the papers. "So chances are if your brother hasn't made it a habit to sending folks to kill you in the past, it's tied up with something new, a debt he owes. And since he's loaded with debt at the Lotus Garden, that means there's a high chance someone at the Rembrandt Company wants you dead."

Liz gave a slow clap as the coffeemaker hissed behind her. "Fantastic detective work, partner."

"How are we supposed to get information from this though?" Renn asked. "I mean, unless they're funding a 'We Hate Kieran Blackmore' campaign, I'm not seeing how we'll be able to draw any connections to Larsen."

"Thankfully we're not relying on your intellect to see us through," Jett muttered as he scanned one of the top pages. "They've got a San Francisco branch to the company?"

"The attacks didn't start until we'd reached this

area." Liz leafed through a couple of pages on her own.

"So the plan is to bust into their offices and start asking questions?" Trevor asked at last, his voice hoarse from disuse.

Liz put her hands on her hips. "Not today you aren't. You've got a gig to play tonight, and I worked hard to book this venue. The Karma Club is a big draw crowd, and the paycheck would be nice."

"Besides, it's mid-afternoon." Danica crooked a brow, leveling her judgment over them. "Most offices will be closing soon, and the lot of you look like you survived a hurricane. That might cut it for playing a rock show, but you'll stand out like sore thumbs if you're investigating an office."

"Who'll go tomorrow?" Kieran asked, his gaze sharpening on Danica. Though Liz swore up and down the woman proved her loyalty, he made it clear he had his reservations.

"You certainly aren't." Danica placed her hands on her hips. "Since you're target numero uno, if Larsen's dealing with someone behind the scenes there, they'll recognize you on sight. Speaking of which…" She paused to rest her gaze on Trevor. "You should sit this one out too, since Rembrandt Company has ties with your boy Alberich."

Trevor's lips pressed into a firm line, and the hush fell over the room again as the boys glanced to one another, everyone feeling the weight of how much the incursion last night messed with Trevor's head. Except Danica, and for that, Liz was grateful.

"Coffee done yet?" She poked behind her to where the full twelve cup had brewed.

Liz handed over a mug, pulling one for herself. "Care to come to a show tonight?" Liz offered, glancing over to Kieran and the boys. If she'd expected protestations from a certain incubus, she ended up disappointed since he remained silent. The intensity in his amber eyes sent a flush through her as she remembered how they'd twined together last night. As much as she fought his overprotective nature, an emptiness ringed the air without his arguments for her safety.

Even as she focused on Danica who began babbling again, his gaze heated her. They might've avoided the conversation last night, however, with Kieran it would come to a head, and they'd have to discuss what transpired between them at some point. For the good of the band, she should nip it in the bud, deal with his ire, and stay the hell away from Kieran Blackmore and his to-die-for voice.

After all, she was the responsible one. The one who thought with her head, not her heart. Liz sipped at her coffee, the dark liquid scorching her mouth. The way the tension percolated through this place, she needed to go for a jog, now. And she had the exact place in mind.

****

Liz spouted off some nonsense about a jog, and even though Kieran frowned like he prepared to launch a complaint, he remained silent instead. As she ran along the sidewalks of San Francisco, the salt-air swiping back the stray strands of her ponytail, she hadn't decided whether or not his lack of fight bothered her. Sweat from her palm printed on the address she had crumpled in her hand.

They'd parked at a fifteen-minute walk away, and if she was going to try and meet with one of her kind, she needed to go by her lonesome. The boys would be at risk.

While no part of San Francisco scared her like run-down sections of New Orleans or some of the other cities she'd visited, this stretch held a few vacant lots and houses on top of more than a couple of nasty glares. It was clear the hunters weren't camped out in Marriotts or Hiltons. She didn't even need to glance at the paper crumpled in her fist—she'd memorized the address the moment Danica gave it to her.

Despite the dose of adrenaline coursing her veins, her stomach soured with each step farther down the sidewalk as she counted the house numbers. This stretch of rowhomes looked well-maintained if not somewhat vacant. Her grip around the paper tightened. What if they considered her a traitor since she worked with the Discord's Desire guys? What if they were included in the fae the hunters wanted to annihilate?

A gray door with the black numbers 235 on it came into view, causing her to halt. This was it.

Words gummed in her throat as she made her way up the steps. Most likely, the first sentence out of her mouth would be gibberish. These hunters had probably grown up together and worked like a family. They couldn't understand her years as an outcast, but they might be able to clarify certain things for her—like the inconsistency of the buzzing in her brain around fae. Or what she was immune to.

Maybe, just maybe, these hunters would've known her parents.

She reached the landing and lifted her knuckles to the door. Liz sucked in a deep breath, unable to calm the nerves rampant inside her. Summoning every ounce of courage, she knocked.

Silence. No creaks of the floorboards from inside, and no rustling. When the silence continued, she reached forward to test the doorknob.

It squeaked but turned. She pushed the door open, her heart hammering in her chest. Liz teetered on the edge of a precipice, blinding, brilliant hope almost in reach—yet the plummet of another lost chance, the descent of another dead-end one misstep away.

No lights were on in this place, and shadows stained every spare surface. The stale air and cobwebs gave off indicators this place hadn't been used in awhile, as did the dust motes floating through the air, illuminated by the rays of light that spilled in from the windows. Liz wandered in, her breath sharpening as she stepped too hard on a floorboard and it emitted a creak.

A porcelain mug sat out on the tabletop in the kitchen, and Liz headed right for the one sign of recent life she'd seen in this place so far. She peered into the mug, her nose wrinkling in disgust right as the tinny scent swept over her. Mold covered the surface of the half-consumed coffee, yet another indicator this place had been long abandoned.

Liz sucked in a breath, trying to ignore the heat behind her eyes as the disappointment sliced into her. She made her way to the door and gripped tight to the doorframe as she surveyed the room one more time.

Another dead end.

Chapter Eighteen

Nothing calmed Kieran like being onstage.

The moment he sang the first notes and cast the melody over the captive audience, a serenity trickled through him. The conversation he and Liz needed to have loomed, but right now he put all those problems aside and sank into the music, feeding off the energy of a teeming crowd filled with folks who were beginning to get rowdy.

He scanned over the masses past the people sucking face, the girls trying to climb onto the stage, and the headbangers near the front, while looking for a certain pissed off hunter. Even if she'd shut him out, that didn't change the way he cared about her, and he sure as hell hadn't stopped worrying over her safety. Maybe his emotions on the subject were too raw to voice at the moment, but he'd leap off the stage and tear into the first fae who looked at her the wrong way. He tapped his boot against the platform to the beat of the music, his voice rising and falling with the tempo.

Most of the time when he gazed out into the audience, a faceless mass spanned in front of him. However, Liz stood out, despite the casual way she sprawled on the barstool with a baseball cap on her head, her ponytail threaded through it, and a jeans and flannel ensemble that worked for him. The girl could wear a burlap sack, and he'd find her devastating. Danica sat by her side, the woman decked in a neon green hip-hugging dress tonight, another flashy choice he'd come to expect from the leannan sidhe.

Liz locked her gaze on him, and the electricity zipping through his veins added one more reason they needed to have a conversation. Soon.

Behind him, Trevor played the guitar with the same pristine precision as ever, despite his brother's shakeup the night before. Discord's Desire started as a gig to sate their needs, but he loved the music. All of them did. The way singing let his troubles melt away. The way it helped him forget for a brief moment his own brother sent hitmen after him. Under the spotlight, up on stage, he wasn't Kieran Blackmore, fuckup of the family. He was the lead singer of Discord's Desire, and there he shone.

All too fast, their set came to an end, the hours flying by in what felt like minutes. To his relief, Liz and Danica lingered in the audience by the bar. He lifted his arms, announcing their exit to dozens of cheers as his eyes narrowed. A couple of guys approached the girls, and the way one of them braced himself against the bar almost on top of Liz set his nerves on fire. With the way Discord's Desire amped their crowds, those guys had one thing in mind.

Once the spotlights shut off, the guys began a quick breakdown of their instruments. Kieran's skin hummed with the need to get off stage and talk to Liz. Now that he wasn't focusing on the music, the urge to rip those guys away short-circuited his brain. He popped the microphone in the holder and brought the stand over, tapping his foot at a too fast beat.

"Go check on Liz," Jett called over to him as he unplugged the amp to his bass. "You're annoying the rest of us."

Kieran gave a fast salute before jogging off the backstage and heading down the corridor to the door. He swung it open, maneuvering past couples making out with loud smacking noises while others engaged in humping the ever-loving crap out of each other. He'd spotted Liz and Danica as well as their obnoxious new friends back by the bar.

Except now the barstools lay empty.

His heart stepped to double time in his chest as he quickened his pace, darting past guys and girls mashed against each other in an overly familiar way. The way he'd left shit with Liz—he regretted it, and Kieran didn't do regrets. He needed to catch up with her and talk, even if their explosion of words ended with her wanting to never speak with him again. That is, as long as she and Danica were safe.

He slammed his palms on the countertop, drawing the attention of the bartender. "Hey, the two girls sitting here—you have any clue where they got to?"

"Got your eye on one of them, yeah?" The big burly guy winked.

"Yeah, sure. Just need to know where they went." Sweat broke out on his forehead. He'd been able to keep his cool while he stood on stage watching over them, but with the couple day interim since the last attack, they were overdue. Not like Larsen would stop sending cronies after him.

"Those guys came to talk, said they had some business." The bartender squinted as he looked to the door on the far right. "They exited out that way."

He started running before the man finished, tearing in that direction. Sure, it might've been some douchebags looking for a good time, so Danica and Liz happened to follow, but he knew for a fact she didn't indulge at their shows. Last night had been the break in a long dry spell for them both. His throat dried as he skidded to a halt before he smacked into the door, shoving his body against it to push the bar open.

Plenty of folks lingered on the streets outside, crowding the sidewalk and leaning against the building, and tufts of smoke billowed out from everyone who'd been waiting until after the show. Vestiges of their set trickled out here, where more folks than average were lip-locked and shedding clothing. Kieran caught the flash of neon green from a block away—the bright dress Danica wore.

Otherworld be damned. He sped up, ignoring the looks his way as he tore down the sidewalk like he'd burst into flame. His brother knew he cared about Liz enough to stake claim, which made her top of the target list—apart from himself of course. Folks near jumped out of the way as he hurtled forward, smacking elbows into whoever happened to not duck out in time. His heartbeat pounded in his ears at an insistent throb at the thought of something happening to Liz.

He skidded to a halt at the end of the block where they'd disappeared to the right, sending a spray of gravel up in the process. A long street stretched out, near isolated apart from a couple walking hand in hand and a lanky guy jaywalking across the street. His hands balled into fists, but nothing jumped out to punch. They'd vanished in plain sight.

Several dark crevasses marked the length of the street—the alleys.

He'd wasted enough time. He had to get to her, now.

Pushing off on his soles, he pounded pavement again, scanning the first alley as he all but darted by.

The bark of gunfire echoed in the air. His blood froze, and for a second he forgot how to breathe. Up ahead. The sound filtered from the alley on the other side of the street. He should've never fucking let her sit in the crowd to watch the show with Danica tonight. So wrapped up in their fight, he hadn't jumped in to argue like he always did, and of course, this would be the night they got dragged off by fae.

Barely pausing to check for incoming cars, Kieran darted across the street, gunning it for the alleyway.

The second he stepped into the entryway, the scent of rotting fish guts overwhelmed him, but what socked him in the gut was the tinny stench trailing in the breeze—of blood.

The group of three guys stood in the alley, cornering Liz and Danica who backed up to the wall. Liz pulled her Beretta out with her finger on the trigger. One of the guys crouched, his hand pressed to his knee, and Kieran's breath rushed out in one big sweep of relief.

Liz glanced up, their eyes meeting as she gave a slight nod, signaling him forward.

He clenched and unclenched his fists as he approached them in the alley. He gritted his teeth as the rage bubbled inside him, begging to spill into violence.

One of the guys whirled in his direction, knife out and flying his way before Kieran said a word. However, human reflexes were nothing compared to his kind, and as the knife sailed toward him, he swerved to the side. The cold metal clattered to the ground.

"Back off, man," the guy shouted. "This doesn't concern you."

"It sure as hell it does," Kieran said, his voice low. Humans, male or female, were easy to manipulate— he only needed one touch. Except right now, the adrenaline churning through his body placed him more in the mindset of punch first, chat later.

"Someone's tailing the guys," Liz called over to him, even though her focus remained on her targets. Danica's hands balled into fists, but she didn't carry weapons on her, at least not any visible ones. Even if the leannan sidhe did have some extraordinary fighting abilities, he doubted she'd whip them out until last resort. The woman held her cards close, revealing little. "They said the creature had a lock on you guys. If we didn't follow, he would turn the joint into a bloodbath." The cold fury in her voice resonated with him.

It was bad enough his brother made his life hell, but those antics were nothing new. However, the threat to the audience and the threat to Liz ignited him in a heartbeat.

"What're you going to do without your knife, asshole?" Kieran closed the distance between him and the knife hurler in a few quick strides, and before the man struck, Kieran's hand clamped around his wrist. "You're going to stop. Now," he purred, with the incubus persuasion of his kind.

A second later, the man's gaze turned dreamy, and he nodded in compliance.

Danica dove forward with her claws out, jumping for the middle guy's leg. In a less than graceful assault, her full body hurl brought both of them tumbling to the concrete, adding some dark stains to her neon dress. Liz seized the distraction and pulled the trigger again on the guy she'd kneecapped. He let out a loud curse as he sank to the ground, blood streaming from his leg. Kieran made a mental note to hide her Beretta at some point, because damn if the girl hadn't gotten trigger happy. Besides, she was a mean shot, at that.

"Who sent you," Kieran said, grilling the guy since the bewitched man wouldn't be able to lie to him.

"Some businessman," the blond murmured, his gaze vacant. "Said to take out the girl and if she wasn't compliant, to take out anyone else in the area."

"Big paycheck involved?" Kieran asked, putting the pieces together.

"Biggest take I've ever seen, and I've been in the

biz for a while." The guy rambled, his body calm while in Kieran's hold, despite the gun being pointed at Danica's guy. Liz's prior target dragged himself out of the alley, palms scraping the gravel since he couldn't walk.

"Who's following my friends? Discord's Desire?" Kieran asked, even though the temptation rode him to snap the bastard's neck and be done with him. They needed any information they could get, so for now smarts would trump.

"Some hulk of a guy, nasty eyes, and weird scaly armor. Wouldn't want to meet him in an alley."

Kieran's grip around his wrist tightened, and his nails bit into the flesh. Had to be something fae to trigger the weird. Human like him wouldn't see shit beyond the surface though. They didn't have any more time to dribble down the drain, and this guy wouldn't cough up any more information if he hadn't even been given names. Kieran let go of the man's wrist, but before the guy came to his senses, he whipped a right hook to the jaw. The man staggered back a few paces, wobbling on his feet. His hands flew for his chin right as his eyes rolled back in his head. He dropped like a stone in the pond.

"Let's go," Kieran said, his veins thrumming with unspent violence.

He barely heard the footsteps from the outside of the alley.

Another human stepped into view, this one dressed in black from head to toe, leather jacket, slacks, and stompers. Unlike the others who didn't look clear of mind, this man's eyes gleamed with pure and unadulterated venom.

"What are you doing to these humans?" the man asked, his voice low with contempt.

"Defending myself," Kieran said, struck with wariness. The predatorial way this human strode into the place, how he looked at him like he saw past all the glamour—Kieran got the sinking feeling Liz might get to meet one of her kind in the worst way possible.

Liz pointed her pistol in the direction of the new guy. "Who are you?" she asked, the edge of desperation in her voice.

"I'm not interested in you," he said. "Get out of the way—these two aren't who you think they are. I'll handle this."

Liz didn't budge. "What, fae? They're exactly who I think they are, hunter," she said, her voice firm this time.

The man's brows furrowed in confusion.

Kieran swallowed, hard. After all this time searching for her kind, this guy was an utter douchebag. He placed a hand on her shoulder. "Did you want to talk with him?" he asked.

"Not at the expense of the two of you," Liz growled.

The last guy left standing snuck out with the distraction, while the other crony struggled to crawl forward. His blood stained the alley in a dark streak. The hunter leaned forward, the platinum knives holstered into his belt glinting in the sparse streetlight. He tugged the blood-soaked man around his shoulder and headed out of the alley.

"You're going to walk away?" Liz asked, her grip tightening on her pistol. "What happened to your whole fae-slaughtering mission?"

The man glanced back, his dark eyes weary. "Our number one goal is to protect human lives first. Always." With that, he continued forward, out of the alleyway and out of sight.

Liz lowered her gun, a troubled look on her face.

Kieran squeezed her shoulder. "I'm sorry," he said, not knowing what else to say in the face of the extreme disappointment she must be struggling with. He'd seen how much she longed for a place in the world, and yet when she encountered one of her own, the guy had been cold, dismissive, and trying to kill him and Danica. Liz's jaw tensed, and she stared out like she attempted to collect her shattered pride from the floor.

Danica jogged beside them. "Use your X-Ray vision to find us, Supes?"

Kieran restrained his smirk at the woman's pop culture addiction. "Sorry, just my magic powers of asking the bartender." Both of them left Liz to brood on instinct, wanting to give her the space to process. She didn't indulge in public emotional displays, ever.

"Where were the guys when you took off?" Danica asked. "Do you think the hunter's going to cause problems for them?"

"Packing away equipment. They've got to be out back where we loaded up." Kieran quickened his pace to a jog again. Sweat prickled on his nape at the constant stream of nerves barraging him from the second he stepped offstage. "Next gig better be at a remote island. Tropical weather, gorgeous beaches, and none of my brother's cronies."

"Don't tempt me, rockstar. I'll start looking up island bars in a heartbeat." Liz forced a smile despite her shake-up.

"If that's the case, I'm becoming a roadie," Danica called out, lagging back. Her heels clacked against the asphalt, keeping her a couple of paces behind as they rushed for the loading area behind Karma Club. The folks leaning against the towering building didn't pay them a second glance this time when Kieran rushed up. First time might've been an odd sight, but San Francisco had seen odder.

His fingers scraped the brick of the building as he whipped around the corner, skidding to a halt in front of the Karma Club's back alley. Kieran's chest heaved up and down. He scanned the area at the same time Liz lifted her Beretta to take aim.

Before he could process anything, Jett strode up to them, scratching the back of his head. If the blood splatters on his shirt weren't evident on first sight, they grew clear the moment the metallic stench invaded his senses.

"I take it you had a distraction of your own?" He winked before flicking a piece of gristle off his open button-down.

"Guess there's no need to alert you guys of a rogue fae." Kieran hooked his thumbs into his jean pockets, stepping past Jett to examine the rest of the loading area.

"Sorry, Ky." Trevor winced as he locked eyes with him. His boot squished into a beyond dead scaled naga, based on the lack of movement and spray of blood coating every surrounding inch. Impaled. By his mic stand.

Kieran marched over to where Trevor did a halfhearted job at freeing his mic stand with pitiful tugs. Giving him an arch look, he grabbed it from his hands and yanked harder. With a squelch that echoed in the quiet of the alley, his mic stand came free. A sigh slipped his throat. After the way the metal bent, he'd need to replace the handle.

"You assholes couldn't have found anything else to use? I put my hands on this thing." Kieran gave them the side-eye.

Renn shrugged as he leaned forward to tug the

body toward the overflowing trash cans and dumpster by the wall. "You've put your hands in more questionable places, so I don't see the big deal."

Trevor fought to restrain his grin.

Jett led Danica and Liz over to where they'd stacked up their equipment, which had survived assault by naga unlike his stand. "At least it didn't put too much of a dent into packing up. Just a minor bloody detour."

"Hope you didn't chip a nail," Liz teased, her eyes glinting.

Kieran's stomach twisted at the sight. Despite the easy way she teased Jett, Kieran understood how much bravado she wielded, how she swore she was okay even when she died inside a little more each day. As much as he understood her, he'd never had smooth sailing with Liz like she did with Jett. Even if half the time they flirted, the other half turned into a fight. The woman would either spell his salvation or his demise.

Within minutes, they'd gotten the instruments, amps, and myriad of other equipment packed away into the RV, and Jett made a beeline for the back, near peeling his dirty shirt off in the process. They'd rolled the body into the dumpster—the best cover up they were going to achieve right now. Not like the creature would register in human records.

Danica slapped a high-five on Liz's palm. "See you bright and early, sunshine." She sashayed out of the RV like a neon whirlwind before anyone else got a word in edgewise.

If Kieran's adrenaline surged before, it was nothing compared to the moment Liz turned toward him, those hazel eyes serious. Neither needed to say a word, because they both knew a confrontation reared on the horizon.

"Want to take a walk? There might be chopped

up naga on the menu at one of the local joints." Kieran kept it as light as he could manage with the guys around.

"Tempting offer, rockstar. Maybe if we're quick enough we'll catch the special." She leaned down to one of the chairs and snagged her hoodie, tossing it over her one shoulder. "Try and keep up." The wink she passed back smoldered, causing liquid heat to flush through him.

Winter's breath, Liz would be the death of him.

Chapter Nineteen

Liz's throat dried before she exited the RV, and a flush of adrenaline prickled her arms. She'd been hoping to dodge around this, but once she caught the confrontational spark in his eyes, it was game, set, match. As they stepped onto the brisk San Francisco streets, she twirled a strand of hair around her finger. His proximity sent a wave of heat through her, the memories of the time between them all too visceral.

She glanced over while they walked in silence. His amber eyes burned with all the intensity of the emotions Kieran Blackmore never tried to hide. Based on the scorching look he gave her, they'd be sailing straight into feelings territory, and that was something Liz didn't do. One good lay didn't make up for a lifetime of goodbyes.

"If I'd known the sexual healing worked both ways, I would've hopped into the sack sooner. I feel fabulous," she said in a deadpan, trying her damndest to stay light and casual.

"Don't," Kieran growled. "Don't continue brushing this off." He stopped on the sidewalk, arms crossed and seething.

She slowed to a halt and turned on her heel to face him. At once, she wished she hadn't. Usually, she sank into autopilot with ease—a slip in the sack with 'wham, bam, thank you, ma'am' efficiency. Yet Kieran, from the day she'd met him, tested those boundaries, whether it be a nudge or the railcar ramming he'd been practicing of late. All of his constant efforts pushed her to this place where she couldn't evade or dash the other way. Not unless she left for good.

He clenched his jaw, and hell, his gaze burned. The scent of cigarette smoke and whiskey enveloped her, causing her heart to quicken. His hair was tousled even though some of the gelled strands held in place from the show. The way his leather fit his lithe frame returned her mind to how he'd pinned her against the wall the night before, and she couldn't help the shudder rolling through her body in response. Yet no matter how much he turned her on, how she longed to indulge in the brief fantasy that she could allow someone in for keeps, she had a lifetime of experience to prove the opposite.

"Sorry," she said with a shrug. "I'm not a happy ending kind of girl." And wasn't that the truth. She jutted her jaw forward, daring him to argue with her defenses, the only thing she clung to against this onslaught. Silken promises weren't enough to erase the stains in her past, and she'd stopped being gullible by the time she turned seven. That foster home had lasted the shortest time and became the first instance of many where she cut and run. To this day, the scent of Listerine made her vomit, because she'd learned then humans could be far, far worse than the monsters lurking outside her window.

"You're not just a one-night stand either," he countered. Based on the dangerous glint in his eyes, bitter, self-deprecating humor filed under brushing the issue off. She was ace at that.

"Well yeah, because you have to see my face the next morning." She pressed her fingers to her lips, blowing him a kiss that attempted playful. Bad plan.

"Fucking hell, Liz. Wanted a taste of an incubus? Don't worry, sweetheart, that's all I'm good for anyway." His temper burst, his voice raw. Old wounds burned in his eyes, ones flooding her with guilt. In avoiding her own issues, she'd unearthed his. She opened her mouth, sharp retort on her tongue, but she stopped.

Running a hand through her tangled strands, she took in a deep breath. Despite being overprotective and stubborn, the boy had a heart of gold and proved time and time again, he'd do anything for her. Time for her to nut up.

"Ky, I'm not playing around with you for kicks." The words weighed heavy on her tongue as she fought to continue. "Yeah, you've been on my mind. A lot. Any idiot can see that. But this is the longest I've stayed in one place, and we haven't even reached six months on the road. You're looking at me with these eyes promising forever, and I'm barely holding onto today." Her chest squeezed tight, and she tugged on the sleeves of her hoodie, agitation flooding her in the wake of the admission.

And he was the type of bastard to promise the world and fight like hell to deliver. But Liz O'Brien fought her own battles—she always did. Hell, it had been the sole way she survived this long.

Kieran didn't hesitate to close the distance between them. He wrapped an arm around her waist, clutching her tight to him against the inferno of warmth, and he tilted her chin up. "One day at a time, babe. That's all I'm asking."

A shiver ran through her spine, and before she could argue, her body betrayed her. The temptation in front of her proved too damn much. She leaned up, grazing her lips against his. The heat between them traveled to her core, and when they kissed, sparks descended to her toes. He deepened the kiss at once, his mouth claiming hers with a hot possessiveness. Her fingers curled into his shoulders as she melted against his mouth, dipping her tongue in to stroke against his own.

Mine.

The urge rolled through her fierce and sudden, one that broke through her drunken haze as the gentle melody of his mouth seduced her. Liz didn't stake claims because wanderers never got to play for keeps. The stubborn bastard found a way to break through her barriers and imprint himself on her, and that spelled bad news.

Even though she wanted to sink into this kiss and see where the night took them, this had gotten too real, too fast. Just like it did last night. She broke the kiss when her swollen lips zinged from his touch. With his hand on her waist, she'd curved against his body as if they were heading for round two.

He pulled back, caution in his eyes.

"Ky, my brain's scrambled fierce right now. This isn't a dismissal, but we're not green lit either." She placed her hands on his arms, not wanting to look into his locked and loaded gaze.

"I can be patient," he murmured, his lips brushing against her ear.

The man was so goddamned gorgeous it placed anyone at a disadvantage. A shiver rolled through her as she clenched her thighs tight. "Yeah, because patience is your strong suit."

"For you? I've got all the time in the world." The way he purred with his sexy as sin voice, she tamped the urge to throw caution to the wind and jump his bones anyway. But with the way things landed between them, that wouldn't be fair to Kieran, and she refused to be part of the lineup of women who'd used him.

"You up to the challenge, rockstar?" she said as she stepped away from his grip.

"Born for it," he said without a pause of hesitation. Once the man made a decision, no doubts lingered, and the way he spoke with a hundred percent assurance, she envied him. Hook-ups were one thing— Liz had perfected the one-night stand. However, relationships, feelings, they brought in all the complicated drama she avoided without fail. Until Kieran came marching in, refusing to back down despite the walls she tried to erect between them.

She slipped her hands into her pockets as the wind swirled around her, sending goosebumps prickling along her arms. He offered heat, hope, and danger in one irresistible package, and as much as she battled against this storm, she fought a losing battle. Because the way her heart sped around him, how she admitted truths she hadn't to anyone else before, and how he pushed her past the discomfort to be real, to be honest, Liz had already lost.

Heartless reputation be damned, she yearned for him with a fervor she'd never felt before. The seductiveness of all his wild emotion overwhelmed her, and for that reason alone, she needed time to process the change.

"I'm going to head back to the RV," she said, scuffing the sidewalk with the sole of her Keds.

Kieran nodded, his serious expression reflecting her sober mood. "I'll be there in a bit. Going to have a walk around the block." He plucked a cigarette from the pack and with the flick of his Bic, lit the end. A tuft of smoke curled into the air as he let out an exhale, even though the embers didn't compare to the way his eyes burned while focusing on her.

She gave him a small smile and tipped her fingers in his direction, saluting before she turned on her heel. Their talks tonight stripped her bare, and she didn't sit well with vulnerability, not with anyone. Her quick paced tread was the best she could swing without breaking into a full run to flee the scene. As she tore across the asphalt in the direction of the RV, she didn't dare turn back. Every ounce of her begged to race to his side, explore his mouth with hers, and let those talented fingers of his captivate her anew.

However, strength came in all shapes and sizes, and Liz, she'd always been steel. He'd always done right by her, and she owed him the effort. Pushing away or drowning in lust would be too easy. Leaving again, as much as she'd miss the boys, would be as well. She'd ditched so many cities and people in the past that the process had become an effortless routine. Even now after finding out what she was, she didn't know if she fit in with the hunters. What terrified her more than anything was the concept of staying. Of trying.

Her tongue dried as she pressed it to the roof of her mouth, trying to swallow. The faint smell of cigarette smoke traveled her way with the breeze, wrapping around her like a caress. And though she didn't glance back, his gaze burned into her every step of the way.

****

Liz set the coffee percolating before Danica arrived. And this time, she dressed to her personal nines in what some might consider business professional. She had to borrow one of Jett's button-downs and rolled the sleeves, since her on-the-road wardrobe consisted of ratty t-shirts, frayed jeans, and form-fitting cargoes. The coffeemaker let out a petulant hiss, but she put up with it. After the way she'd left things with Kieran last night, her body hummed. So loudly in fact, she hadn't managed a wink of sleep.

It didn't help she heard when he shuffled in later and sank into his bed with a creak. All the while she lay in her own bed, wishing she could take those heavy steps to cross the distance between them and slip into his. Which meant the second the sun rose over the horizon, she gave up on her farce at sleep and began dressing for the day. Because they got to pretend to work in offices, the very thing she hated.

Once the coffeemaker stopped spitting, she grabbed the handle to pull it out.

"That skirt would look better on the floor." His silken voice glided into her ear, almost causing her to drop the coffee.

Her grip tightened around the handle, trying not to let on the heady dose of desire that rolled through her with his lips so close to her ear and the hot words on his tongue. Whatever, two could play that game.

"Where's the mystique there?" she flirted, turning around to face him with a smirk. "Much more fun for you to guess whether or not I'm wearing panties."

"Not. Fair." He groaned, leaning against the kitchen counter. His gaze sparked with need, which encouraged her teasing smile.

"All's fair, rockstar," she said, pouring herself a mugful. She tilted her head to the coffee, and he nodded, so she pulled and poured another. Before she indulged in the steaming goodness, a knock sounded at the door, guaranteed to be their leannan sidhe friend.

"We'll continue this later," Kieran said as he strode to the door, a cocky smile on his lips.

Liz rolled her eyes in response, even though she couldn't help the surge of desire filtering through her at his words. Because hell, she wanted to lick the length of his body before the night was through. Yet the pesky feelings equation held her back.

Danica followed Kieran up the steps, dressed in the most subdued clothes Liz saw her in since they'd met. No neon skirts, colorful accessories, or even spiked heels—this navy pantsuit and cream blouse stated business.

Danica caught her stare. "If we're nosing around and asking questions, we'd best be forgettable."

"I should be going," Kieran argued, crossing his arms over his chest.

Liz didn't bother restraining her smile, a wash of relief flooding through her at the return of his normal argumentative self. As much as he was a stubborn annoyance, she wouldn't have the incubus any other way.

"You're the one Larsen's targeting, so that would be a resounding hell no." Danica gave him a level glance back, not ruffled in the slightest.

"Catch up on your beauty sleep," Liz said. "Better stay pretty for your adoring fans."

"Didn't know you cared so much," he drawled, his gaze sparking as their eyes met.

Before she responded, Jett strolled in, wearing a stark white shirt, matching silver cufflinks, and a crimson slash of a tie with the same efficiency as Danica. He straightened a few strands of his coiffed 'do as he came to a stop in front of them. "Ready to do this thing?"

Danica glanced behind him to the bunks in the back of the RV. "Broody and the Slut staying in for the day?" Even with her normal inquisitiveness, something in her tone struck Liz's curiosity.

"Broody and the Slut—new band name, called it," Kieran said before taking a sip of his coffee.

Danica had fixed herself a cup with cream while they'd been talking, and despite the heat curling from the surface, when Liz glanced over, the woman's cup was half empty.

"See you lot on the other side. Sooner we pump some information from the secretaries, the sooner we can put a kibosh on back alley naga visits." Jett delivered one of his business slick grins in response.

Liz groaned. "Of course, that means you're going to sleep with the whole batch."

A smirk on his face, Jett didn't respond as he strode to the front of the RV.

"Stay put," Liz warned Kieran, even though based on the mischievous look on his face, he'd ceased listening.

He pointed to himself, brows lifted. "Not a dog."

The impulse struck her, and she leaned in, her breasts brushing against his rock-hard frame and her fingers trailing along his neck. "Then why can I hear you panting?" she whispered before spinning around and quick-stepping it after Jett. A giddy grin struck her face, and she didn't bother turning back.

Danica followed suit at once, and all three of them piled out of the RV, making their way up the street for the steps leading underground to the light rail.

This early in the morning, swarms of suits bustled along the sidewalks, heading in and out of the skyscrapers looming overhead. Liz led the charge down the steps to the rail, ignoring the flickering overhead light. People flooded in and out of the place, from punks clutching their skateboards to the crew of had-to-be lawyers straightening their suitcases. Out of all the cities she'd been to, this one had one of the most efficient public transportation systems, and in a matter of minutes, the car screeched to a halt, the doors hissed open, and they entered the train.

Danica plopped into one of the open seats, and Liz followed suit while Jett clung to the pole, edgy like he always got in crowded spaces.

"So what's with the long looks between you and Kieran?" Danica murmured, her chocolate eyes gleaming with mischief.

If she wanted to tango, Liz was game. "I'm a little more curious as to whether Broody or the Slut has you interested," she dished back.

"You're good, darling," she purred, a feline smile rolling to those full lips.

Liz pitied whatever boy she pursued, because a woman like her was a formidable force. As fast as they'd gotten on, the train lurched to a halt at their stop.

"Quit wasting time," Jett said, weaving his way to the doors. The crowds had him at his most snappish, so they were best moving past them as quick as possible. The moment they emerged at the top of the steps, sunlight poured on them in buckets, a result of this gorgeous, cloudless day. It glowed off the surface of the nearest building, a glass monolith glittering under the sun.

"Their offices are in there," Danica said, shielding her eyes against the glare. "Who's ready to play pretend?"

"Do it every day." Jett winked, puffing his chest forward and putting his chiseled profile in full display. No wonder the panties dropped around him. Liz had fallen victim before.

"We're from the bank, wanting to clarify certain transactions to the Lotus Den, yes?" Liz reached back to straighten her ponytail. They hadn't even stepped in, and nerves jittered through her. Maybe she should've stayed back with the guys. Offices struck the match of memories she no longer wanted burning.

Danica lifted the suitcase she carried. "I even printed logo stationary and statements for the occasion. Let's get our whammy on."

The bone-white steps were on display from where they stood in front of the glass doors. Jett leaned over to squeeze her shoulder, as if he sensed the anxiety dripping off her. "You've got this," he said.

She forced the grin, returning her plastic mask into place. After all, they had too many close calls with these assassins Kieran's brother kept sending. Any chance to put the kibosh, she'd take it.

Danica grabbed the glass door and opened it. "After you," she said, gesturing inside.

Sucking in a deep breath, Liz ignored the memories crowding in her mind and put on a brave face. She was one of the openly declared enemies of the fae walking straight into their territory. No big deal.

Chapter Twenty

"Color me shocked," Trevor drawled, pacing in front of Kieran. "You listened for once?"

A cocky grin played on Kieran's face as he leaned into the booth, arms spread out on either side. "Who said anything about listening? I'm giving them a head start."

No way in hell would he leave Liz to stride into the place by herself after how jumpy she'd been in Danica's office. He wasn't blind—the girl had her share of damage, and she, like Jett, fit in the repress it and forget it camp. However, everyone on board this RV had damage. If anything, his past gave him more of an impetus to embrace life to its fullest. What better way to spit in his parents' faces than by finding happiness?

"What do you have in mind?" Renn stalked into the room, his hair a mess and half-dressed as usual with his shirt off and his cargos struggling to cling to his hips.

"Well I'll be damned," Trevor said, his grin reaching his eyes with a knowing gleam. "Liz is going to murder you." Despite the couple day setback, Trev managed to quash the whiplash of running into his old master and made quick headway in returning to his usual calm self.

"She can try. We'll be too busy playing distraction. Who's going to pay attention to a couple of bankers when rockstars are visiting?" Kieran hopped up from his seat, retrieving the messenger bag that slumped in the corner beside him. The several knives in there should've been enough armament, but in case his incubus charms didn't work right, he slipped a pistol in the waistband of his jeans.

"Renn, you want to meet some hot secretaries, right?" Kieran baited, knowing he didn't need to ask. None of the guys were the sit at home with the candles burning sort.

"As much as we want the ladies melting, I'm thinking you're best putting a shirt on, brother," Trevor said, casting a glance over to Renn who poked around the kitchen cabinets sans-shirt.

With a shrug, Renn strolled to the bunks, and a crash followed the bang of a drawer as he wrestled himself into clothing.

Trevor reached into his pockets and pulled out a butterfly knife, followed by a few checks to the boot knives he carried before popping them into place. "Can't wait to see the faces Danica makes when we come crashing in on her well-constructed plan," he murmured, a slow smile rolling to his face.

Kieran arched a brow but didn't say anything as he marched his way to the front of the RV. The second Renn skidded out of the back with a rumpled button-down on, Kieran hopped down the steps and broke out into the beautiful sunlit day.

Time to go stir up shit.

****

The stale lighting of the Rembrandt Offices wasn't doing any favors for his tanned skin, though Kieran never needed perfect lighting when he could seduce with his voice or a single touch. Not like he intended on bedding the folks he used his mojo on. The talk with Liz last night strengthened his convictions. She had a bucket of reservations and logical arguments against why they would never work, but desire burned in her eyes every time she stared his way.

The woman might be immune to his abilities, but he'd always been able to sense desire. After he stopped devouring chi during casual flings, he'd been fueling up at shows even if he was a little hungrier than normal. Until he locked lips with Liz O'Brien. He'd never burst with this explosion of energy in his life.

Trevor and Renn kept pace with him as he strode down the paisley carpeted corridor. Ahead, a set of glass doors spelled out Rembrandt Company in white vinyl lettering. He more than prepared to bust the door down and put on a show, even if he didn't have a clue as to what story they were rolling with. Kieran never worked well with drawn-out plans anyway. He'd drop in, follow his gut, and go with the punches.

Hand on the handle, Kieran opened the door. In the foyer, a cream desk spanned most of the reception area with several chairs along the walls and magazines piled high on side tables as if he'd stepped into a doctor's office. A corridor stretched out in both directions, leading to the individual offices, though he hadn't spent much time researching into what this company did. He probably should've.

Four women sat at computers behind the tall desk in the foyer, one of them on the phone. The second the three of them stepped into the room, all eyes honed their way and not because ripped jeans and piercings weren't office appropriate. Lust dripped from the women's gazes upon approach, and Kieran took full advantage of the attention, walking up to lean on the counter.

"Not wanting to be a nuisance, but I came to clear a family matter." He flashed a ladykiller grin, one that worked a thousand times in the past. For a fae-run company, these ladies were as human as they came, and a slight flush broke out on the cheeks of the brunette he talked to.

"What can we do to help you?" she asked, her voice coming in a bit breathy. The woman tucked her curly hair behind her ears while the other receptionist spent a couple of minutes tugging her V-neck into place to reveal a slip of cleavage.

"Do you happen to know who my brother's been consulting with here? His name is Larsen Blackmore. I was confused with him when I went out the other night, and I wanted to make sure there's no trouble going on in the family." He leaned forward a little closer and lifted his hand with a mock whisper. "I think he's got a gambling problem."

The brunette tilted her head to the computer screen at once, and her fingers flew, clack-clacking on the keypad. A loud laugh came from the girl next to her at whatever Trevor murmured, and based on the way the woman on the phone kept turning and gaping she wasn't paying any attention to whoever talked on the other end.

"He's been meeting with Jay Vandermere over in loans and consolidation," she said, before looking up. Her eyes gleamed with hope, but unfortunately for her, he didn't need an energy drink pick-me-up. Renn drew an audience at this point as the two other girls both focused on him and Trevor, their batting lashes and hair twirls the tip of the iceberg. If his boys went their normal route, in seconds, buttons would pop, pencils would drop, and they'd be making an excuse to head to the bathroom.

"We'll be in touch with you once we consolidate our files. However, that will take some time." A loud male's voice carried their way as several pairs of footsteps clacked in their direction.

Kieran froze, his palm pressed to the desk, praying no one would recognize him. He needed to act fast. "Look, sweetheart, can you do me a huge personal favor?" He leaned in, stroking his fingers over her hand. Forget attraction, she became putty in the face of his incubus mojo. "If you can get your hands on those transactions, I'm going to print them up and show them to my folks so we can do something about my brother's problem. Here…" He paused to pluck a pen and notepad from her desk before scribbling his email. "Just send them here."

She nodded, her gaze warm and devoted, like she'd jump off a cliff if he asked her to. Though with the extremes his touch inspired in people, it wasn't a far shot. Most times, the complete control left him feeling like he needed to take a shower to scrub the filth away.

The group stepped into view, walking in their direction. A strapping selkie who wore the hell out of a suit and tie led them, followed by three very familiar faces. When he locked gazes with the group, Liz's mouth opened, Jett heaved a sigh, and Danica's brows narrowed. They had to wait to yell at him, since right now they wouldn't risk blowing their cover. Kieran took full advantage of it, nodding in their direction as they were escorted to the door. The selkie passed him a grimace when he walked by, and Kieran knew they'd run out of time.

"Quit flirting with these lovely ladies, boys. We've got a show to get ready for," he said, trying to get Trevor and Renn's attention. Both of them picked up what he put down, wrapping up their conversations quick. "See you later." He winked at the brunette before turning on his heel and slipping his hands into his pockets. Before he took another step forward, he bumped straight into the selkie who crossed his arms and fixed him with a glower.

"What are you harassing my staff for?" the man rumbled.

"Hoping they'd pass around a flyer for our show tonight, but no dice." Kieran met his gaze with a challenge, not pausing for a heartbeat.

"Unregistered visitors aren't welcome in these buildings," the selkie ground out, emphasizing visitors since they both knew he meant fae. Kieran's hands balled into fists, ready for a fight with the way the man eyed him down. "You won't mind sitting with our security officers so they can ensure your motives, would you?" The guy's eyes flickered with a glint, since he had them pinned.

Shit. Maybe this was why Danica hadn't wanted them to tag along. He glanced to Trevor, who paled. Once those bastards questioned him, Trev's name be up for sale to Alberich, and whoever tried to eliminate him would know he sniffed around, blowing any advantage they might have.

The selkie crossed his arms over his chest, a smug look spreading over his face at their hesitation. They needed to make a call, and fast.

Kieran glanced to Renn and Trev, nodding slowly. Based on the gleam in their eyes, they rolled on the exact page as him.

"Run," he said in the same instance he rocketed past the selkie, hurtling for the door. Footsteps followed him in the same mad scramble when he slammed into the glass door, sending it flying open. The selkie's shouts sounded, but he paid the man no mind while he raced down the corridor. One glance back told him all he needed to know—Trevor and Renn raced behind him, keeping pace. A smile ripped across his face at the thrill of the chase.

Three figures stood waiting, but Kieran waved upon approach, not coming to a stop.

"May have stirred up a bit of a ruckus," he called as he dashed by them, the other guys in tow. Jett shook his head and raced after them.

"I should've known better." Liz called out from behind as they ran for the elevator. "The moment we told you no, you *had* to rebel."

"Aww, it's like you know me," Kieran said as he skidded to the elevator.

He slung an arm around her shoulders to bring her in close while they waited. His heart thudded faster from the sprint, and his nerves jangled to keep running, but the elevator decided to take a thousand years.

From the end of the corridor, the selkie's shouts echoed, but he wouldn't chase after them without his guards.

Liz rolled her eyes but to his satisfaction leaned into him. The way she curved against him was a sure sign her surroundings made her uncomfortable, though the woman would never admit it. Pride bubbled in him at being any safety line for her.

"What the hell do you guys think you were doing?" Danica hissed out, even though she kept her voice under control.

"Sorry darling, all the sitting around back in the RV, and we got bored," Trevor said, jumping in before Kieran. He felt the steam emanating from the leannan sidhe as she tried to keep her temper under wraps.

The elevator door dinged open, and Liz peeled herself off him, jumping in first.

"I was waiting for you guys to show." Jett cast him a sideways glance. They stood next to each other in the elevator as it let off a ding at each floor. "You're the last person to listen to orders."

The elevator door clicked open again after they settled onto the ground floor. Sunbeams cast alluring patterns on the slate flooring in front of them. Liz burst out and quickened her pace to the exit. The rest of them followed suit, bolting past the doors before anyone from the Rembrandt company could find and question them.

"At least tell me you found out something," Danica grumbled, her arms crossed in front of her chest and those plum lips pursed.

"You guys first," Kieran said. "Let's hear how the professionals got it done."

"Food first. I'm starving," Liz said, undoing the top buttons of the oversized button-down she wore. In seconds, she'd shrugged it off to reveal a luscious amount of her tanned skin with the maroon tank top she sported.

"I know a spot," Renn said to everyone's surprise as he took the lead. This close to Fisherman's Wharf, restaurants littered the streetsides, offering a buffet of options from Mexican to sushi. After a couple of turns, Renn pointed to the end of the street where a neon lit sign marked Fred's Diner out on the landscape. "They've got good shakes and a place to sit quiet." Renn shrugged.

Jett lifted a brow. "The epitome of epicurean taste. I can see it on the Zagat reviews list: good shakes, now shut up and eat your meal." That elicited a snort out of Liz.

Renn gave Jett a lazy shove. "No one gives a fuck about your fancy ratings."

Danica's heels clacked against the sidewalk as she took the lead, the woman walking as if her skirt lit on fire. She flung the door open and plunged into the dim entrance, not waiting for the rest of them. Kieran sauntered beside Liz, her clean citrus scent floating his way and reminding him of memories he'd be happy to relive. Hell to hunting down people and hell to an audience, he wanted to slam her against the wall and explore her mouth all over again. He wanted to spend hours teasing her, watching the gorgeous expression on her face as she rode those blissful waves.

Her eyes met his, the molten desire there mirroring the heat burning inside him. "Down, boy," she whispered in his ear, the brush of her lips against his skin igniting his veins.

Trevor glanced their way, suspicion in his gaze as they strode into the diner. Not like anything between them remained much of a secret with all the busybodies on the RV. Living in such close quarters made privacy a near impossibility. The door thudded behind them as they entered the bright restaurant, neon blue lighting underneath the mirror paneling along the walls. The vibrant red leather booths and black and white checkerboard flooring bordered on obnoxious, but Kieran didn't give a damn about the décor if the food was good.

With the six of them, they didn't fit in any of the booths lining the side, so instead, Danica claimed the nearest corner booth and scooted in. The guys piled in right after, followed by Liz, and then Kieran. A waitress sauntered over, black polo on and a bored expression on her face as she click-clicked a pen against a pad of paper.

Until she stopped in front of the table. Her eyes widened with interest, and her hands made a beeline to smoothing out her hair. "What can I get for you?"

"We can all agree on coffee, yes?" Kieran piped up, casting a glance to the table.

"Fuck off, you're not ordering for us," Liz said, her palms flattening on the chrome surface of the table. "I want a milkshake. Can you do peanut butter?"

"Sure thing." The woman nodded, jotting it down. "Coffee for the rest of you?"

Trevor lifted a hand. "Coke for me." As she finished writing the order, she dipped extra low to drop the menus on the table, giving a full flash of her cleavage. Renn and Jett leaned forward with a familiar spark in their eyes.

The second the waitress sashayed away, Danica jumped in. "Is it always like this with you guys?"

"Always," Liz muttered in a deadpan. "I've gotten every shade of nasty glare on the planet."

"Not like you've got anything to worry about, gorgeous," Kieran said, the flirting compulsory. He waited for the push back, the eye roll, or whatever witty comment perched on her barbed tongue. Instead, she surprised him by tilting her head to the side and sinking into thoughtfulness. His brows rose in response, not daring to embrace the fragile hope she might be coming around to what they'd discussed last night.

"He's right, Obiwan, you've got the looks and attitude to back it up," Danica said, passing her a wink.

"If my looks reflected my attitude, I'd be some big, surly linebacker," Liz joked, the moment passing. The service on the coffees was lightning fast and the Coke soon followed, so they quick flipped their plastic menus open, making a decision on meals. Kieran settled on a burger smothered in mushrooms and Jack cheese, planning on polishing the whole thing off.

To no one's surprise, Liz went for a plate of nachos.

"Continuing your quest?" he asked, elbowing her in the side to get her attention.

"Someone needs to find the perfect nachos. Might as well be me." She gave him a wan smile, which made her hazel eyes glow. Whether she realized it or not, the girl had softened her ice exterior, and the longer she stayed with them, the more she'd let him in. He didn't blame her survival instincts—she'd needed them after the life she'd lived. However, he'd made it his mission to break the defenses of Liz O'Brien. To prove she didn't need to remain so alone.

"Alright, so dish." Danica interrupted the

conversation, demanding everyone's attention. "What did you guys discover while there? We got them to send over their financials involving transactions paid to Lotus Garden. If Larsen isn't feeling a fire up his ass, he will be soon."

"Yeah, the guy we talked to had a sour frown on his puss the second we brought that up," Jett said.

"Aren't you happy I worked my mojo then," Kieran said, a smug grin playing on his face. He couldn't help it—after all the hubbub about staying back, he'd gotten further than all of them. "Because I got the name of the guy lending money to Larsen. Meaning we can pay Jay Vandermere a personal visit."

Jett's brows tightened together as he scratched his chin. "The name sounds familiar, but I can't quite place it. Definitely fae."

"Lucky for you guys, we've got the magic of the internet." Danica whipped out her smartphone, plugging away the information at once. "One Jay Vandermere at your service, and he's a suburbs boy."

Trevor shook his head. "The speed you found that is downright disturbing."

"Entertainment is my business," Danica said with a shrug. "Means I have to keep up with the pop culture trends and stay with the times, electronics and all. My clients trust me for my expertise, and the subtle nudge my powers give their abilities—all while their energy keeps me looking this lush and youthful." She batted her eyes, those long lashes a quick flicker.

"You can have your fancy trends. I want my milkshake." Liz made a face as she glanced over to the waitress who left the cup on the counter and sat chatting with another server. One of the curses of being viewed as competition. Kieran hadn't missed the dirty glance the waitress passed her. He tapped his fingers on the countertop.

"Looks like tonight we've got a dinner date with Jay Vandermere. Hope he's ready for company." Because Kieran had put up with his brother's torture for too long. It was high time he nailed the bastard in the eyes of the very Court he worshipped so much.

Chapter Twenty-One

The afternoon was agonizing.

Between the long, lingering glances between them, the constant brushes against each other, and the dirty whispers, Liz was ready to drag Kieran by the belt over to her bed. Every time she tried to remind herself she needed to keep her distance because reasons, her libido stomped in and frazzled her brain. Hell, being in the same space as him short circuited her wiring. All those well-built, logical defenses crumbled when even her nipples perked to attention the moment his fingers brushed by her arm accidentally on purpose.

And of course, everyone decided the best way to spend their time before sunset was loitering around the RV. The crowded space grew so stifling she prepared to hang out the window for a breath alone. They drove out to the suburbs and camped out in a nearby parking lot about a mile away from Vandermere's digs. Sweat beaded her temple, and she plucked her shirt off her chest to let some air in.

Kieran's grin widened, and he shot her a wink.

To make it worse, Jett and Renn had begun arguing again, and Danica joined into the fray.

"Just because you can fit five clementines into your mouth doesn't mean you *should*." Jett slammed his hands on the table, getting way too heated over such an idiotic argument.

"It's not going to score you any points with the ladies," Danica said, jumping in. "Cramming balls into your mouth seems to be a cred you'd pull out with the other team."

"Devil be damned, the lot of you're all enough to

give me a migraine." Trevor stalked to the back, shaking his head.

Liz tapped her finger against the countertop, staring out the window at the streaks of crimson coming to claim the horizon. Sunset meant go-time, and it couldn't come soon enough.

"Who's ready to forget we ever devolved to talking about Renn's lack of a gag reflex and head the fuck out?" Kieran rose from his seat and clapped his hands on the tabletop, the sound drawing everyone's attention.

"Yes, please," Liz muttered, rising as well.

Trevor glanced between them before one of his molasses sweet smiles rolled to his lips. Not like they hadn't gone toe to toe on the subject of what existed between her and Kieran. Ever since the conversation last night with him in the wake of the powerful emotions he'd unlocked, her justifications came across flimsier and flimsier.

"Couldn't get me out soon enough." Jett gave a lazy salute on his way to the front of the RV and strolled out the door. Liz quick-stepped it behind him, and without waiting for the others, they headed in the designated direction. She shifted her hips, adjusting her Beretta into place, because she sure as hell wouldn't go to this guy's house unprepared. After the number of times she'd fired her baby in the past week alone, she didn't feel comfortable going anywhere without it.

"Caught all those longing looks, Juliet." Jett hooked his thumbs into the belt loops of his slacks. "You and Romeo going to invite me to the wedding?"

Liz shot him a look so hard her eyeballs threatened to abandon ship. "You know better than to mention the 'W' word in my presence."

"Sorry, sorry," he said, lifting his hands, unable

to hide his cheeky grin. "It's not a one-nighter for you though is it?"

"Damnit, Jett. Not you too with the heavy hitting questions." She rifled a hand through her hair, which had grown sticky with sweat from being holed in the RV for too long. Her stomach squeezed with discomfort at sailing into this emotional territory again so soon after the last time. Jett was the one she relied on to skate the superficial with her, not get mired in all this feelings bullshit.

"Come on, Lizzie. You're vacillating between sexually frustrated and pissed off due to the chaos in your head, and everyone's terrified. Trevor was clutching a teddy bear in the back and crying," Jett teased.

Liz shook her head, amusement welling up inside her. "Ky's so intense, and I don't do that. I don't stake claims on forever, because hell, I've never stayed with a group of people for this long. Cut and run's bred into my bones, and I won't put him through that." She didn't glance up, expecting Jett to argue with her the way Kieran did.

However, he remained silent instead as they cut through a strip mall, making their way to the green street signs ahead in the residential areas. Behind her, the guys and Danica caused enough of a racket that any covert operation would be busted in a heartbeat.

Jett broke the silence between them. "Let Ky be him. He's always going to launch himself into anything a hundred and ten percent, and that's never going to change. You try to keep up with him, and you'll make yourself crazy. Be yourself, Lizzie. If you care about him in a big way, don't sit there harping on the future and what might happen, because fuck, you never know. You're both adults. Even if shit goes foul in the end, you sure as hell aren't getting ousted. We hired you as a booking manager before Kieran set his sights on you."

Her heart ached in response to Jett voicing the exact worries she'd buried. She'd traveled all across the states, lived in random apartments, and worked odd jobs her entire life, but not until she joined with the guys of Discord's Desire did she first feel like she had a home. And the one thing keeping her from jumping off the precipice with Kieran was the fear that burrowed deep inside her. Because for the first time, she didn't want to run.

Liz let out a hiss of a sigh. "Holy hell, J. Slice right through me, why don't you?" She managed a lopsided half smile in the wake of the emotional bomb he'd detonated. The voices behind them grew louder as the others closed the distance. Liz squared her shoulders, clearing her mental state of mind to hop into the swing of it with everyone else.

"Font of eternal wisdom, here," Jett said, jerking a thumb toward himself with a grin.

"What are you guys gossiping about?" Kieran asked, stepping in line with them as he butted into the conversation.

Liz didn't mind in the slightest—she never minded. His puppy dog persistence had endeared her from the start, and she'd never been given more attention or care in her life.

"Liz here is comparing penis size and technique." Jett's eyes glinted. "You know, since she took a tumble with both of us."

Kieran's hand rested on her shoulder at once, Jett's taunt prodding the incubus's eternal competitive streak. "Depends on which performance merits a second round." Heat crept into his voice, and she enjoyed the way his fingertips skated along her skin. He stepped behind her, his rock-hard abs pressing against her back and making her forget reason. "You know where my bunk is, babe," he murmured into her ear. His velvet voice drove her wild.

Danica chose that moment to surge beside them, pointing a finger at the sign ahead. "We're close, guys. Let's quiet down."

"Should we do a split up sort of deal?" Trevor asked from behind them.

"Our divide and distract seemed to work well before." Liz shrugged. "Though either way we should scope out the house beforehand. If he's got a horde of fae assholes living with him, we'll need to come back another time."

They made it to the street corner with the lonely green sign and began walking down the lane. This part of the area, the ocean lay nowhere in sight. Trees towered overhead, brushing against the roofs of these three-story houses with fresh shingles and coats of paint, windows in good repair, everything that screamed normal and suburban. Nothing pointing with flashing lights 'evil fae lives here.' Like they'd be so lucky.

All the casual chatter died to a minimum once they stepped onto the shaded streets of this quiet neighborhood. Liz's hand crept to her side to brush against her Beretta, ready to draw at a moment's notice. Knives glinted as Jett palmed one, and Trevor slipped his own out.

"He should be at the one on the right," Danica said, her voice breaking through the hush surrounding them. She pointed to a house with blue shutters and two cars in the driveway, a Toyota RAV and a slick black Mercedes.

Perfect suburban house in the perfect suburban neighborhood, yet the same sinking feeling welled in her stomach as the night they headed into known danger at the Lotus Garden. Liz O'Brien had learned from an early age the worst sharks in the sea were those who appeared the most normal.

At this point, the sun had set, and a few lone streetlights cast dim beams along the path. With the night came cool breezes making her wish she'd brought her hoodie along. Stars glittered overhead, visible across a velvet horizon unstained by smog. Plenty of normals lived in this neighborhood, unaware a fae set up shop here. None of these humans realized how many of the fae worked and wandered among them, and how often their lives were influenced and toyed with by these powerful creatures.

"Ready to face your arch nemesis?" she murmured to Kieran, who brimmed with tension beside her.

"I'd love to find out what this guy's fixation with me is. I mean, I assume he and my brother are conspiring to form my biggest fan club. Oh, the perils of fame." He placed a hand over his forehead in mock agony, grinning afterward.

"Poor rockstar, what a tough life you've got," she said, tugging the Beretta out from her waistband the nearer they got to the mailbox. The lights were visible through the windows, meaning folks were home. As much as the impatience in her veins begged her to storm to the door and question the asshole, scoping the place seemed wiser. With the funds being extracted to send these hitmen after Kieran, Vandermere wasn't his biggest fan.

Fireflies flickered by the bushes in the distance, drawing her attention as they veered around the side. They stayed near the dark pools of shadow created by the tall trees surrounding the place. From where they crept through the grasses, even with the glow of lights from the windows and the movement inside, quiet reigned apart from the hum of cicada and the buzz of other insects performing their summer symphony. Goosebumps prickled on the back of her neck the closer they inched, and the tension threaded through their entire group.

"Let's head to the window to check and see if anyone's up and walking around," Jett suggested as he crept toward the large window offering a clear view of the adjacent room lit with an amber glow. From the glimpse of long couches, big lazy chairs, and the figures sitting inside, that had to be a den or living room. Regardless, it'd be the best vantage point of gauging who waited for them inside the house.

One by one, they veered away from the silver spotlight illuminating half the side of the house while staying in the shadows. Without a clear line of who sat inside, Liz had no idea what fae might be waiting for them or what their abilities were. The grass whispered against her boots, and each footstep sent a prickle of paranoia through her that someone might be watching, waiting in the darkness. She nudged her way to the forefront of the group, edging against the wall until her fingers fumbled with the windowsill.

She lifted herself up until she peered over the sill into the tinted glass. The kitchen coated in darkness spanned larger than the average one, all dark marble countertops and shiny chrome fixtures. Even without the lights on, the Kitchen-Aid, impressive metal freezer, and wide island in the center of it marked this place out as money. Jay Vandermere wasn't short on cash.

Kieran pushed in beside her, and Jett squashed her in on the other side as they all peered in through the window, making sure to stay as low out of sight as possible.

Three figures sat in the other room, sprawled on

the couches and armchairs decorating the living space. Kieran's hands balled into fists, and when she caught sight of the man on the left, she understood why. She hadn't seen the smug mug of Kieran's brother since the night of the Court function, and she'd been relieved of that.

Larsen leaned back in one of the armchairs, a cigar hanging out of his mouth while two other big guys chatted with him.

Another man, if you could call him one, hunched over. His longer than average bones stretched the skin on his frame and gave him a ghastly look. The dusky skin tone resembled ash, and his body tensed at the ready, even while they sat and chatted.

If Liz placed any bets, the guy on the couch was Jay Vandermere based on the crisp white button-down he wore and the suspenders leading to his fitted slacks. Like Larsen, the man had slick businessman looks with the sort of trimmed hair, square jaw, machismo leaking fuel to draw ladies in like moths to the light. He sat with a stack of papers in front of him, leafing through a few while passing the occasional glance to Larsen.

She leaned up, trying to press an ear closer to the cool glass and hear what they were talking about inside. The murmurs were low, so she could only make out wisps of their conversation. Mumblings of the Rembrant offices and unwelcome visitors. The reason Larsen showed up here tonight became clear.

While they outnumbered those guys, they'd be the ones breaking and entering if they found their way inside. And neither the fae Courts nor the human police would swing in their favor. Jett's fingers tightened on the windowsill as he heaved himself higher to peer at the kitchen counters below them. Stacks of papers had been left there as well, and if they managed to snag any of them, they might find themselves less in the dark. Because right now, they were wading through shadows.

A creak drew her attention, snapping her focus to the living room. Long and lanky stood from his seat and with fast, efficient paces crossed the living room.

Heading straight in their direction.

Chapter Twenty-Two

At the sight of his brother, Kieran's blood boiled. Here they were, fighting for their lives on a daily basis while the smug bastard sat back with a cigar, rubbing elbows with some assholes from one of the big fae-run corporations. He squinted, focusing on the guy leaning on the couch, a blond man whose face looked familiar. Even though he couldn't quite figure where he'd seen Jay Vandermere before, at once he pinpointed the incubus energy. One of his kind.

Except before he tried to read their lips, the big, ugly guy stood from his seat and headed in their direction. And he could've swore those limpid eyes flickered to the window. Winter's breath, he hoped not.

"Duck," he whispered, as he, Liz, and Jett all crouched. They couldn't risk peering inside, not while that thing gunned for the kitchen like he'd caught sight of them. Instead, he pressed his back against the wall the moment the rest of his crew made with the same idea. One glance from the ashen beast and they were screwed, but as long as the creature didn't start surveying the area from the window, they might escape unnoticed.

The uneven bumps of the wall pressed into his back, needling him as he tried to regulate his breaths, making them more even and focusing on quiet. A shuffle came from inside the kitchen, the tread of heavy footsteps, followed by rustling around. The noises traveled closer, and for a moment, his heart stopped in his chest. Liz pressed against him, her focus on the tall cypresses ahead while she kept her cool mask in place. He reached down and brushed his fingers against hers before squeezing her hand.

She passed him a wan smile, and those hazel eyes gleamed in the spare moonlight. Another sharp thud from inside the kitchen startled him.

Danica's brows furrowed as her gaze kept flitting upward with constant movement even though the rest of them made every effort to be as still and silent as possible.

After a few seconds of it, Trevor reached over to her and placed a hand on her shoulder as he passed her a look. He received a glower moments later.

A trickle of ice cascaded down Kieran's back. He didn't dare look up, but menace radiated from the creature's presence, so close, and still. It stopped rummaging around, and if he had to place a bet, it stood right by the window looking out to the tree line. His breath hitched in his throat as seconds stretched to ages while he burned holes into the cypresses before them with his gaze, trying his best to remain invisible.

Until the footsteps started again with a creak to the hardwood beneath. After several seconds of movement, the sounds faded as the creature left the kitchen. Kieran let out a slow exhale as his muscles relaxed, and Liz's hand dropped from his.

After a couple of minutes, Jett broke the silence. "What about checking his mailbox?" he murmured.

The creature inside was dangerous and in Larsen and Jay's employ. Kieran wished he could remember where he'd seen Jay Vandermere before. Deep in his gut, he knew the connection was important.

"Yeah, we'd best save breaking and entering for when he's not home with company," Kieran said, keeping his voice low. Tilting his head toward the road, the rest of the crew took the cue. One by one, they slipped away from the sill as the lot of them tiptoed their way through the well-maintained lawn. Longer tendrils of dandelions brushed his boots while he focused on the road ahead. Because until they obtained solid evidence to lobby against his brother, goading Lars proved a dangerous game.

He quickened his pace, walking through the side of the driveway slicked with shadows. Every ounce of him longed to bust into the house and start slinging punches, but his ever-tenuous grip on common sense tamped those urges.

He cast a careful glance to the door as Jett jogged to the mailbox and fiddled with the latch. In seconds, he managed to snag a couple of envelopes and jammed them into his pocket, crinkling the paper.

"As we add to our enemies," Liz muttered. "Now the postal service will be after our asses."

Kieran didn't bother restraining his grin. As of late, their enemies multiplied at an unsettling pace. A rattle in the distance froze him in his tracks. He whipped around in the direction of the house. The slight movement was the one giveaway—the front doorknob started to turn.

"We've got to get out of here. Now." Kieran kept his voice low and controlled as he sauntered forward, leading the way. Though his body screamed run, in a suburban neighborhood like this, no one would blink twice at a group taking a leisurely walk. A bunch of people on the run would toss a red flag right in front of the bull. His heart sped in his chest, but he didn't look back and forced a measured pace as their group strode away from the Vandermere house.

His throat dried at the distant click of a door shutting, but already, they'd made it a few houses down where the trees and shadows obscured them. The sound of their footsteps echoed in his ears as loud as the regular march of his heart. Danica sped up a bit with her normal anxious tread as she assumed the lead, her hands balling into fists. As for the guys, each one of them had become pros at putting on a stage face, so Kieran didn't worry in the slightest.

A couple of twigs crunched under the heavy tread of his boots, but Kieran wasn't listening for that. Since he couldn't whip around and check the entrance every five seconds, he relied on his hearing. The sound of an ignition starting sent another flush of anxiety through him. The Mercedes in the driveway most likely belonged to one Larsen Blackmore—he knew his brother's taste.

The purr of the car as it set in motion made Kieran clench his fists. He refused to run. The street sign stood out a couple of houses away, and once they made it to the end of this road, they could turn off in a different direction than his brother. Except, cars moved faster.

Tires clicked across the street, the sound approaching quicker than he liked. Even though his focus should've remained on the road ahead, he couldn't help sneaking a look to the side. The sleek black car accelerated, picking up pace as it zoomed past them.

Kieran glanced in the direction in the same second the Mercedes whizzed by.

The same moment Lars chose to scan at the group from his window. Their eyes locked, and his brother's widened in recognition.

But the car revved into motion, whizzing by as it reached the street sign and whipped around the corner to the right.

"He saw us. Run," Kieran commanded, his legs snapping into motion. The breeze swept strands of his hair across his forehead, and the energy pumped through him while he raced ahead, galvanized by the flash in his brother's eyes. He didn't trust the bastard for a heartbeat. As he increased his speed, he passed by tall, towering cypresses right before he whipped to the left in the direction they'd come from. The beat-up strip mall they'd passed resided at the top of the hill and beyond that lay the parking lot they stationed the RV in.

Liz kept up with him, her cheeks flushed and determination in her eyes as her ponytail bounced with the movement. Danica surged ahead, the woman's survival instinct something else. Asphalt pounded under his tread, and at this point, his heartbeat thundered in his ears. Any moment, his brother might be turning the car around and coming for them. Except that would be direct involvement, something Lars never did.

Sweat trickled from his temple, crawling down his cheek. The breakneck pace grew more challenging with the increased slope of the hill. After several minutes, they burst onto the blacktop of the strip mall.

Many of the shops had closed for the night. Kieran listened, but no rev of an engine and no hum of tires cut across the pavement from behind. Even when he glanced back, stray leaves skittered across the street they'd just raced along. If his brother had been wheeling around after them, he would've caught up at this point.

He slowed his pace to a jog. The rest of the crew followed suit as soon as they noticed, even though Danica continued booking it across the parking lot like someone lit her ass on fire.

"Did your brother catch sight of us?" Trevor asked as he walked in time with him.

Kieran nodded, his face grim. "That can't spell good news. The fact we're closing in on his trail might push him into desperation, and people do stupid things when they're desperate."

Jett shrugged, catching up with them. "Stupid things, yes, but sometimes desperation works in our favor. If he's making mistakes, he'll be easier to catch in the act."

Kieran slipped his hands into his pockets. "Either way, let's haul our girl back into the city proper. I'll feel better when we're not parked alone in suburban central."

****

Kieran pulled the RV into the parking lot and braked so hard the whole vehicle shuddered. He ignored Jett's complaints behind him. Renn joined in the whining as well, for once the two agreeing on something. They'd dropped Danica off in central San Fran, but since they didn't have a gig tonight, the idea of bar hopping again didn't strike his match. So instead, he pulled into one of the lots inside Golden Gate Park. Twofold idea on that one anyway—they'd be much tougher to track here in case his brother sent fae after them.

Trevor didn't argue with him—his brother loved the outdoors and would take any chance he could get for some solace. And to his surprise, Liz had been uncharacteristically quiet all day. It pushed him to the edge of discomfort, because after the silence came the inevitable rejection. His own family didn't want him, so why would she?

"Both of you can shove off." Kieran addressed Renn and Jett as he rose from his seat. "Enjoy the night. If you're desperate for a drink and a fuck, catch public trans and troll the town. I'm going to enjoy not jumping at every shadow for a hot minute."

Trevor strolled past the lot of them to the door. "I'll be enjoying myself on a hike. After spending so much time crammed into the RV with you lot, I'm taking my breathers where I can get them." He gave them a wink before he pushed the doors open and exited, tossing a hand up in the process.

Liz stepped to the front of the RV, muscling past Jett and Renn. "Want to take a walk?"

Kieran's throat dried at her invitation and the serious air around her. That couldn't spell good news.

Jett nudged her forward, a knowing look in his eyes because she'd probably discussed things with him.

"Yeah, let's get some air," he said, the RV growing more confining than ever. Without waiting, he hopped out of the driver's seat and clattered down the steps. Orders dried on his tongue as he glanced to Jett and Renn who both did a terrible job of restraining their amusement.

"I'll keep the savage in check," Jett said, casting a less than amused glance over to Renn who glared at him. Kieran gave a lazy salute before opening the RV door to be greeted by the brisk night air in the Golden Gate Park. Liz hopped out behind him, rubbing her hands along her bare arms the second she exited the RV.

He lifted a brow. "Sure you don't want to grab a hoodie or something?"

"A little breeze is good for me," she grumbled, being stubborn on purpose at this point.

He shook his head, not bothering to hide his grin as they walked down the paths leading to the deeper woods. Tall trees reached up mingling with the rolling hills that spanned far into the distance. The night sky took on a purplish hue, making the silver stars shine even brighter. However, not even the most beautiful vistas drew his attention from Liz for long.

The shadows cast her full lips in stark relief and intensified the determination in those hazel eyes. Even walking alongside her, the urge to close the distance between them and claim her burned inside him, heating him in spite of the cool night. She rubbed her hands along her arms again, because she should've brought a hoodie. Kieran rolled his eyes and shrugged his leather off. He placed it around her shoulders, which drew her gorgeous gaze.

"I'm fine," she said, fixing him with a flat stare. All the unsaid words hummed between them, the buzzing reaching an unbearable stage.

"Look, spit out whatever you want to tell me." He ran a hand through his hair as he stopped in his stroll, agitation pushing him something fierce. "I can make a guess based on the serious and brooding. Don't worry about my feelings. I'm a big boy, and I've already been cut out of my own family. Do your worst." He stood a half second away from pacing a hole into the ground before them, because as much as he talked a big game, this would devastate him.

From the moment he'd met her, Liz had a hold on him he didn't want to give up, a calm to his storm. But the hope burning between them grew painful, the hope that for once he might have someone who accepted him—knew his flaws and gave a fuck anyway. As much as he didn't want to admit it, the way his parents cut him out of the bloodline and how his brother treated him like raw garbage made their mark on his psyche.

Liz slipped her hands in her pockets, a small smile on her face as she shook her head. "You think you've got me all figured out, do you? Nice try, rockstar."

Kieran's brows furrowed as he tapped his boot against the lawn. Her scent wrapped around him, the clean citrus that had turned into an aphrodisiac. He could barely stand the distance between them, which widened by the second.

Liz let out a sharp exhale, her gaze skating the ground. "Look, I figured something out today. I made a lot of excuses, but in the end, that's what they were. Being aboard the RV as your manager, this is the first time I've found somewhere I considered a real home, and

I'm petrified anything could take it from me."

Kieran nodded, understanding hitting him full force at her hesitation. After all, if things imploded between them, it would make their close quarters a torture. He couldn't imagine waking every day to the wreckage of their relationship, and his past ones had gone up in flames. However, Liz was a different case, since he'd formed a friendship with her first, one he valued and treasured. As much as it might be painful to interact with her every day knowing she wasn't his, he wouldn't begrudge the place she'd earned.

"You've always got a home here, no matter what happens between us. The day I claimed you at the Court function, I made that promise."

She met his eyes, the serious look there arresting him on the spot. "I know. And look, I'm never going to be comfortable with the share and cares—I'm emotionless, remember?" She joked to hide the discomfort as she nudged her Keds against a patch of grass. "But, I want whatever the hell this is between us." Her voice lowered to a near whisper, but her gaze marked him with the same intensity he'd been feeling all along. "I want you more than I can stand."

Her words burned a brand in him he'd never forget, in all his years. The soft vulnerability in her tone, the yearning in her gaze, and the stark bravery of her confession impacted him in a fierce way. His heart ached to completion.

Closing the distance between them, Kieran wrapped his hands around her waist and dipped down to claim her lips.

Chapter Twenty-Three

All this time, Kieran had been holding back. His lips descended on hers with an unparalleled ferocity, leaving her breathless. She sank into the kiss, her hands twining around the nape of his neck while his hands gripped firm to her hips. She'd spent so much time arguing the explosive chemistry between them, but as she indulged in the kiss, her chest raw from her confession, she couldn't imagine living without it.

The sounds of a summer night echoed through the park from the trills and chirps of all sorts of critters to the soft rustle of leaves from the strong breezes gusting through this place. Liz drank in everything: the glow of the sky above with hazy, ringed clouds, and his scent of whiskey and leather, the same one that intoxicated her every time. She memorized the details of his face, the messy strands of his dark hair, the possessiveness in his amber eyes, and those delectable lips as he descended on her again.

She moaned, the sensation of their lips brushing together sending another thrill through her. As she explored his mouth, the tip of her tongue ran up and down one of his fangs. He let out a low growl, his hands beginning to roam the length of her body. The heat from his skin when he slid his hands under her shirt to press against her bare waist made her shiver. As much as she could kiss him forever, at once the contact wasn't enough. She needed more.

Letting down her defenses like that, the unguarded rawness of what happened between them pierced her to the core. To her surprise though, in the hollow of her fallen defenses arrived a fierce self-possession when it came to him. After keeping him at a distance for so long, Liz was ready to ride the storm.

Her fingers traveled the length of his chest along the hard muscles beneath his black wifebeater until she seized on the hem. Heat curled into her core at the sensation of his skin, and her gaze met his with a challenge as she yanked up. A grin spread on his face, wide enough his fangs poked out as he shrugged out of the shirt.

"Right here? In front of everyone?" he murmured against her mouth. "My modesty."

Liz snorted. "Like you had a shred of it."

His hands wrapped around her hips again until they circled around her ass. With one swift move, he cupped her ass, lifting her around his waist. Her legs twined around his back as she pressed tight to him, the graze of the length straining his jeans enough to drive her wild.

"Maybe I want you all to myself for once," he whispered in her ear as she gripped on tight.

She let out a squeak of surprise as he walked forward, crossing through the field. Leaning up, she captured his mouth again, teasing him as she swept her tongue inside his mouth. She bit his lip and dove back in again.

He groaned, the sound reverberating against them as he pressed his length against her core.

Her panties were soaked from the sweet sensations rolling through her, and she itched to toss her pants aside. She wanted to lick him head to toe, feel his skin under her fingers all over. They'd waited so long for this. No barriers, physical or emotional. This couldn't be excused away as a one-night stand or late night healing sesh. All of the desire that brewed between them culminated into this powerful night.

He came to an abrupt stop, which dragged her attention to their surroundings. Kieran lowered her to the ground, her ass hitting a cold marble step. A half globe spanned overhead, segments sprawling out to reach the elegant columns on either side of this temple. Behind them, the steps rose to a platform for this ancient looking performance stage. Of course, he'd bring her to the music concourse.

"Maybe I want to hear those screams amplified," he murmured in her ear, his eyes dancing with mirth. She shook her head, unable to keep the smile off her face as she reached for the button of his jeans. "Not fair," he said, shifting his hips out of reach. "You've got way too many layers."

Liz didn't put up a fight as those skillful fingers of his flicked open the button of her cargos and slipped them down her ankles. She kicked her shoes off in the process. She was down to a tank, his jacket around her shoulders, and her panties, which at this point were getting in the way. The breeze wrapped around her bare legs, causing prickles up them. Despite the chill, her core ignited when Kieran set his gaze on her.

She moaned as he nipped at the inside of her thigh, moving his way closer and closer to her center. "Dammit, Ky," she ground out, "fuck me already."

He smirked, his eyes dancing. "I'm just starting to have fun." With another deft motion, her panties hit the ground. His hot breath puffed against her bare folds, causing her thighs to clench in anticipation.

Kieran gripped her ass as he leaned down to torture her more.

The second his tongue flicked against her clit, she let out a gasp, surprised by the thrill rising up her spine. Except she didn't have a chance to register as he dove in for more. Kieran had a talented mouth for more than one reason, which he proved over and over again. He licked and sucked at her with such precision she was in exquisite agony. Her breaths came in shorter as bliss rolled through her in undulating waves. Every time she let out a moan, he'd increase the tempo, thrumming against her clit.

The sight of him between her legs as those amber eyes glanced to her was sexy as anything, and her grip tightened against the steps behind her as he drove her to the edge. The sensations were so sharp and radiant they neared painful while riding so close to release. His tongue glided over her sensitive skin again before his fingernails dug into her ass, and he devoured her anew. Her toes curled at the sight of his tongue darting across his lips before he dipped down again.

This time, the slight sweep of his tongue sent her over the edge.

Her breath hitched as she shouted out his name, the sound reverberating through the building surrounding them. The fierce spike of pleasure near blinded her, and she sank into the orgasm as it traveled through her entire body. A flush of heat reached her cheeks as she leaned up to grab onto his shoulders. His eyes danced with a smug smile on his face, all cocksure and wicked. Damn the bastard, thinking he got the upper hand.

"Pants, off," she demanded in a firm voice even though her insides fluttered from Kieran's more than expert attention.

"Yes, ma'am," he said, making quick work of sliding his jeans off those toned legs and kicking them and his boots to the side. As Kieran faced her without a stitch on, her insides twisted tight with a vicious spike of desire. Despite the fact he'd made her cum, those hard abs, his more than impressive erection, and his muscular arms caused her core to hum all over again.

She licked her lips, anxious to get a taste of him. Besides, turnabout was fair play. Liz wanted to wipe the cocky smile off his face. Before he could do anything, she crouched in front of him and ran her tongue along the length of his erection.

His palms clapped onto her shoulders, fingers sinking into her skin as she enjoyed how his thighs stiffened every time her tongue darted out to tease him. His one hand moved to her hair, gripping into her tangled strands as she enclosed her mouth around his cock.

He let out a low groan as she moved her mouth up and down his length, sucking in as she picked up speed. His balls tightened in response, same as his grip in her hair, the second she trailed her tongue along the bottom of his shaft as she went. Liz reached her hand around the base, working him with her hand and her mouth at the same time as she enjoyed the sounds coming from his lips, a music in itself. This turned her on all over again, and wetness pooled between her legs.

"Fuck, I'm going to cum if you don't stop," he managed to get out, his voice low and husky.

Liz quirked an eyebrow at him but pulled out to tease the tip of his cock with her tongue.

He seized the opportunity, dropping to his knees in front of her.

"And I was just having fun," she complained with a smirk on her lips, licking the extra moisture from them.

"If I'm going to cum, I want it to be inside you." His husky voice whispering by her ear set her veins on fire. The way he looked at her promised forever, with the intensity he'd gazed at her from the start. Except this time, Liz didn't run away. Instead, she lifted her head to press her lips against his to drink in the taste of sweat and sex. She shrugged off his jacket at last, and seconds later her tank top and bra went flying to the side as well.

Even though the night breezes swept her way, dragging several strands of her hair aloft, the cold couldn't disturb the way her body burned for him. The first time was all fury and need, but this time she drank in their surroundings, treasuring every second. No matter what the future held for her, she'd hold this memory dear.

Kieran prowled up to her, his arms on either side as she perched on the top step with her bare ass against the chilled stone.

She sprawled her legs open as he leaned over top her. Her nipples pebbled as the tips grazed against his warm skin, the sensation igniting her core.

Kieran reached for one breast with a firm grip as he lowered his mouth to the nipple. His talented tongue went to work again, and in seconds, her clit throbbed, and her folds were soaked. Hell above, she needed him inside her. His cock brushed against her opening while Kieran teased her other breast, sending a sharp pulse of need.

She grabbed him by the hip, pulling him forward. "Enough playtime, rockstar," she murmured, her voice hoarse with desire.

"Sure you can take it?" Even with his infuriating grin, Liz understood him well enough to read the seriousness in his eyes and the tender way he said it. This wasn't some quick alley fuck or something to dismiss away in the light of day.

"Try me," she said, challenge heating her gaze. A satisfied smile curled onto his lips, and his eyes softened with a sweetness she never expected from the fierce and furious leader of Discord's Desire.

His lips brushed against hers, and his hands grabbed her hips as he lowered himself into her. The tip plunged into her opening, but the slow glide was sweet agony as inch by inch he brought himself in to the hilt. She bucked forward, filled to completion with him. He brought his lips to brush against her neck and then nipped at her ear with his fangs as he shifted back and forth. She moved with him in unison, their dance so natural and their motions in time.

The scent of whiskey and sweat all around her enhanced her arousal, and she moaned into his ear as their pace increased. His hot length slid into her with a quick rhythm that had her panting in minutes, and each time he retreated, she thrust her hips toward him again. Her nails scored his lower back when he drove into her, hitting her sweet spot with breathless accuracy. Sweat pricked on her forehead and slicked his arms, drops trailing down his back as he rammed into her, again and again.

Her ass bounced against the stone behind them, but she didn't care anymore, so addicted to the way their bodies danced together. Kieran's hand moved around to her low back, his mouth on hers, demanding and urgent as she tasted the salt from his sweat. Her hands roamed along his sweat-slicked skin in desperation for the feel of his heat against her fingertips. His animalistic growl as he increased speed vibrated against her lips.

He plunged into her faster while she got slicker by the second. Each time they crashed together, she floated higher and higher on a painful edge. His grip tightened on her too, his hot breaths a whisper against her mouth between his demanding kisses.

Again, again, again.

Liz's core burned for him, her pussy squeezing tight with each thrust as she neared climax. He drove into her with his temper put to good use. The pressure mounted, expanding inside her until she neared bursting. Her nails dug into his shoulders as she bucked forward, desperate for release. Kieran thrust in even deeper this time, and when he hit home, she cried out his name.

Her second orgasm came even stronger than the first, rolling through her like the crash of the tides. Stars flashed in front of her eyes as her pussy quaked with the release.

Seconds later, Kieran plunged in again, his cock stiffening before heat spilled inside. His breath exploded in gasps as he emptied himself into her, pressing his mouth to hers again while he came. Kieran shuddered against Liz when he finished, before their bodies relaxed in completion.

She leaned onto her back, the coolness of the stone blissful against her sweat-soaked body.

Kieran rolled with Liz, not pulling out as he braced himself with his forearms on either side of her.

Liz basked in the hazy satisfaction, unlike the other night where she'd scurried to put on clothing. In this place with him, for the first time in her life, she wasn't on edge. That in and of itself was utter ecstasy. Her bones felt like jelly in the aftermath, and her skin grew sensitized from the sheer amount of attention Kieran gave her. He pulled out and rolled onto his back, arms stretched over his head as he stared at the dome above them. The distance lasted for a second before he looped an arm around her shoulders, tugging her against him.

"Gross," she murmured as she pressed her mouth against his chest with a kiss.

"You're the one getting your sweat all over me. I was pristine," he teased, squeezing her tight. Kieran might be an impatient hothead on the tamest of days, but she adored the strength of his affection.

Liz sat up, bringing her knees forward as she scanned the area ahead of them. Though they lay in shadow, the rest of the park spanned acres ahead of them, all lush tall trees and rolling meadows. The sky glittered with a blanket of stars, and a full moon cast silver rays through the clearing. The breeze filtered by again to bring the sweetness of the flowers surrounding them. Kieran's fingertip traced lazy circles on her lower back, the motion making her shiver.

She glanced at him. His tanned skin was edible, wild strands of his dark hair plastered against his forehead, and a satisfied smile curled his lips. Her heart squeezed tight in her chest, the emotions so strong they stole her breath away. The hollow of her chest ached with how perfect this moment was with him. How she wouldn't trade this night for anything.

Liz stared at the moon above, those cool beams skating along her skin and mingling with the shadows. For so many years, she'd stare at the sky, and the delicate loneliness there would blaze through her in the way it did down below. However, for the first time as she gazed at the night sky, though distant, it didn't stir the ache in her chest. Instead, she watched the way the shadows kissed those cold rays, making them all the stronger.

And in that single, beautiful moment, she understood.

Chapter Twenty-Four

The next gig would take place at the Cat Club, a joint catering to a more alternative crowd and, from the hearsay, a mixture of fae. Kieran wasn't going to lie, he'd grown paranoid about any place heavy with his kind after his brother caught sight of him tracking them down. On top of that, a hunter could be lurking in any alley wielding a platinum knife with his name on it—they meant business and he'd be stupid to underestimate them. He leaned down to lace up his ten-hole boots and then straightened, casting a glance to his bed.

Liz lay under the rumpled sheets, strands of her wavy hair pressing against her cheek. Those long lashes of hers fluttered, but despite the motion, she remained asleep, her fist clutching tight to the pillow. Her full lips were kissable, and Kieran restrained the urge to dip down and wake her up. After last night, everything changed between them. He hadn't believed it possible to be soaring this high, and it took several tries to wipe the dopey smile off his face.

Their night under the stars ended with her curling up with him in bed, and falling asleep by her side had been everything he'd hoped for. The woman made him crazy in the best way. However, after the look in his brother's eyes, he couldn't rest easy, knowing Liz would be watching them from the audience and vulnerable to attack. Though he'd give anything to stay and hop back in bed with her, he headed toward the front of the RV.

Jett leaned back in the booth, reading something on his tablet at the kitchen table. As Kieran approached, he glanced over. "Someone was busy last night," he said, before taking a sip out of his mug. Based on the murky complexion and the fact it was Jett, the contents had a fifty-fifty shot at being whisky or coffee.

"Shove off, siren." Kieran fastened a knife inside his boot and crouched to their locked cabinet to pull out a pistol. He shoved it in the hem of his waistband.

"Touchy, touchy. Aren't you supposed to be basking in the afterglow?" Jett smirked at him from his seat.

"This is me basking," Kieran said, pointing to his chest. He couldn't restrain the smile for long though, and after a second he shook his head. "She's something else."

"Yes, she is," Jett said, his tone growing serious as he drummed his fingers on the tabletop. Kieran straightened in his stance, wondering if he'd missed something big. "And since there's no one else to do it, I'm giving you the big brother speech. You hurt her, and I'll slit your throat."

Kieran's forehead wrinkled as he snagged a banana from the bunch lying on the kitchen counter. "The big brother who banged her? Little incestuous don't you think?"

"Who am I to deny my gift?" Jett joked before his eyes traveled to the bulge at Kieran's side. "Why the heavy arsenal?"

"Going to scout out the joint for tonight. Don't want any nasty surprises, not with our girl in the audience." Kieran made his way to the front of the RV before peeling the banana and popping it into his mouth.

"Want backup?" Jett asked, calling to him from his seat.

Kieran stopped and shook his head. "No need," he said between bites. "This is a simple in and out with a side of breakfast." Without waiting, he hopped down the steps and out the door, bursting into the bright sunshine of another beautiful day in San Francisco. After rolling his shoulders and tossing the banana peel onto the pavement, he took off at a brisk jog toward the nearest subway terminal.

****

The front of the club was painted black with a simple vinyl sign, featuring none of the glitz or neons the other clubs tried. 'Now Playing' posters plastered the windows, the current one featuring the subterranean blue image of him and the others they'd taken by the waterside. Even though the club wouldn't be opening for another couple of hours, he tested the knob of the front door—open. Some form of staff would be bustling around setting the place up.

"Hey, I'm here to check out the space," Kieran called in as he entered the club. Though at night, the club would be filled with people, music, and pulsing lights, right now, the black paint job on the platforms was slapdash, and the wide spanning dance floors collected scuff marks and dents.

"Who's there?" a female voice called from the other room.

"Kieran from Discord's Desire," he called, striding through into the adjacent area. A short lady with blonde pigtails adjusted the latch on the cage in the center of the room, a dirty rag hanging out from her front pocket.

"Scoping before your set tonight?" she asked. As she glanced up, disinterest in her eyes, her look changed the second she got a once over of him. Human girls were putty in his hands with the exception of one. The one woman in the world who wasn't spelled into attraction, who viewed him as his real self, not the incubus, and not the rockstar.

"Yeah, I'll be out in a second," he said, strolling past this room into the next. He didn't need some broad trailing him around. Each of these rooms was enclosed except for this last one with more stains marring the floor than the others, which must lead to the loading dock. Unfortunately, no upstairs balconies for Liz to get a birds-eye view of the place. With the bars split in the different rooms too, she'd have to at minimum stay in the same one they played in. He strode over to the back door where black wooden planks plastered over the big monstrosity and the oversized handle didn't quite fit.

In the alley, cigarette butts littered the ground, making it obvious the place became a smoker's haven at night. It led down and to the right where the corridor emptied out onto the road since the honks and whirr of tires sounded from where he stood. Kieran jammed his hands into the pockets of his leather as he strode forward. Better he dodge out this way than have the girl inside puppydogging around him.

The breezes whipped around, this time bringing the slight smell of burning charcoal. Kieran lifted his head, glancing around in both directions. However, he didn't spot any rooftop terraces or smoke trailing into the breeze. Not like his senses weren't in overdrive, what with the handful of fae they'd been fighting the past couple of weeks. This stacked up to more than the usual bar brawl.

He whipped around the corner, ready to get the hell back to the RV. To Liz.

Until heat and smoke blinded him. Too late, he caught the gigantic fist hurtling his way, promising lights out.

Chapter Twenty-Five

Liz awoke to a persistent flick to her ear. Before her vision came into focus, the scent of whiskey and cigarettes wrapped around her, a reminder of last night and her monumental decision. She made a low grumbling noise in response to the flicks, but they didn't let up.

"Come on, Lizzie. I'll drag you out by force next," a voice that wasn't Kieran said from beside her.

She sat up, shunting the blanket off as she wiped her bleary eyes. "Chill, J. I'm moving," she mumbled.

Jett stood by Kieran's top bunk where she'd curled up with the incubus last night. He leaned on the frame of the bed, draping his arm along the ledge. "He should've been back an hour ago." The sharp note in his voice woke her at once. Jett glared at the ground, a scowl on his face.

"Kieran went out?" she asked, hopping off the top bunk and down to the floor. She made quick work of tying her long hair into a messy ponytail before following Jett out into the kitchen. Renn's snores trailed in from his bunk, but Trevor sat at the black leather booth, leaning toward the open window with his cigarette.

"You haven't heard from him?" Trevor asked, blowing a stream of smoke out the window a second later.

Liz shook her head, her stomach sinking. She snapped her phone from the table, but no missed calls or texts flashed for her attention. Even though the logical part of her brain came up with excuses, she couldn't ignore the hollowing in her gut. With Larsen sending hits after Kieran, he wasn't safe in the slightest, and if anything happened to him—Liz clenched her jaw tight.

"Where did he go?" she asked, tapping her foot as she tried to keep her tone under control. Indulging in her worries wouldn't help anyone right now.

"Went to scope out the gig for tonight," Jett said, pressing his palms against the counter as he sank into a hunch. "Mother Hen wanted to make sure you had a safe vantage point to watch the show."

Of course he did. The idiot placed her safety before his own every time. "And you let him go alone?" Her voice came out sharper and more critical than intended. At the following dark look from Jett, she regretted the lapse. He must be beating himself up enough. "I'm sorry," she said, beginning to pace. "I know how stubborn he can be."

"Maybe the train's not running regular and he got held up," Trevor suggested without much confidence.

Jett shook his head. "His phone's going straight to voicemail."

Panic pricked the back of her neck, enforced by the bottoming out in her stomach that she couldn't shake for the life of her.

"What're we waiting for?" Trevor tossed his butt out the window, snapping it up tight. "If he went to scope out the club, then let's head there."

Liz didn't respond since she'd begun walking to the back to get changed. After rummaging through her trunk for a half second, she tugged on a pair of black cargoes and a wrinkled maroon tee. Not like her ensemble mattered—time was of the essence if something happened to Kieran.

"Renn, get the hell up!" Jett hollered at the top of his lungs, projecting his own anxious energy into his favorite activity of antagonizing their drummer.

Renn shot up from his deep sleep, whipping

around with a snort and tossing his fists up. "Wha?" he said, lowering his fists once he realized it was just Jett being loud.

"Get some clothes on. Kieran's missing." Jett didn't waste time cracking jokes and reached to the pile of Renn's dirty laundry, grabbing a fistful of shirt and pants and tossing them his way.

To Renn's credit, he woke fast, throwing on his clothes with the speed of a lifetime of quick changes.

Liz slipped into her Keds and popped her Beretta into her waistband. The last couple of weeks, the thing had been her lifeline. Her brain buzzed, but she focused on the task ahead rather than indulging into a spiral of worries so fierce they'd crush her.

She strode to the front of the RV where Trevor waited.

He white-knuckled the driver's seat with a grim expression. "He's never disconnected right before a gig. Ky's always running point, practicing, and chatting with folks at the venue. I'm not liking how this silence sits." Trevor's gaze flicked to where Renn and Jett approached.

Liz nodded, but she didn't trust her voice at the moment. Fear spread through her like a sickness at every second longer with no word from their intrepid band leader. The air around them sank to subterranean depths as Trevor opened the door, and they set out to the Cat Club.

****

Liz near leapt from the light rail once the doors slid open and raced up the steps, anxious to get to the club. The ride on the train had been silent with a couple of attempts at jokes that fell flat in the face of their fears. She stepped to the sidewalk, teeming with everyone from dreadlocked rastas to the blazer and skirt combo from the lady ducking into the health food shop. The small storefronts along this street splashed the place with color, between the big vinyl signs outside some and painted letters on others.

"If he's sitting there jawing off with the workers indoors, I'm going to slug him," Trevor murmured, even though he didn't sound like he believed his own words for a heartbeat.

"Or he picked a fight with the first bastard who eyed him the wrong way and doesn't want to slink back home with a shiner right before a gig." Jett indulged in the fantasy, even though they all knew it was wishful thinking. He glanced to her with bitter knowledge in his eyes.

Liz sucked in a deep breath, understanding what he attempted. Game face. "He could've gotten lost. You know how bad his sense of direction is." Her stomach tightened, but in mouthing off, she kept the swell of fear at bay. Until they found any definitive hint of what might've happened, the what-ifs would drown her alive.

Renn let out a sharp laugh. "And Ky's way too stubborn to ask for directions."

The black walls and doors of the Cat Club stood out along the streetside, the windows plastered with Discord's Desire posters Liz had sent in earlier. The boys had grumbled about doing photoshoots, but someone needed to whip them into proper marketing shape. The faint smell of smoke lingered out here, and a few buckets out front filled to the brim with butts made it clear more than a couple of folks hung back after hours.

Renn's nose wrinkled upon approach, a sour look on his face.

Liz walked straight to the door and tested the knob. Open. She didn't bother knocking and instead slipped inside the air-conditioned building.

A clank came from the bar to the right, and a

blonde, pig-tailed chick stood from where she'd been rearranging bottles. "Can I help you?" she asked, her gaze honing in on the guys at once.

Not like Liz hadn't gotten used to it—when she walked around with those walking talking sex machines, she may as well have been invisible. "Did anyone swing by earlier?" she asked, stepping up to the bar. "Our friend was heading here to check the venue out before they performed tonight."

The blonde squinted while she placed several bottles of Grey Goose on the countertop. "From Discord's Desire? Yeah, he poked around earlier, gauging setup."

Liz's heart thumped a little faster. So he at least made it to here. "Did he say where he was headed?"

The woman shook her head as she jerked a thumb in the direction of the other rooms. "He scoped the place and left out the alley."

"Thanks, beautiful," Jett said with a wink, charming her while they headed in through the other rooms.

Blind as they were, all they could do was try to find whatever traces of him that surfaced. Unfortunately for them, San Francisco was a huge city. Liz raked a hand through her hair, hating how her insides buzzed. After setting a quick pace through the rooms, the black slatted door with the oversized handle stood out, the one leading to the alleyway.

The second she burst into the alleyway, her nose crinkled from the sharp scent of smoke. Not the tang of cigarette smoke, although butts littered the asphalt out here. This reminded her of the acrid stench of scorched coals or a bonfire.

Trevor took the lead, stepping in front of her. He'd closed his eyes at this point and walked in a slow, measured pace. Until now, the banshee kept his abilities under wraps. However, his skills involved more than predicting deaths.

"He's able to see the imprint of past trauma or violence. If anything happened here, he'd register it bright and clear," Jett whispered into her ear.

Liz leaned against the brick wall, wanting to ram her fists against it. Even though the stones were heated from the bright overhead sun, none of the warmth pierced through to the depths her insides plummeted. "Why haven't we tapped this yet?" She raised a brow.

Jett shook his head. "Because half of the time, our boy Kieran was at the forefront of the violence—no need for a report when he'd fill us in on his exploits."

Trevor stopped at the end of the alley, his brows furrowing even though his eyes remained shut. His fingers trailed out into the air until he crouched to the ground and pressed his hands to the cement.

"What—" Liz started to ask, when Jett clapped a hand on her shoulder.

"Let him do his thing. You're not going to reach him while he's tranced out." Jett watched him just as carefully.

Renn stepped up a couple of paces and squinted at the ground closer to where Trevor crouched. "Is that blood?" he asked, pointing to the dark splotches in the asphalt.

Liz bit on her tongue until she tasted copper. Her deep breath came out in a slow, unsteady stream as she crossed the distance to where Renn indicated. Crouching near Trevor, she leaned down to examine the near-dried liquid on the pavement.

Trevor blinked a couple of times as his eyes came into focus again, leaving the trance behind. She leaned down to sniff the substance when he placed his hand on her shoulder. "He got knocked out, but as far as I know, they took him alive."

The sinking in her gut didn't increase with the delivered news, because she'd known from the get-go. With the way Larsen sent goons after his brother the past couple of weeks, it would've been an impossible coincidence for his disappearance to have been caused by anyone else. Instead, a jolt of rage shot through her, a cleansing fire that scorched her systems.

"Who took him?" she asked, her voice low. Calm.

"A couple of Unseelie bastards, including the big nasty we spotted the other day at Jay Vandermere's house. They knocked him out as soon as he rounded the corner, and then they hauled him away." Trevor's eyes held a fury she'd seen once, at the Lotus Garden when his nightmarish old owner showed up.

"Fuck." She let out a low curse bordering on a growl. Unless Danica made some vast strides with whatever Rembrandt industries sent her way, they had no clue as to why Jay Vandermere was after Kieran. "I'll bust into Vandermere's house and wring him alive." She palmed her Beretta, ready to march down to his place and demand retribution.

"I want answers as bad as you do, Lizzie," Jett said, remaining the calm one since her own sense of reason had been scorched away. "However, we've got to play smart. Let's get Danica to meet with us back at the RV, and we'll go over the mail we stole last night. There has to be something we're overlooking."

The idea of heading to the RV while Kieran remained out there in the hands of the enemy dosed her with anxiety, but she fought the urge to snap at Jett. After all, if they didn't track down the bastards who took him, they might never get him back.

"Fine," she said, her voice terse, "but I want first

dibs on the big nasty who took him."

Chapter Twenty-Six

The stench of mildew reached him at once, further evident by the damp chill along his bare arms. The second scent he picked up was an all too familiar one, a roasted coffee aroma that failed to stamp out all the wrongness here. Kieran let out a wet cough, his eye aching, his jaw throbbing, and patches of intense pain lining his arms and legs.

He had no idea how long he'd been here, but not only had his one eye crusted over, but the other swelled too much to open all the way. As he tried to bring his hands forward to clear out his eyes, pressure restricted him from the wrist, snapping them into place again. Kieran let out a shallow breath. Fuck, he'd been restrained, which eliminated one of his greatest assets, the ability to touch and influence. Whoever took him here had prepared to lock up an incubus.

All he remembered was brimstone, heat, and a big ass bastard looming over him when he'd turned the corner. If memory served him right, two malevolent Unseelie had been waiting in the wings behind the main guy. Which meant he would've been boned either way.

He blinked the crust out of his one eye and managed to squeeze the other one open enough to get a gauge on the room. Darkness surrounded him except from the couple of ochre beams spilling in through the small square window by the ceiling. So he hung in a basement of sorts. With his luck, it'd either be his asshole brother's digs or the idiot who'd helped him, Jay Vandermere.

From the slow beams ambling through the place, he caught a glimpse of wire racks in the back lined to the brim with pressure-sealed five-pounder coffee bags. His brow wrinkled in confusion as he scanned the rest of the room. Apart from the shelving laden with brown Kraft boxes, the room lay empty. A black desk sat in the corner, and the earthen floor hadn't been finished, adding to the musty smell down here.

He tugged at the manacles strapped to his wrists, causing the chains to jangle. These weren't the average restraints either—the way they ached around his wrists meant they must've been forged with platinum bands. Pure platinum was a tool of the Unseelie and would've scalded a Seelie-born like him, even without claiming his allegiance to any courts or proprieties. Glancing at the beams above him, Kieran balled his hands into fists, trying to concentrate through the pain.

Jay Vandermere—he'd seen the man before in earlier years. Hell, he could've sworn he even shook the man's hand after being introduced, but all of those fae functions blurred into the past for him as a parade of hated memories. The burns along his arms throbbed, but he ignored the pain, focusing in on the walls.

The realization struck him like a punch to the gut.

The basement door creaked open from the long stairwell leading up—to escape. Footsteps pounded along the wooden steps, the weight causing the planks to groan. Kieran's insides squeezed tight until the rage coiled inside him like a beast begging to prowl. His gaze didn't leave the steps once, waiting for the intruder to approach from the shadows and confirm his hunch that now seemed all too clear.

"You've finally woken up," a familiar voice murmured. "I thought you were going to sleep the day away."

The woman slunk toward him with the poise she always radiated, her hips swinging side to side. Jett had joked she carried a flame for him, but Winter's breath, he hadn't believed the siren, until now. A smile curved her lips as she came to a halt in front of him, placing her hands on her hips, as if they were having a normal conversation and he wasn't chained up.

Jessa stared at him, the cruelty in her gaze a foreign thing from the woman he'd once loved.

"Nice, sweetheart. Because this isn't coming across desperate," Kieran drawled. Despite the bite of the cuffs around his wrists and the pain radiating through him, his rage triumphed over all of that.

Jessa's eyes narrowed. "You goddamn asshole. Like we both don't know you cost me my place in the Court. I would've risked it all for you, but when you dumped me, they treated me like a leper, a pariah."

Kieran snorted. "Welcome to the club. I've been a pariah from birth so don't expect too much sympathy from me. Not like your family disowned you."

"They would've. But with the upcoming hunter threat, Tiberius promised a position of power to anyone who could bring more numbers into the fold by recruiting their unaligned. Fail to do so and you're excised from Court protection. With our family businesses tied together, my family's at risk too." Jessa folded her arms across her chest with a haughty look in her gaze as she scanned him up and down.

The possession stark in her features sent a shudder of revulsion through him. As if he didn't know what her addled brain had in mind with his disappearance. He'd been wrong pegging Misandra as a psycho, because her betrayal didn't come close to this level of insanity.

"You can't force me to align—that's not how it works," Kieran said, trying to focus on needling her rather than the way his body ached or the slow trickle of dread at how deeply in trouble he was. "Tiberius will find some other reason to discredit you and your family instead. Face it, Jessa. The Court is preying on your desperation, and Winter's breath, you reek of it."

Her brows furrowed, the twisted anger turning those pretty features into something ugly. As he goaded her, he scanned the room, looking for a nearby tool, furniture, or some way to get out of there. With her front and center, he couldn't start testing the chains, and the chairs, a stray wrench, and other items lay at least several feet away, meaning he wouldn't be able to tug anything forward with his feet.

"Big talk when you're reduced to a prisoner down here," she said with a sneer, walking closer to him. "Being aligned is essential for your own protection. But until you've come to see reason, I'll enjoy breaking you." The hunger in her eyes as she stared him over spelled out what sordid future she had in mind.

Bile rose in Kieran's throat, but he didn't let his mind wander too far ahead. Indulging in those fears would cripple him. The lust-filled look in Jessa's eyes and the thought of how he'd left Liz sleeping in his bed made him too sick to bear.

However, Kieran would get the hell out of here, no matter the cost. He wouldn't be reduced to the hellish future Jessa envisioned. "Sorry, Jess, psychos are a turn off. I've had enough of your ugly mug to last a century," he said.

"Once your hunter girl is out of the picture, you'll have no reason to remain out in the cold." Jessa's eyes flashed with anger as his words hit home. "Who knows, maybe Tiberius will even reward me for killing one of the enemy."

Kieran's eyes narrowed. "Don't you dare do a thing to her," he growled. His hands balled into fists, wrists straining against the heavy manacles. If she laid a finger on Liz, he wouldn't hesitate to shoot her cold. In all of his disorientation upon waking up and encountering Jessa, he hadn't thought to check for his weapons. Nothing weighted his waist, but he shifted forward, pretending to surge out of anger toward her. Cool metal brushed against the inside of his boot—the bitch hadn't removed his butterfly knife.

"Touchy, touchy." Jessa resumed her level of calm, cruel, and collected as she tapped the side of her face. "Maybe I'll bring you her head as a souvenir."

The idea of anyone trying to hurt Liz made his temper skyrocket in a fierce way. He treasured those memories last night with her so much they ached in his chest. The way Liz dropped her guards and welcomed him in—being with her was like after a long journey, returning home. Kieran thrashed against his bonds, the chains jangling with his motions and the manacles biting deeper into his wrists.

"The more you struggle, the more you'll injure yourself," she said leaning in close to him. "And we both know I won't be able to heal you in the way you need." Her gaze fixated on his lips.

Kieran squeezed his stomach tight to bite back the revulsion and played into it. He switched on the gaze he'd delivered to a thousand girls before who he hadn't given a damn about. Sure, he'd healed and energized, but they never reached his heart, and they'd never connected with him.

Jessa's eyes widened, and the greedy bitch leaned forward to kiss him.

Her mistake.

Kieran reared back, slamming his forehead against hers. The crack resounded around the room, but before she staggered backward, he thrust his hips forward to lock his legs around her torso. He'd sleep with her over his dead body or preferably hers. Pivoting with his hips, he used his legs like a clamp and given the momentum, shoved her body forward.

Reeling from the sudden onslaught, Jessa whipped around at an off angle and lost her balance. She went flying forward, spreading her hands out as she crashed onto the ground.

She hit the floor with a smack, her side absorbing most of the blow. He'd been hoping the attack would've knocked her out but no such luck. She let out a groan as she shook her head, wincing at the motion.

Kieran braced himself for the backlash, because stirring the pot with someone as batshit as Jessa would have consequences. In their year together, he'd never seen this side of her, this sadistic and desperate streak. Selfish and spoiled, sure, but he'd looked past those traits during their relationship.

She pushed herself from the floor and smoothed the skirts of her long paisley dress. The woman took her time with each meticulous stroke to the starchy fabric, even though she brimmed with rage the entire time.

She straightened her stance until her gaze met Kieran's, those dark doe eyes glinting with a vicious gleam. "You won't be pulling a stunt like that again." Her voice iced over as she walked to the desk on the opposite side of the room. Her heels clicked against the hard-packed earth as she crossed the chamber. When she reached the desk, she pulled open the drawer, retrieving several long, thin knives. "I can be patient," she said, the leaden tone unnerving.

Kieran clenched his jaw, refusing to look down. She could torture him all she liked—he wouldn't break. His brother had done a number on him every time he found happiness, his parents had beaten him in their fights for submission, and he'd gotten into so many brawls growing up that he didn't fear a little pain. The only threat with any weight was the one against Liz, because he couldn't bear to lose her, not after what transpired between them.

But if Jessa wasted her time torturing him, she wouldn't be trying to eliminate Liz.

"Bring it, bitch," he growled.

Chapter Twenty-Seven

Once they leapt off the light rail and raced up the steps of the underground tunnel on their way back to the RV, Liz yanked out her phone to make the call to Danica. Each passing moment with no word from Kieran and no leads allowed her imagination to take hold, and that became a dark and terrifying place. Her Keds slapped along the pavement as she set a quick pace, though with the way their nerves rode them, the guys kept up.

She pressed Danica's number and lifted the phone to her ear, waiting for the clever leannan sidhe to pick up as the ringing began. Her breath caught in her throat. She gunned for the RV like a lifeline, as if she'd arrive there and Kieran would be waiting. Like nothing ever happened. Like he hadn't been beaten and dragged out to wherever the fuck the bastard who wanted him dead or alive kept him. This entire situation reaffirmed her healthy fear of the fae from the start—despite the ones she cared about, the rest of the lot were a menace.

"Hey, Obiwan," Danica's cheery voice came through the phone loud and clear.

"Kieran's been snatched. Did you get those emails? Do you have any lead as to who the hell might've taken him?" Liz fought to keep her voice level as she relayed the information, even though urgency leaked through anyway.

A sigh came through the speaker. "That sucks, but I'm outtie, chica. Our alliance was to take Larsen down, and right now, I'm delivering his head on a platter to the Court. Bastard will be behind bars once they get a gander at these financials. Everyone's got their panties in a twist about recruiting their unaligned, whether it be family or business associates, but I wouldn't worry—it's not like anyone can force the decision." Danica spoke with the same brisk, business-like efficiency as always, and before Liz fit another word in edgewise, the line went silent, because Danica hung up.

"What did she have to say?" Renn asked, lagging a pace or two behind them.

Liz blinked, unable to register what had just happened. She tucked her phone into her pocket, and her brows furrowed, but she couldn't piece together how fast someone she'd believed to be a friend dropped them in their time of need. The entire excursion yesterday hadn't been about Jay Vandermere—Danica must have gotten what she needed from the financials they'd scoured over during their visit to Rembrandt company. A sharp shard needled her chest as the realization sunk in from betrayal she hadn't felt this fiercely in a long time.

"She's out," Liz said as they neared the parking lot.

"You're fucking kidding me," Trevor growled. "Why the hell is she bailing out?"

Jett's gaze flashed to ice with understanding. "Because she got what she needed to from us. She never signed on to solve a mystery or help Kieran—she stated her intentions from the beginning: to take Larsen down. And once she got the ammo to do so, she no longer needed this alliance."

"Fae lawyering at its finest," Liz spat out. Rage burned in her something fierce at the sharp needling in her chest. She'd believed Danica to be a friend, thought she was more than a convenient alliance. And now in two foul sweeps, her so-called friend got the hell out of dodge, and the man she'd finally let in was missing with no leads. "Fuck," she cursed, her voice ragged. If anything happened to Kieran, she'd never forgive herself.

"Cold-hearted bitch," Renn said, shaking his head. The storm cloud around their group increased at this news, since the one hope they had snuffed out.

Liz's throat burned, but she didn't let her emotions triumph. Though her incubus would fight like hell the moment he woke up, if his captors wanted him dead in the end or were trying to extract information from him, she didn't want to think about the torture he might endure. The idea made her ill.

"We can't let that deter us," Liz said, the calm person she projected sounding foreign in her ears. "Priority number one is getting our boy back."

"Right, the mail we stole." Trevor took the cue and jogged ahead. While they'd pieced through the letters last night for a brief scan of anything startling, everyone had been too exhausted to fine-tooth comb it with the sleuthing that seemed to be Danica's specialty. They'd come to rely on her too much, not realizing the woman served herself, and that was it. Liz tugged on the end of her ponytail, frustration riding her in one consuming tidal wave.

"What did she say?" Jett asked as they made their way to the RV.

Trevor opened the doors and near dove inside.

"That she was 'outtie.' Seelie and Unseelie families are coming out of the woodwork to push those unaligned to take a side or the rulers will dole out consequences. Not like she couldn't be bothered to help out," Liz said, not trying to quench the bitterness. She should've expected this one—after all, she'd spent a lifetime not trusting people. However, being around these guys changed her, and they'd left their mark in an indelible way. She'd found people she trusted with her life. For the first time, she had a home she didn't want to leave.

"Hmm," Jett murmured, sinking deep into thought.

Liz hopped up the steps to the RV right as Renn slammed a fist into the side. The ferocity of his punch left a dent, but she didn't have the heart to argue it or even care. The exact same frustration coursed through her.

Trevor sat at the kitchen table where the letters they'd snagged lay open across it. He pored over them with the same intensity he applied to playing the guitar, so absorbed he shut out everything else.

She snagged a couple of the flyers from the top— junk mail that came with any route. Except this consisted of the normal suburban tripe of lawn cutting services and a local restaurant opening.

Trevor scanned over a banking document, which by the seven or eight pages in it proved to be a lengthy read.

Liz tossed the papers to the side while Jett snagged a chair beside them and plucked another piece of mail from the bunch.

Under the flyers lay an official looking envelope with a return address featuring none other than the Blackmore family. She tore the thing open. A bill for services. The thing was all numbers and menial bullshit, the sort any company might send to another. "At least we know why Larsen wants him so badly now," she muttered. "Associates of undeclareds are getting the black mark."

"Just families, or business as well?" Jett eyed her, his tone sharpening.

Liz's pulse quickened at his sudden attention, hoping beyond hope he could sort this better than she managed. "Business as well."

Jett seized the bill from her hands, eyeballing it as

if it burned. "I should've realized when she urged him to align," he said, his voice hoarse and low. He let out a groan as he flung the invite to the ground. "We've been idiots. It's been right under our noses the entire time. Danica even hinted at it—the Saudertons are business partners of the Blackmore's. Their name is at risk so long as Kieran's not sworn to the Seelie to stand against the hunters."

Liz barely dared to breathe. "Who is it? Who has him?" The hope in her chest hurt, not daring to believe they stumbled on a lead. That they might have a chance at getting Kieran back.

"A certain owner of Perfect Percolation," Jett said, shaking his head. "The motives are all clear as day—after Ky dumped her, her status in the social circles took a nose dive, and she's never gotten over him despite the fact he moved on the second they split. Her family must've put her up to it once Tiberius made the decree."

"The bitch plays a good game, but seems to me the best litmus test with the fae is how they treat humans." Liz's blood boiled, and her hand reached to her side for her Beretta on instinct. She was ready to march out and take the coffee shop by force. "After all, she was stone cold to me from the get-go. I wouldn't doubt for a second she's capable of those levels of crazy."

"So what are we waiting for?" Trevor's voice sharpened like a knife. "Let's head to her goddamn coffee shop and get Ky back." The banshee stood from his seat, ready to storm off at a moment's notice.

Jett shook his head. "We've got to play this smart. Retrieve him, and we have no way of pinning this on Jessa apart from the word of four folks who don't follow the Court and one of the enemy—sorry, Liz. He'll be in as much danger as before if not more."

Bile rose in Liz's throat at the thought of Kieran

in the hands of that bitch, Jessa. She hadn't liked her from the start, and her gut feeling wasn't due to the woman being Kieran's ex. The way Jessa regarded him, like a favorite toy or lost possession—Liz saw it back then in her eyes, and the look made her hackles rise on the spot. And with Jessa's unhinged personality, throw her into a temper and deadly mistakes happened. They couldn't afford to wait any longer.

Renn approached, his forehead shining with sweat from the anger he'd been channeling into punching the RV, the ground, and anything he could get his hands on. "What's your suggestion, Jett?" he asked, to everyone's surprise. All the aggression spent must've granted him the level head Liz and Trevor didn't have at the moment. Jett, she didn't worry about—he always stayed cool, no matter the situation.

"She has to be caught on an infraction of Court law—though I guarantee we can find something to pin on her. And all the better if we can verify in front of a witness of worth." Jett passed Renn a meaningful glance.

He nodded in response. "My cousin's in the Otherworld. He can catch a slipstream to here in no time."

"Will he come though?" Jett asked, knowing something Liz was in the dark about. Based on the wrinkle on Trevor's forehead, he hadn't a clue either.

Renn shrugged. "Given proper motivation, sure. He's a stickler for the rules, and I rarely bother him, so he might be inclined to take this seriously."

"Who the hell is your cousin?" Liz cut in with the burning question she wanted an answer to. If they were going to risk waiting, risk Kieran's life and sanity on this, it better be for a damned good reason.

"He's one of the guardians of Tiberius, so I guess pretty high up on the food chain. High up enough to be exempt from this unaligned decree." Renn didn't seem impressed, but if he'd played in the sandbox with this guy, she could see why that wouldn't be a thing. "If anyone could validate a violation on the spot, it'd be that asshole."

"Go contact him." Jett shooed Renn off, who rolled his eyes in response as he sauntered toward the front of the RV. Liz's hand curled around the handle of her Beretta, ready to charge out the door. Jett turned to face her, placing a hand on her shoulder. "You guys won't be sitting idle, Lizzie. Trev and you can go scout Perfect Percolations. Stay out of sight, but check the back entrances and look for any hidden rooms or areas they might keep him. If it's no dice there, I know where the bitch lives—though a condo on the top floor is a lot more difficult for storage than your own personal business."

Liz exhaled a shaky breath, letting Jett's plan sink in. She could hug her best friend right now. He would wait behind with Renn, letting her and Trevor take point duty because he knew how out of their skin they both were while their band leader was held captive. She trusted his level head right now more than her own, because the very idea of Kieran in the succubus's grasp made her homicidal.

Trevor plunged into their safe, strapping on a pistol, a few knives, and slipping his breaking and entering kit into his pocket. After his experiences in cages, the man learned every tool of escape. Liz packed her arsenal, and with the rage welling inside her, she invited the opportunity to tear the woman apart with her bare hands.

"Go," Jett urged them. "Make sure he's safe." He turned to his phone, dialing a couple of contacts himself and setting his plan into play.

Trevor locked gazes with her, the wordless

understanding there. Time to head out.

She took the lead, striding to the front of the RV and exiting past the glass doors.

Renn stood out front in deep concentration with his hands at his temples as if he telepathically connected with someone. Liz didn't dare disturb, not with so much riding on this operation. She and Trevor kept pace with each other while they strode across the parking lot, heading straight for the station they'd departed from. The banshee buzzed with rage as his gaze blazed, and each step was tight and controlled.

Liz's own fury grew into a stoked blaze. She'd let it build and build until she got Jessa Sauderton in her sights and unleashed hell.

"She better not have touched a hair on his head." Trevor's voice came out a low murmur. Despite the rage, fear burrowed behind it, the fear they both shared for Kieran. After all the time she'd spent keeping the incubus at a distance, now that she'd let him in, she couldn't imagine her life without the hotheaded, loyal, and stubborn man.

"We'll wait as long as we can for Jett and Renn, but if it comes down to it, we're getting Kieran the hell out of there tonight, plan or no." Liz met Trevor's gaze, an understanding blossoming between them. Jett had known what he'd been doing in sending them to Kieran, because if anything fouled up on their end, Trevor and Liz wouldn't hesitate in putting Kieran's safety first, damn the consequences. And the moment she got Kieran back, she'd burn Perfect Percolation to the ground with Jessa in it.

Chapter Twenty-Eight

"I think you've had enough for now." Jessa's voice broke through the haze of pain. Kieran's body ached to begin with, but now he bled from open wounds, so that was awesome. Jessa frowned at the knives, which were covered in his blood. He'd like to say she got creative with them, but the only thing taking wild leaps of fancy were her delusions, because she'd delivered the typical stab and jab routine, with a couple stripes down the arm. Nothing compared to the punishments his folks doled when he'd rebelled.

"Getting tired, Jess? Didn't realize torture could be so exhausting," Kieran said, not giving a damn if she started over again. He'd grit his teeth and bear it. "I thought you were trying to tickle me with those things."

She fixed him with a glare. "The point is to break your spirit, not your body. I've got plenty of use for your body, and if you think I'll be marring that up in any permanent way, you're wrong. I need you nice and compliant for your formal introduction into the Seelie Court."

"Great job you're doing there. I'm brimming with energy." He delivered a taunting grin, despite the way his arms radiated pain from the long stripes down them and aching wounds from where she'd stabbed his chest, avoiding the vitals.

All the while, he shut out the future she kept depicting, because that line of thinking would break him. He'd been a used-up object before like half the girls he slept with, and he didn't want to return to that. Not after he'd found Liz and experienced the difference the brilliant and real connection between them offered. One taste of her, and he never wanted to quit.

"Don't worry, we're just getting started." Jessa bit on her finger in the coy way that brought men to her bedroom. The sight made him nauseous. "After all, I've got a certain hunter girl to target and maim—let's see how mouthy you are after that. Falling for one of them is pathetic."

"You think bringing me into the fold will help your family earn Tiberius's good graces? You're getting played like a pawn, Jess. You're no different from how Lars uses Misandra—the insane, expendable one to throw into a hopeless case. You and I both know I'd be a nightmare in the Courts." He pushed her as far as he could, because the second she stopped paying attention to him, she'd switch her attention to tracking Liz.

"Shut the hell up," she snapped, her eyes icing over. "You don't know my family or what we've been through."

Kieran lifted a brow. "Oh, I know them plenty, like I know you've always been the shame of the family." He pushed hard, knowing how much being different from the rest rotted into your bones year after year.

A flush hit her tan skin as her fists tightened around the knife handles she held. "You're one to talk, Kieran. The Blackmores disowned you, yet you parade around with their last name. Who do you think you're fooling? Everyone knows your damage."

"I don't hide it." He delivered his response, calmer than he thought possible given the fact he hung from manacles, leaking blood, and aching all over in the basement of a coffee shop.

Knowing what a twisted, broken creature Jessa was gave him an understanding he'd been lacking before. In accepting his past and the damage it caused, he'd given himself the power. The control. Yet this pathetic woman clung to the opinions of Court, living in the delusion they'd some day accept her, psychopathic tendencies and all. That she might have status and position beyond a pawn in her family. The whole thing was laughable and sad.

The second he got out of here, he'd expose Larsen and Jessa to the Court for what they were—pathetic toadies with no backbone. Both groveled after the same power to the point they let those desires own them.

"You're nothing, Kieran *Blackmore*," she said, her eyes flashing with anger. "You're worth nothing."

"To the eyes of the Court maybe," he said, a serenity reaching him despite his position. "But they were never the ones who mattered, anyway."

Jessa gripped the knife handles so tight her knuckles whitened, but she didn't respond. Instead, she turned and headed for the steps. "We'll see if you're saying that after your girl's gone." The succubus marched up the steps, determination in those insane eyes as she headed to seal Liz's fate.

Kieran hoped Jessa let her crazy leak out—because with the way Liz's hand jumped to her Beretta, she'd shoot the woman down.

He squinted, looking at the window. Dark orange light streamed through, the shadows increasing with the coming nightfall. By now, the band would've realized he was missing for sure with a gig lined up later tonight. Kind of hard to perform without your lead singer. The copper stench of his blood flooded the room, mingling with the mildew and packed dirt. Kieran glanced to the manacles around his wrists, which grew bloody and raw from all the chafing on top of the throb of diluted platinum against his skin.

If he got to the knife at his boot, he might be able to try and pick the manacles, or at least he'd plunge the blade into Jessa's chest the next time she paid a visit. He shifted his weight forward, trying to swing momentum as he lifted his knees. The balanced weight placed an unbearable strain on his wrists to the point he was half a shade sure they would separate at the joint. Kieran gritted his teeth, switching to another tactic.

He dropped his one leg and lifted the one he wanted, tilting his boot closer and closer to his face. Ducking his head, he tried to make a grab for the knife resting at the top. The movement shifted the knife toward him, but once he dropped his leg it would slide right back to the base. Even though his leg burned and his body weakened from the hours of Jessa playing slice and dice on him, he channeled every ounce of energy into holding the limb aloft.

Closer. His hip screamed, and his knee begged to be released, but he inched his foot closer to his face, straining his neck as far as it would go.

Another inch.

His wrists screamed as the manacles scraped against them, the tension increasing as his broken body begged to sag onto the ground. But Kieran wouldn't give up. He needed to get the hell out of here. Had to keep Liz safe.

He leaned in and snapped his jaw at the hem of his boot. The edge of the butterfly knife clinked against his tooth. Kieran nudged it forward with his tongue until he clamped down, his teeth getting a firm hold on the outside. The second he got it in his grip, he stopped straining, lifting his neck and returning his leg to the ground.

The cool metal of the butterfly knife's casing pressed against his lips, but he refused to let go of his grip on the thing. If he found a way to get the manacles off, he'd fight his way out. Troublemaker like him, Kieran had plenty of experience picking locks.

He let go of the one side, circling his neck around to swing the knife free. Nudging the end with his tongue, he shifted the placement on his teeth so they gripped the handle, the naked blade pointing to his left. Wincing, he glanced to his left arm where the manacle clapped around the wrist. This next movement would hurt, big time. His fingers grazed the chains, tugging them to test the give—not much. Joy.

Tilting his body to the left, he strained to bring his manacled wrist closer to his head. Though his head could rest against his biceps, trying to reach for the wrists would be a much harder task. Kieran gritted his teeth and tugged his arm toward him, his nerves screaming at the pressure on his raw, damaged skin. He pushed himself up on his tiptoes, but even straining with his neck tilted up, inches separated him from the manacle.

The rustle of footsteps pounded above, the denizens of the coffee shop walking around, unaware Jessa created her own personal torture chamber underneath.

His vision shuddered in front of him, blinking to black and back. He let out a sigh as he sank into place, his muscles screaming from the pain and ready to give. If he didn't allow a half second break, even if he escaped he'd be useless. Despite the energy high he'd gotten from his night with Liz—and he hadn't floated so high, ever—the adrenaline crash from Jessa's hack job at torturing and from being knocked over the head, chained up, and injured took its toll.

Truth be told, he was in shit shape and needed to feed, badly.

A loud scraping noise from outside drew his

attention. Kieran's gaze snapped to the window. Shadows smothered it, snuffing out the paltry light. His heartbeat raced in his chest, a burst of hope flooding through him he couldn't quite smother. He gave up on his attempts at dragging the manacle down, focusing on the movement by the window.

A small tap came from the window again, followed by a splintering crinkle that echoed through the entire room. The glass fragmented out from the center like a disjointed snowflake, until pieces tumbled inside to hit the floor. A large nail protruded through again, someone guiding it from the outside as they tapped the larger shards surrounding the edges in to fall to the ground as well.

The commotion snared Kieran's interest at this point. After all—none of Jessa's cronies would be breaking and entering into her secret lair.

Once the shards were cleared away, a face poked in, though it took a couple of seconds before Kieran could identify any features with the way the shadows clung. His heart raced in his chest at the sight, the familiar long chin, the sharp eyes behind the glint of glasses he sometimes wore, and silver hair he should've gotten trimmed a few states back.

Trevor.

Just as quick, the banshee moved out of sight for the other person beside him to duck their head in. He'd recognize her anywhere. The messy brown hair tied into a ponytail, the stubborn jut of her jaw, and the spark of ferocity in her hazel eyes as she locked gazes with him. Kieran's heart near burst in his chest with relief at the sight of Liz. It had been mere hours since they'd been apart, but those hours were a veritable nightmare.

Except she'd walked right to the gates of the insane woman who wanted her dead. He jerked his head to the side in an 'out' motion, hoping she'd catch the hint. However, as fast as their eyes met, she had already set to motion. Her hands gripped the top of the ledge, and she inched her way through, feet first. Next, her legs pushed through, then her hips, until she hung by her outside grip on the window with her arms stretched to full length as she gauged the distance below.

With a foot drop, she let go to thud to the floor. The second she dropped, Trevor inched through the window with the same quickness. Liz didn't hesitate. Once her sneakers hit the ground, she rocketed toward him. She skidded to a halt in front of him, taking inventory of his wounds. Hell, he wanted to spit out the butterfly knife and kiss her into oblivion, but she couldn't be caught down here. Not while Jessa hunted for her blood. A click sounded from behind them, but the sound came from Trevor approaching.

Liz plucked the butterfly knife out of his mouth, her eyes glistening in the darkness. The woman would never admit to tears, but he caught the fear and concern shining there, and it filled him with a deep, unreserved affection he'd never experienced before. He cared about his brothers in the band to the point he would kill for them, but Liz had merged her way deeper into his consciousness. She was with his every breath, every thought, and the way she made him feel gave him the strength to endure.

"You need to get out of here," he said, trying to warn her. As much as their departure would slay him, he didn't like the idea of Jessa running into Liz.

"Shut up, you stubborn bastard," she said, her voice low and hoarse. Leaning in, she pressed her lips against his. She brushed them against him in a soft way, a nectar he'd become addicted to. And as she dipped her tongue in to stroke his own, energy trickled through him.

Her lips caressed his mouth with a melody he couldn't try and emulate, a healing sweetness that was all her own. As she deepened the kiss, her body trembled against him.

"Is this all about healing, or some pleasure too?" he murmured against her mouth, trying to distract her.

"You idiot." She delivered one more fierce kiss before pulling away.

Trevor reached for his manacles, his lockpicking kit in full use. If anyone understood the humiliation and pain of being chained up, his best friend did. One of the manacles dropped to the ground, and at once, his hand slammed down to his side. Kieran winced at the flare of the raw skin exposed. Trevor passed him a sympathetic look as he set to working the other hand free.

Liz held up the butterfly knife. "Looks like you didn't even need rescuing, Rambo."

"Next step would've been strangling Jessa with her own manacles when she came back down." He shrugged his free arm, rolling the stiff shoulder. A second later, Trevor freed the other wrist, allowing him full range of moment. A knot unfurled in his chest at the freedom. He hadn't even been imprisoned for long, but folks rarely got the one-up on him—Kieran didn't give them the chance. He'd fought the chains of his parents and the chains of his birthright for too long.

Pins and needles flooded his arms, and he flexed his fingers, rolling the joints to get the blood moving faster.

Liz handed over his knife. "Better if you're armed. Is she up above?"

"Not sure. She was on the warpath for you." Kieran passed her a glance. "One of the perks with hooking up with me includes jealous exes. Aren't you overjoyed?"

"Thrilled. Can I shoot her now?" Liz's gaze burned with a deep rage. She hadn't been trembling out of fear but molten anger.

"Love this new fiery streak in you, babe. What's next post jailbreak? Arson?" Kieran's lips curled into a smile. A deep ache resided in his chest at her overflowing concern and at how she'd hunted him down. Her care shone on her face. The normal Liz O'Brien would've taken efforts to hide her emotions under a cool veneer, but as she stood in front of him, trembling with rage, her raw feelings for him were on clear display.

"Don't let her deny it, she spent the entire time over muttering about burning this joint down," Trevor said, a smirk on his face.

A creak sounded from outside, followed by a rapid pounding of footsteps from above. Kieran clenched the handle of his butterfly knife as the groan of floorboards traveled in the direction of the door.

Jessa was coming.

Chapter Twenty-Nine

When she said she'd burn this place down, she never spoke a more serious truth. Especially after finding Kieran chained up, mutilated, and tortured. Heat burned behind her eyes, and rage scorched her soul at seeing the burn patches along his arms and the long, ragged slices of red. At the soaked red patch in his shirt, the dirt and scratches marring his features, and the ugly bruises. And she'd never loved him more than when he'd brushed all of it off like what he endured was nothing—teasing her to bring a smile to her face.

The door slammed from the top of the stairwell, and not one, but two familiar figures appeared at the top. Jessa strode down the steps, followed by the worker they'd seen behind the counter the other day.

Liz pulled her Beretta forward and aimed the pistol in the direction of the women.

Except, Jessa had thought ahead, and she turned the muzzle of her own gun their way as she took her time creeping down the steps. "Oh look, the prey made my job easier by coming to me," she said in a low purr, the same coldness gleaming in her eyes as the first time they'd met.

The woman hadn't intimidated her then, and all her haughtiness didn't now. "You know, the humans-are-beneath-me shit is old news. I mean, thank god you have powers—who the hell would hook up with you if you couldn't force them into it?" The words left her mouth before she thought about them. She wrinkled her nose and glanced back. "Sorry, Ky."

He shook his head, a grin on his face. "We've all made our mistakes. She's her family's."

Jessa's gaze darkened. He'd hit a sore spot with his comment, making it all the clearer why she might've kidnapped him. As much as Liz wanted to rush out of the place, she needed to keep them occupied while Jett and Renn headed their way. If they did. She hadn't checked her phone since they'd arrived, and though Jett would've preferred the scene preserved, she refused to let Kieran hang in those chains a moment longer.

"You're outnumbered, Jess," Trevor said, lifting his gun in the process. Kieran brandished his knife, and based on how his jaw tensed, he was more than ready to use it.

"Yet we've both got targets at the ready, and you know I'll shoot." Her muzzle pointed at Liz, to no one's surprise. "You haven't been introduced to my employee, Eira—one of the huldafolk."

Liz's forehead creased with her frown, all the while keeping her Beretta focused on Jessa. "Is that supposed to make me shake in my boots or something?"

"Not like a *human* would know," she said the word as if she'd uttered cockroach, "but out of everyone in the room, succubus, incubus, and banshee, she's the one with external offensive abilities worth a damn. Worth more than the little pistol you keep clinging to, girl."

"See if you're still saying that when my pistol's shoved up your holier-than-thou ass," Liz spat, ready to fire, damn the consequences. She sucked in a deep breath, tapping into the composure and survival instincts that kept her alive all these years. A level head was less likely to end in death, death, and more death. Kieran might be the lunge in and start slinging type, but he could also indulge in a hot make-out session to heal wounds. From their brief kiss, the ribbons along his arms had begun to seal.

Eira smiled beside Jessa as she lifted her palms. Flames blossomed on both of them, which spelled all sorts of bad news for their crew. With guns loaded, flames at the ready, and some mighty mean stares flying around, the tension thickened in the air like smog.

Liz waited, watching.

The first person to move would be the idiot who everyone targeted, and with the way everyone focused on each other's weapons, the bubble of violence expanded and expanded until it was ready to burst.

Jessa's finger twitched like she itched to pull the trigger, and those dark eyes fixated on Liz with an intensity veering on obsession. Well, after the way the bitch left Kieran, she jumped at the bit to pull the trigger too. However, the second the woman's eyes narrowed. That confirmed it—she was going to shoot first.

Except Liz wasn't the only one who noticed.

Kieran dove in first, his butterfly knife at the ready as he lunged for Jessa. Making himself the idiot who everyone targeted.

"Fuck." Liz let out a low curse, ready to strangle Kieran for always trying to put her safety first. With the way he leapt into her line of vision she couldn't shoot, and Eira whipped in his direction, those flames burning bright as she reared her hands back, ready to toss them forward.

Trevor didn't sit idle though. His finger squeezed the trigger as the first shot fired, the bullet zooming straight for Eira.

At the last second, the fae noticed his attack and whipped around in his direction, her aim sloppy while she lobbed those fireballs. Since she moved from her initial spot, the bullet didn't score her in the vitals, but instead, burrowed into her shoulder, causing a low growl from her in response.

The fireballs landed on either side of him, crashing to the ground to hiss on the packed earth before extinguishing. Trevor circled around to a different vantage point as those orbs sparked to life in her palms again.

Though she hated how he put himself in danger, she had to admit Kieran went for the smart play. Jessa might hurt him, but he was the one person in the room she'd hesitate to kill. He thrust the butterfly knife forward, aiming for her stomach as she kept her muzzle trained on him. When he got close enough, she whipped the pistol toward his face.

He'd been waiting.

His hand darted out as he grabbed hold of the muzzle and yanked forward, causing Jessa to struggle with her grip. Not letting go, he used the distraction and sliced in with the butterfly knife.

Jessa let out a low hiss when the blade scored flesh. With a fierce tug, she snagged the gun out of his grip and staggered back a few paces, her one hand popping to the fresh slice in her stomach.

Kieran pivoted, moving lightning fast out of the way. Liz didn't miss the look he shot her either. She was ready.

Liz squeezed the trigger, aiming for the woman's shoulder. Right as the bullet cracked from her pistol, Eira skidded into the way, trying to evade a shot from Trevor. Kieran lunged to the ground as said bullet whizzed overhead. It grazed Eira's shoulder before continuing on to plunge into Jessa's arm, farther down. There, it wouldn't incapacitate, just make things real annoying.

The graze sparked Eira's attention—literally.

Before Liz could switch focus and pull the trigger, one of those fireballs came hurtling her way. She dove to the ground as it soared toward her, the crackling resounding in her ears. Sliding forward, she pulled herself out of the trajectory.

At least, until the other one followed.

Liz rolled away as fast as she could manage but not fast enough. White hot pain radiated through her when the blaze crashed onto her left leg. She slammed it to the ground at once to snuff out the flames, but even after, her nerves screamed, and she gritted her teeth to keep from howling.

Before Eira took another step forward, Trevor kept her in check, sending a bullet whistling through the air toward her.

The woman let out a low grunt as it thudded into her hip, but she switched her focus to Liz a second later.

"This the one you want dead, boss?" she called out to Jessa who struggled against Kieran's relentless attacks.

"And buried," Jessa hissed while she fended off a swing from the butterfly knife.

Like hell. Liz rolled onto her back, ignoring the searing pain of her left leg. She might not be able to stand fast, but she could do one thing.

She only needed one second to line the shot as the woman lifted her palms in the air, ready to sling.

"Left yourself wide open, bitch." Liz squeezed the trigger.

The bullet sailed through the air, burrowing into Eira's chest. Fluid burst from the huldafolk woman as Liz's shot hit bullseye. Eira staggered back several paces, the fire in her hands snuffed out. A second later, the woman dropped to the ground, her jaw working while she tried to summon fire in her hands once more.

Trevor came to the rescue, rushing in for the double tap.

Liz pushed herself from the ground, ignoring the

burning sensation all along her skin. Focusing on what an ugly, charred mess her leg was right now wouldn't help anyone. Right now, she had a succubitch to kill.

The second Eira went down, Liz's gaze flicked to Jessa. The succubus realized they outnumbered her, and she wouldn't win against them. Jessa soaked in her surroundings with a cold calculation, her focus on Liz.

Her stomach sank when their eyes met, because she knew what desperation did. It made people unpredictable, and it made them dangerous.

Kieran thrust the blade forward, scoring along her arm, but Jessa didn't bother to defend. Her focus narrowed to taking Liz out.

Before Liz lifted her Beretta, the succubus hurtled toward her at top speed, pistol out and finger leaping for the trigger.

However, Kieran had been paying attention.

The second Jessa began to move and her finger latched onto the trigger, his expression darkened, his amber eyes vicious, and his jaw clenched tight. She didn't get a couple paces before he spun around and stabbed her in the back. Right beside the already leaking shoulder blade.

Her arm dropped from the sudden attack, and the gun tumbled out of her hand.

Kieran kicked the pistol away from her reach, stepping in front of Jessa.

"You don't ever touch her," he growled. "Ever."

A slam sounded from above, coming from the coffee shop, followed by the heavy tread of multiple sets of footsteps.

Trevor approached, aiming his pistol mere inches away from Jessa. "Don't even think of moving."

Jessa stared at him, chilling hatred in her gaze while she balled her hands into fists. Her neck grew taut as she tensed, looking for an opportunity.

Liz limped up to them, her finger on the trigger. "Game over," she murmured as the door to the basement creaked open.

"Hope we're not interrupting a party." Jett's familiar voice called from the top of the steps. Relief cascaded over her in a fierce wash. Although from where they stood, holding their gun to Jessa, she appeared more the victim than Kieran. Renn approached first, his brows crinkling as he surveyed the damage. Jett trailed behind him, and after that came a taller than average satyr packing enough muscle to put the whole band to shame. The man wore street clothes, but the pure gold adorning the vest over his button down and the tailored way his threads fit suggested money.

"These gentlemen have explained the situation and handed over the financials," the satyr said to Kieran as he approached. "However, I find it hard to believe this defenseless woman could have done so much damage."

Trevor stepped in front of them, handing over his phone. "We freed him. Here's what we found upon entering. Only one who would've known about this place is the owner and proprietor of Perfect Percolation, Jessa Sauderton. While I know unaligned aren't under Court protection, the fae mercenaries that Blackmore and Sauderton money bought were in your care."

"Go to hell." She spat on the floor as she glared at them.

The satyr gave a slow nod of appraisal as he looked at the picture Trevor snapped while Kieran hung, and then over at Jessa. "You realize this is a grievous charge, yes?"

"My family required it of me," she said. "To enter into their good graces, I needed to force Kieran Blackmore's allegiance."

"In the wake of this new threat against us, we require the noble families to bring their unaligned into the fold. You failing to do so isn't our problem. The fact you wasted viable soldiers in a time of war is." His incredulity broadcasted clear as did his insufferable arrogance. Liz came to the decision she didn't like him, another stuffy representative of the type of fae she hated.

"And my brother collaborated with her. Jay Vandermere was funneling him money, and in return, Lars and Jessa bought out their employees to kidnap me." Kieran jumped in with surprising composure given the hellish day they'd all had. The steel grit in his eyes told that he wouldn't allow his brother to weasel out of this one. Not this time.

"The Blackmore family has gained another black mark on their record due to Larsen's dealings with the Rembrandt company," the satyr confirmed. Kieran's brows shot up in surprise. "Danica of the Maslanka family has surfaced the records of the finances used to fund the assassination attempt on the King. They came from Jay Vandermere with the Rembrandt company, working in conjunction with Larsen Blackmore. The arrangements with Jessa Sauderton must have been enmeshed in this attempt."

"What will you do with Larsen?" Kieran asked as his hands balled into fists. Liz bit her lip, the anxiousness welling inside her as well. If they let the bastard roam free after the hell he'd put them through, she'd lob a fist through the drywall.

"Larsen Blackmore and Jay Vandermere will be imprisoned for some time, or at least until the King has grown bored with them." The satyr didn't blink, but Renn shuddered. Liz could imagine whatever playtime the leader of the fae had arranged, it would be nightmarish.

"What will happen to me?" Jessa dropped the rage and attempted to play the pity card, trembling lip and all. Liz let out a groan of annoyance.

"You'll join your partners in crime. You understand in a time of war, punishments meted out will be harsher for those risking our soldiers in the fight." The satyr continued in his low monotone. He must be a roaring delight at dinner parties. He snapped his fingers and glanced to Jessa, the expectation clear.

To Liz's surprise, the woman obeyed, rising with a whimper.

The man surveyed them before continuing. "I take it you lot can excuse yourselves? I'll send a detail to clean this mess later."

"We're good, cousin. Thanks," Renn said, giving the man a lazy salute.

He regarded Renn with a nod before marching towards the stair, as if he were in full military uniform.

Jessa trailed behind him, but not before shooting daggers at Liz.

Liz rolled her eyes, since the woman couldn't do anything to her behind bars or in the Fae King's personal torture chamber.

"Who's ready to get the hell out of this shithole?" Jett asked, wrinkling his nose as he scanned over the blood splatters and Eira's dead body on the floor.

"Think you guys are up for playing the gig still? You might be able to slide in, just in time," Liz said.

"Cruel taskmaster. I was tortured. Tortured! And you're going to make me head up there and strut my stuff?" Kieran teased her, a glint in his eyes. Liz leaned against him, her leg aching as she tilted her head up. He met her lips with a kiss that made her spine tingle, the exact sort to leave her breathless.

"I'll make sure you're well healed up before

then," she said, her voice husky with need.

"Does that mean you'll wear a nurse outfit?" He winked, squeezing her tight to his side. "What about your leg?" he asked, glancing to where her calf began to blister in an ugly way.

Liz let out a sigh. "I suppose we can make a stop off to the hospital on the way home. Get the good drugs."

Trevor shook his head, leading the way up the steps. "Come on, guys. Let's go home."

Chapter Thirty

Kieran stood on stage at the club, basking in the crowd that accumulated during the night. "Everyone enjoying themselves?" he called out into the microphone as they prepared to launch into their last song.

Screams and hollers resounded through the room in response, and he basked in their energy. Between his healing session with Liz beforehand and playing a show, his wounds had begun to heal. Scratches closed over, cuts and deep gouges scabbed, and the severe exhaustion disappeared.

Liz sat at the bar along the back wall, crossing her legs as she perched on the barstool with an elegant casualness like she hadn't spent an afternoon fighting his nightmare of an ex. Her one leg had gotten wrapped up on their hospital trip, but she didn't complain in the slightest despite the nasty burn she'd gotten.

Pride burned in his chest as their eyes met, and she shared a small smile with him. She wasn't showy, loud, or boisterous—she left that to him, but the woman proved her worth a thousand times over. She'd fought for him with a ferocity he'd never forget.

"I'm dedicating this song to a very special lady in the audience," Kieran said, a grin on his face as he pointed in her direction. Some groans sounded from the chicks, but a few other folks clapped in response. Trevor shook his head, and Jett fought and failed to hide a smile, while Renn gave a drill on the drums in enthusiastic response. "Our booking manager, Liz O'Brien is the reason we're here tonight. But more importantly, this woman is one of the most amazing people I've ever met, and the love of my life."

His voice boomed out over the audience, but his eyes weren't on them, just her. Liz scowled at him, arms crossed over her chest, but he caught the flush in her cheeks all the way from where he stood on stage. The scowl dropped, and she shook her head as a smile bloomed on those perfect lips. Kieran's heart swelled close to bursting while he nodded to Trevor who began strumming at his guitar. He tapped to the beat of the music, clutching the microphone and sinking into the song.

The melody surrounded him, sinking into his bones, part of this beautiful thing he'd created with his family—not the ones who wrote him off or the ones who abandoned him. No, these guys who fought by his side and this woman who'd captured his heart, they'd become his real family. Unlike the Courts who spent so much time on bloodlines, Kieran would happily shed his. In leaving the past behind, he'd become someone he could be proud of.

He'd learned to be a leader, a fighter, and learned the worth of opening his heart. Those lessons were the ones he'd take to the grave.

Kieran finished the song with one final note that resounded through the room, echoing back to greet him as the other instruments died down with the ending. Roars and applause exploded through the room from the crowd, at least from those who weren't making out on the floor.

"Thank you," Kieran called out into the microphone. "We are Discord's Desire!"

The spotlights dimmed while the screams and hollers continued, making his bones buzz. Liz would be so pissed with him for pointing her out, but he didn't give a damn. He felt so amazing right now he wanted to share his joy with the world. Once the sounds died down and the other peripheral lights had dimmed, he switched his microphone off and dragged it away from center stage. The glow of fainter red lights around the corners of the room switched on, turning the place back into a regular club vibe.

The second he stepped off stage, Liz waited for him, arms crossed and brows raised. "Really, rockstar? Like I need more death threats from your fangirls," she said, fixing him with a wan look.

He placed the mic stand down, coming to greet her with a kiss. She melted into it as his tongue began exploring her mouth, and he tasted her sweetness. Her lips caressed his as they sank into a rhythm, shutting the world out around him.

An elbow checked his side. Well, almost shutting it out.

"Come on, asshole. You're not getting out of packing up because you got a girlfriend," Trevor said, a smile on his face as he walked by with one of the amps.

Kieran ran a hand through his sweat-slicked hair, unable to hide his smile. "Suppose we better pick this up later?"

"Hold on there a minute. You're not going anywhere until you explain why the hell you were dropping 'love of my life's' on stage." Liz cocked her hip to the side, placing her hand on it.

Kieran shrugged. "Because I felt like it?" That earned him a swat to the head. He grabbed her hands, drawing her attention to front and center. His heart sped a couple of notches, but he didn't shirk from his feelings. "And because, Elizabeth O'Brien, I love you."

She smirked as she tried to restrain her smile, even though those hazel eyes of hers shone in response. The woman would never be the gushiest person on the planet, but he'd come to treasure those small gestures, his counterbalance in every way. "Well, I love you too," she murmured, almost too quiet to hear.

"What was that?" He leaned in, his hand to his ear.

"Shove off, jerk. You know what I said." She grinned in full now, smacking him in the shoulder. "Let's go help the guys pack before Jett comes back to yell at us."

He beamed, watching as she jogged over to the others to help them with another one of the amps. When Liz O'Brien first entered their entourage, he'd been fine with it because they needed organization, and she'd provided that a thousandfold. However, he'd fallen for the woman hidden behind the cool mask she showed the world, the one that cracked piece by piece the longer she'd been with them.

And she'd shaped him as well, shown him a future he'd never believed could belong to him. She tempered his rage with her patience and was unafraid to lend the unparalleled strength and steel core that defined her. Liz had become the eye of the storm amidst his hurricane.

Despite the torture Lars put him through and Jessa's attempts to break him, Kieran had become stronger than ever. Because he'd found the place he belonged, people he loved, and a joy so incandescent it could never be extinguished.

The End

www.katherine-mcintyre.com

CAPTIVATING MELODY

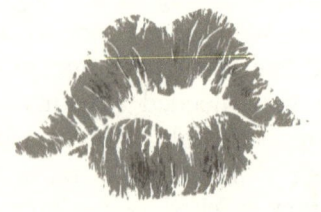

EVERNIGHT PUBLISHING ®

www.evernightpublishing.com